⊹

ON LINE

In the
River
ce

✠

In the
River
Province

STORIES BY
*L*ISA
SANDLIN

✠

SOUTHERN
METHODIST
UNIVERSITY PRESS
Dallas

Requests for permission to reproduce material
from this work should be sent to:
    Rights and Permissions
    Southern Methodist University Press
    PO Box 750415
    Dallas, Texas 75275-0415

Cover art by Catherine Ferguson
Jacket and text design by Teresa W. Wingfield

Library of Congress Cataloging-in-Publication Data

Sandlin, Lisa.
    In the river province : stories / by Lisa Sandlin.—1st ed.
      p. cm.
    Contents: 'Orita on the road to Chimayó—Everything
moves—Beautiful—The career of Saint Librada—Another
exciting day in Santa Fe—Night class—I loved you then,
I love you still—The saint of bilocation.
    ISBN 0-87074-488-7 (alk. paper)
    1. New Mexico—Social life and customs—Fiction.
2. Christian pilgrims and pilgrimages—Fiction. 3. Christian
fiction, American. 4. Christian saints—Fiction. I. Title.
PS3569.A516815 2004
813'.54—dc22   2003067384

Printed in the United States of America on acid-free paper

10   9   8   7   6   5   4   3   2   1

✠

✣

Acknowledgments

Sources for "The Saint of Bilocation" were Alonso de Benavides's Memorial of 1630 and its following notes: Paul Horgan's *Great River*; Marcelin Defouneaux's *Daily Life in Spain in the Golden Age*. Information on Sor María de Ágreda came from Clark Colahan's fine study *The Visions of Sor María de Ágreda: Writing Knowledge and Power*. The story is inspired by Benavides's historical interview; however, personalities, additional characters, details, and outcome of the interview are inventions. Information on Santiago came from Marc Simmons's fascinating essay "Santiago: Reality and Myth," in *Santiago: Saint of Two Worlds*, by Joan Myers, Marc Simmons, and Donna Pierce. Grateful acknowledgment to *Shenandoah* editor Dabney Stuart, who published "Everything Moves" and "'Orita on the Road to Chimayó"; to Bill Henderson and *Pushcart* for including the latter in their *Pushcart Prize Volume XIX*; to *Southwest Review* editor Betsey Mills, for printing "I Loved You Then, I Love You Still." To friends who read versions of these stories—Laura Hays, Joette Hayashigawa, Frances Kean, Carolyn Stupin, Carolyn Kenny, Susan Guillaume, Barbara Schmitz, Gretchen Ronnow, Neil Harrison, Jim Brummels—thank you for your precious time. I am indebted to Dr. Alan Bruflat, David Briggs, and Maria Cristina Lopez for Spanish-checking; to Eddie Elfers for cover ideas; to Wayne State College for sabbatical leave; to Kathryn Lang for her grace and expert editing. And for his *audace, encore de l'audace, toujours de l'audace*, I fervently thank David Samora.

✜

✛

Prologue

Good Friday could fall in March. It could fall in April.

Perhaps you start out in La Villa Real de Santa Fe de San Francisco de Asis, as the Spanish named Santa Fe, or—its native name—Bead Water. Perhaps you start out by the highway access to Tesuque, Dry Spot. Perhaps you begin at El Rancho or Pojoaque or Cuyamungue or Nambé, and you walk all the way to the Santuario de Chimayó on Good Friday. The day a broken body was changed for a whole one, an old for a new. Your feet on the dirt, your feet on the gravel and blacktop, praise that change.

Before dawn you'll be cold. The full moon over the Jemez will light your left shoulder; Venus will glow on the right rim of the sky above the Sangre foothills. Out on U.S. 285, sheriff's cars cruise the lane next to the pilgrims, slowing down speeders. In Nambé the trees talk, dogs bark. The sleeping hills are black.

The Sangres roll. Sunburst pierces the clouds, reveals the flesh of the hills, tinged with red and shadowed with violet, endlessly folded, clutched by the roots of piñon. Out of black-and-white morning sharpness, earth brown houses appear, blue doorways. There's not much gravel shoulder to walk on. You slip, the little rocks skidding beneath your feet. Maybe you have blisters. Certainly you've had a pebble or sand in your shoe. Maybe your hip joints ache or your tailbone or the small of your back, or your calf and thigh muscles have stiffened. A yellow finch dazzling a tree tip reminds you that your spirit rides the top of your head like a bundle.

Take a donut, a slice of orange, a cup of hot coffee from the people along the way who've set up trays and coolers to feed you. If it snows, hunch your shoulders, tuck your face, and keep walking. If it's fair, you may tie your coat-arms around your waist and feel your skin tighten with sunburn. Your mind may be busy—or clean, as though you had no home to go back to. For this one day, the road is all the home that is necessary. For this one day, you do not make the mistake of feeling alone. So many people, so many stories are walking beside you.

I

✤

'*Orita*
on the Road
to Chimayó

WHEN GOOD FRIDAY fell in March, it often snowed, and next day the *New Mexican* ran photos of pilgrims trudging into the white flurry, heads bent, cold hands shoved up their sleeves. But this Friday landed three weeks into April. The sky glowed like a turquoise bowl, from the Sangres to the Jemez mountains, over the piñon hills, over the tiny, toiling people. They streamed from the south, from Pojoaque and Santa Fe, even Albuquerque, walking the sides of the highway to keep out of the way of cars.

Back here, on this particular jog of a shortcut off U.S. 285, they had to keep out of the way of three young firemen who were running to Chimayó. The firemen wore gym shorts and football jerseys cut off at the ribs. One wore a turned-round LOBOS cap. They had dark, slim-muscled legs without much hair, and their stomachs were flat now, but not for much longer. Their barrel chests would plump out. They called to people *Gangway!* or they ran around them so close that people jumped aside, stumbling and sliding on the gritty shoulder.

The firemen hadn't yet caught up to Catherine Sachett, a woman with the long, sad face of an El Greco count. Catherine was dedicating the first mile of her pilgrimage to the exorcism of her ex-husband. She was well now, except for those traces of Pete. Her sickness and the loss of her breasts had just . . . erased him. First to go was his great jackass laugh, then eye contact, then his voice faded so that she kept after him, repeating, "What, babe?" He had managed to make love to her after the operation, give him that. And it wasn't that he turned her around; she liked it that way. It was how he touched her—his hands fast, lifeless, quickly withdrawn. Pulling up the sheet, she'd leaned against the head-board and asked him, "Where's my husband?" A few days later Pete

3

disappeared for real, giving Catherine, in a backhanded way, her lone advantage: her rage at him outweighed the fear of cancer.

She used to dress up in dreams—sequined minis, always Caribbean Blue—slip in the C-cup breast forms, and go kill Pete. Shooting him was good for her, she found: fury and pain swarmed from her belly, her forehead, from far down beneath her scars. She woke up with a wetness on her body, broken through the skin like dew.

Catherine sighed and shooed her ringless hands around. *Out of here, out.*

She'd promised her second mile to the sick people she visited now. To Loretta, Erlinda, and Roy, curled like children in wide white beds. And the third mile was for . . . In Mexican Spanish everything little— *chico*—can be made even littler. *Chiquito, chiquitito,* that just means something's really there. Catherine Sachett hardly knew it, but she was walking a part—*lo más chiquitito* part—of the third mile for herself, because she was still alive.

Sweat from those running firemen flicked on Benny Ortiz, and he hurled them a few words. Benny was good-looking but jittery, a twenty-nine year-old weightlifter with no Life Plan. Sometimes, really pumped, with four or five guys psyching him, he freaked himself—glided from under the iron and spread into the mirror's thin brightness. His mother thought he was walking the pilgrimage because her folded hands guilted him into it: let his father come back to them. Right. What Benny really wanted—what he'd ask for in Chimayó's little *santuario*—was the guts to tell his mother to give it up. Tune in. Get some strength. The old man wasn't ever coming back. Once, when Benny was still dumb, he'd gone to a house where his father was staying with a girl and her baby. He'd brought a bear for the kid; hey, it was his brother. And the girl—Benny could still picture her dead spider eyelashes—told him not to come around again. His father shrugged, winked, like he'd fix it later. Who's asking? Benny knew the rule: don't ask your father for nothing. He shot a swift finger to fireman number 19's back.

About that time, as Benny's finger still goosed number 19, the wind jacked up. Light started sliding from the blue bowl sky.

⁜

Because the sky had darkened, it was easy to see the man fly up as the car veered to the shoulder and caught him. He was wearing a white shirt and a white straw cowboy hat like a real Mexican, and he sailed up in a gainer except his arms weren't tucked but flung out. He landed on his back well off the road, on a piece of ground tended by a tall piñon. The driver wavered, but then nosed the car—a low-slung Buick, metallic green—back onto the road and hit the gas.

Two of the firemen pirouetted in their tracks and took out after the Buick. The third, once he wasn't mesmerized by the flying man, spotted a roadside cross held up by some decent-sized rocks. Should he EMT the poor guy now or bust that fucker's back window? Smoke one *pow!* right down the pipe. "Hold on, don't move him!" he called, scooped up a rock and ran off.

Catherine Sachett found the victim first, on a hard swell of ground behind the piñon. She knelt beside the hurt young man, a boy really, of eighteen or nineteen. The next person to run up, a man about Pete's age but with an easy brow, took one look, repeated after Catherine, "Ambulance," and sprinted out toward U.S. 285 for help.

The hip was mangled, but worse, the boy seemed not to feel it. He didn't respond when she pressed her palm to his groin, through his raveled jeans, which were growing wet and red. He gazed up at Catherine as to a face in an alarming dream.

Aquí está, oh no, Brother Teo the historian, whom he'd always displeased. Though Brother begged him to memorize the blessed lives, the boy could never remember which saint had burned, which had been ripped by lions, which had her breasts sliced off, which sat old and feeble in the temple door repeating to the heedless, "Love one another." Brother Teo reported him to his mother. Then they exchanged expressions: Brother, eased, departing to coach the soccer team, and his mother's face drawn long and sad. When he saw how sad she looked, the boy thrashed.

With one hand, Catherine stroked his chest until he calmed and even smiled at her. With the other, she pressed a clean handkerchief to the bleeding. She didn't know much first aid, but growing up in south Texas had taught her some Spanish. The wind was rising; she bent close. "*¿Dime, chulo, cómo te llamas?*"

The boy told her, his tone straining a beat, urgent, and he gestured. Verdiano, his name was Verdiano. When he flashed a nervous smile, his kid mustache looked even wispier, like a teenage Zorro's, and he stared up at her with eyes that were big, dark, and clear. But he didn't know

'Orita *on the*
Road to Chimayó

where he was—she could see that. Other pilgrims discarded their staffs in the ditch, tracked over from the road, and gathered by the piñon, asking questions. One old man, his cheek stapled in on itself in a deep scar, crossed himself and hunkered down at the boy's head. "Hey, let's get the wind off him," he said. Those who'd happened to be on this shortcut shuffled together, elbow to elbow.

Turning his head slowly to take them in, Verdiano murmured, "*Frío, hermanos.*" He spoke so familiarly that people hurried to pull off sweatshirts and windbreakers. When Benny Ortiz stripped off his MAN-POWER T-shirt, a couple of women raised their eyebrows. The staple-faced man, already squatting, took it on himself to receive the clothes, duckwalked a step and spread them on the boy. He tucked some gray sleeves beneath the boy's worn-down Chihuahua heels.

Swiveling his head again, Verdiano addressed them "*Gracias . . . gracias.*" He fixed on Catherine. Her hollow cheeks, how lines were worn all around her eyes but not her mouth, made him comfortable. Catherine told the bystanders, "He says he could have lived in the trailer with the others, but to save rent he slept in the restaurant's storeroom, so then the only thing anyone tells him is what table to clean. He says he hasn't talked in six months."

"Yo, Ms. U.N.," Benny growled, "save the translation." Benny didn't usually put himself forward, didn't pay. But he was ruffled. He was up-set. Who died and left her boss? Pectorals bulged as he knelt down, squinting at the Anglo woman. Bony, they never stopped dieting. Raw eyelids. "You a nurse?" he asked her. To keep focused, he really bored in on her. Because there was one little more thing—the way the boy said *Cold, brothers* barbed his chest. Benny'd been hit by an urge he didn't know what to do with: to make sure the kid got warm now, got an ambulance, got a doctor with some brains.

"I'm not a nurse," Catherine said. Benny craned around at the by-standers. "Anybody here a doctor or a EMT?" They all shook their heads. "Bunch of plumbers," he muttered; Catherine heard. She cocked her head at him, asking, "Look, you know first aid? You want to do this?" Benny jerked back—hey, not him. And for making fun of how he didn't know anything, he'd give her the needle back. He jutted his chin at her. "You got a pretty good hold of his privates there."

She spread her fingers so the blood seeped through, then closed them up again. People winced and murmured over the injured boy, whose olive face was a shocky white, like they were seeing it by moonlight. The handkerchief was soaked. A woman in a sunhat offered another.

Benny passed the handkerchief, then spoke into the kid's ear. He couldn't keep the Anglo woman from hearing, but he could let her know she wasn't included in any way. "Bro. Ambulance'll be here soon. Don't talk." The kid nodded at the English, smiled, turned his head until he located Catherine's sad face, and began to talk.

They were startled by the boy's thanking them for listening. "*Es que . . .*" he felt like talking, he said. He looked from Catherine to Benny, and his eyes softened and he choked. The onlookers flinched, but no blood came up. He just cleared his throat and started to talk again. He told them about his family back in Mexico, his four little sisters and his mother, who was tranquil now that an aunt had died and left them two rooms in her house. He told about his *novia,* his sweetheart, who was sick. She coughed too much and when the wind blew, she had to lie down. Her name was Ana Luz, and she sewed Ford seat covers, Verdiano said, and though he had family, she had no one but him. "Thank you, señores, but I'd better stand up now." *'Orita,* he said, meaning he'd stand right this second, in this tiny bit of now. His head lifted as though the rest of him would follow, but it didn't and his mauve lips formed an O. For a moment, they thought he might cry out.

Verdiano knew he had something urgent to do, but not what it was. Then Brother Teo's exasperated voice lanced his confusion. Staving him off respectfully with *Sí, hermano,* oblivious of his own fingers rising in a jerky ripple, Verdiano cast about in his jumbled mind for a saint to report on. Who came to his aid, inching forward with eager, earthy hands, but the least likely of luminaries—Simplicio.

Simplicio was a kitchen worker, just like him. Simplicio was a kitchen worker to the priests, but he took no vow himself because he loved a girl and wanted her, and besides, he was mostly Indian and couldn't read.

Benny, who'd ordered Verdiano to "C'mon lay back, man," recoiled at the sight of the kid's hands. They reminded him of caught fish quivering. "Hold here," the bony woman urged him to take over. Why'd she do that if she thought he was so stupid? Benny held his breath when he received the rag, feeling the trickle, the suggestion of a beat *thum . . . thum . . .* under his pressure. The woman captured Verdiano's hands and smoothed them

'Orita *on the*
Road to Chimayó

7

down. She asked the whole crowd to go through what pockets they had left for another handkerchief and then resumed pressing the wound. She passed the soaked rag to Benny, who couldn't help squeezing it and shuddering before he threw it away.

"*Una vez,*" Verdiano said, when the cook's knife slipped and cut the back of his hand and the little strings there, Simplicio put down some carrots and clamped the cook's hand between his. When he let go, the strings were whole, and the bloody cut sealed pale pink like baby veal. "*Hijo,* like veal!" exclaimed the staple-cheeked man, and the boy turned up his eyes toward the voice and smiled. "*Sí,* señor," he said. "*Y otra vez,*" the cook's helper spilled boiling fat on his shins and feet. Simplicio knelt down and blew on the burns. He rubbed some spit on the blisters. They went away. That time, the cook told the head priest, who told the bishop, who called Simplicio before him and ordered him not to do those things anymore.

Wind tossed a piece of Verdiano's hair on and off his forehead until Benny licked his fingers and combed it back. Every so often, another curious pilgrim would cross to see what was happening behind the piñon, see the boy on the ground, and stay. At first the people had shifted foot to foot, anxious. They'd scanned the sea of hills, the piñons, the arroyos, stared hard toward the highway they knew was on the other side. But then they'd just crept in closer to hear the story. What else could they do? All run off in a crowd to get an ambulance? If somebody didn't hear a phrase, Catherine repeated it in English. Verdiano would wait for her to finish before he went on. Talking calmed him, though the corners of his mouth crusted white.

One day when Simplicio was coming back from the garden with onions and garlic, he heard a scream from the church wall where some masons were plastering on a scaffold. A man was falling, so Simplicio stopped him. He didn't save him because he'd been forbidden. He just stopped him upside down in the air.

"How did he do that, Verdiano?" asked the woman in the sunhat.

"*Lo mismo,*" the boy said, licking his lips. The same as before. It was good to hear his name called. He breathed in deeply, breathed out deeply, like a fat man after a fine dinner, and said it again, "It's so good to hear my name." The little wind-tears flying out of his eyes roused a world in the sunhat woman's head. She should have had children this boy's age.

Those children, her own blood, now found themselves alone, hurt in some strange land, like this boy. Tenderly she promised, "Listen, Verdiano, we're here." The staple-faced man asked, "So what happened? Did Simplicio save the mason?" The woman jabbed him with her elbow. "Let the boy save his strength."

Verdiano meant to gesture as he spoke, but his hands moved apart from his words; that frustrated him. He shrugged and laid them on his chest, as though they were gloves he'd taken off.

Simplicio had to go ask permission to save the man, Verdiano told them. He was only a kitchen worker. So the mason stayed in the air upside down while Simplicio found the bishop. When he doffed his hat, he saw how his hands were dirty from the garden; abashed, he hid them behind his back. He would obey his superior. Yet . . . he wanted to save the mason. The man surely had a wife and children to feed. And then. Then he craved . . . Say the truth, Simplicio: you crave the time during these occasions when all runs out and all flows in.

Simplicio lowered his head and advanced. "Do I save this man, your grace, or let him fall?" he asked the bishop.

"I told you to stop doing these things," the bishop said.

Simplicio begged, "I can't help it, holiness, they go where I do."

"Nevertheless, you don't have qualifications."

Verdiano took a long time saying that word cal-i-fi-ca-ci-o-nes; once he'd gotten it out, he seemed spent. His lids fluttered, showing the whites of his eyes. People groaned.

Benny cursed, thumped Verdiano's chest, hollered at the woman across from him. "Fix it, fix it, lady, get a new rag or somethin'!" She looked at him—híjole, what eyes, like bruises—unzipped her yellow sweatshirt, reached under a t-shirt, and handed him one of two round pink jobs with pooches like sofa buttons on them. She applied the other to the bleeding—it fit perfect.

Connection, Catherine knew too much about why people stick around not to sense a connection. She'd seen them, patients who'd become friends, holding on at seventy-nine pounds, waiting for the grandbaby, the son on the midnight plane. Catherine cupped her free hand to call him back. "Verdiano!" She had to yell. "Verdiano! This long story! Do you mean you left your novia in Mexico waiting for you?"

Verdiano returned. "But that's it," he said. "Ana Luz, I left her in

'Orita *on the*
Road to Chimayó

9

Mexico, hanging in the air." The chalk corners of his mouth frowned in dismay, stretching the wispy mustache. The clear brown eyes spilled.

Catherine understood the beauty of resignation—a way to go forward—but now she found herself coughing up its other half, the beauty of not being resigned. As a plain matter of fact, she would not allow this situation to exist. "Do something," she commanded to no one in particular. The wind whistled; a fat, wet snowflake landed on the piñon. She looked at the muscled man across from her.

Benny's features had gone a little slack after he verified to himself what exactly the woman had given him: the pink job was supposed to be her breast. The woman's gaze seared each bystander and returned to the staple-faced man at Verdiano's head. "Do something for this boy!" she shouted.

The crowd began emptying their pockets, but because they were pilgrims that day on a route with nothing to buy, they didn't have much money. Benny nodded gruffly toward Catherine, so they stuffed the money for Verdiano in her yellow sweatshirt pocket.

He said, "Look, bro. That's for your girl," but Verdiano didn't understand so he put it in Spanish, "*Pa tu novia,*" and then Verdiano tried to touch his white cowboy hat in thanks, but it had blown away long since, and besides, his hands were gone. He only closed his eyes, showing how long and thick his black lashes grew, and opened them again.

The old man with the scar still wanted to know about Simplicio, did he save the mason or not?

Benny crowded the narrow old face. "Cost you to find out, *viejo.* How much you got?"

The sunhat woman raised a dyed eyebrow and said about the old man, her husband, "*¿Ése?* He owns seventy-nine apartments in Santa Fe."

"*Cállate, mujer,* what does that have to do with anything?"

"And five houses all on the same street. *Y* one *por acá* way up on the hill. That one has a historical plaque."

The old man blinked and shifted a little in the wind, like a stunted piñon.

Benny pulled out his pockets so the wind would flap them. "Anybody else here got money?" Everybody said No, Uh uh, that was it. They'd given it all. For a minute, like he was straining at the limit—275 pounds of iron chin high and wobbling—Benny couldn't figure what to do. But then *Eeee, this is it I'm a genius,* he loomed over the old man. All the shivering still didn't make his muscles look any smaller. "Give him a house, Mr. Monopoly."

"A house?" The old man looked at the people, and they looked back at him. "Give my house? That I worked all my life for?" He thrust out his hands so they could see the pad of callus from gripping the trowel, but that was years ago and the people saw only smooth skin.

"Well, let him live there, then. Give him some rent."

"Yeah, rent." "Rent's okay." People's heads were bobbing.

The old man's eyes got slick and his face as chamisa green as the spring roadside. He held his stomach down with both hands. All the time his face was working, rubbery, like the staple was being pried open.

"Evaristo, *qué pasa?*" cried his wife. "What's happening with you?"

Coughing, Evaristo managed to sputter, "A year's free rent."

Benny gave him some breathing room, smiled. "No, you don't get it. As long as he wants."

Evaristo grunted. "It hurts like I swallowed a cleaver, five years," he said.

Everybody rumbled approval. Catherine informed Verdiano, whose face, by now as white as a Japanese dancing girl's, didn't change. Two more spring snowflakes lumbered down. The bystanders hugged their own arms. "Look, take this." Catherine gave her sweatshirt to Benny, who tugged it on, the cuffs hitting him midarm. He zipped it up tight and by main force did not look to see how level the pocket on her T-shirt lay.

Once he'd made the hard decision, old Evaristo's next one was surer. "He can live in the little *casita* on Scissors Street, the first one I bought. Let him bring his *novia* there. *¿Cómo se llama?*"

All the rest had gone past Verdiano like so much chatter, like restaurant conversation; he couldn't quite attend to it. But *novia,* Verdiano heard. "Ana Luz," he said.

"No, not that house!" Evaristo's wife had his number. "That one is falling down."

"Hey, a little mud." Her husband threw out his arms. "I will provide." Saying it, he was an actor, but with the little sentiment echoing, bouncing off people's impressed faces, he began to believe, *un poco, un*

'Orita *on the*
Road to Chimayó

poquito, you know? He liked how it sounded. He cleared a single snow-flake above Verdiano's head. "I will provide."

"They'll have children, Evaristo." His wife enlarged the world—now Verdiano and Ana Luz had dear little babies the ages her grandchildren should be. "Get them a new roof, a washer-dryer. Some carpet, *entiendes?* Some of that champagne color, it goes with everything."

Evaristo's half-face bloomed out. "No problem."

Benny grumbled, "Okay, you paid, you can ask now."

The old man was blank. Ask what? Ay, the curse of old age, he couldn't remember anything he needed to know. "Ask what?" he said.

"The story. Did Simplicio get the mason down or not?"

So they turned to Verdiano and asked him, and he was about to answer when the car drove up.

✣

A green Buick with the back window smashed coasted to a stop by the ditch. Those runner firemen, they'd caught up to her. One scared her foot off the gas with a rock hurled through her rear window; the other two ran alongside until the car stopped rolling. They had to make her raise her head off the wheel and hear what they were telling her. They had to get her to unlock a door. They had to talk her into unclenching her fist and giving them the car keys. It took some time, but finally they'd made her do all those things. Then they slid in and turned the car around.

Three men in wet gym shorts lunged out the doors and dragged over a girl by the tender part of her arm. The crowd melted back, all except Evaristo's wife, who pointed a red finger, "*¡Mira!* Look at that busted headlight. Look at the dent! It was her, all right." A hissing noise came from the people, and just then a cop car approached and they cheered. "Hey! Hey! Here they come," people yelled, and, "It's about time," and, "Where's the ambulance?" but even though a fireman loped out from behind the piñon, semaphoring and whistling, the cop car drove right by. "Eeee, those guys are more stupid than dirt," the fireman said. He left the girl and took off chasing the cruiser.

Another fireman hauled her through the crowd of people right up to the hurt boy. She took a lot of little steps because her white lace mini cut any natural stride, and her white high heels made her sink and trip over the uneven ground. A second after the girl stumbled by, they could smell her. She smelled like piña coladas and peach daiquiris and crème de menthe with shaved chocolate and amaretto sours with extra cherry juice. She stared down at Verdiano, her huge brown eyes smudged all around with flicks of mascara.

Nobody said anything. Some of them stood on their toes to see what she was going to do. They thought the girl would fall on her knees in her white Easter mini, clench her hands, and cry. Say she didn't see him. Say it was an accident, she didn't mean to hit him. Never in a million years did she . . . that's what they were expecting. But the girl just curled her lip, breathed through her mouth, and tried to back up. Her wide eyes kept jerking away from the boy on the ground to the people around her. She twisted her head like someone was poking her with a stick.

Finally a fireman narrowed one eye and nodded his heavy head two or three times to show how serious he was. "If he dies, you're a murderer," he pronounced to the girl. The bystanders agreed with him. They had some names for her, and they weren't just mumbling. They were making sure she heard. Somebody reached past the fireman and shoved her. "Hey, don't do that," another person said and shoved her back. Evaristo's wife dug two red fingernails into the girl's lace shoulder blades, giving her a pinch. This one here, this very girl broke her children, never even looked back as they bled on the road. "Little *puta* hit and run," she accused. The girl whimpered.

The girl and the whimper made Benny Ortiz kind of sick. Couple a years ago it might have been fun to shove her, but not now. The kid was still going to be lying here with most of his blood leaked out, wasn't he? Benny made the first speech of his life. "Hey, back off," he told the bystanders. "She's lost it. Like if your dad was poundin' your mom and you climbed up in a chair and clocked him with the steam iron, then when he woke up you swore you didn't. I mean, you stared at that iron, and you truly believed you didn't. It's too big to handle. Look at her, man, she ain't got her lights on."

But nobody paid much attention. "*Mira*, kid," a fireman hooked his thumb at the girl and spoke past Benny to Verdiano. "This is the one did it to you." People stopped muttering and watched to see what would happen.

Verdiano opened his velvet eyes on the girl. Pink, the most delicate pink, a drop of red in an ocean of white, tinged his cheeks.

'Orita *on the*
Road to Chimayó

13

"Ana Luz," he said.

The fireman yelled in frustration. "No, no, man, wake up! *This* is the one hit you!"

"Ana Luz, I can smell your cough syrup."

The girl surged back, but the fireman had her clamped.

"It's good you drank it because the wind is blowing."

She shook her head, her pretty face contorted.

The sunhat woman cried, "Little bitch hit and run! You ought to get down on your knees and beg him you're sorry." With that, the woman stepped up and pushed her to her knees, so that when she fell forward the girl's black-streaked cheek touched the boy's white one.

Verdiano's eyes glittered. His chin was trembling. Here she was, his *novia*, all dressed up. After a grinding day shift, she must have sneaked in at night to make this dress. He could see how it must have been. Ana Luz with her bowed neck, hiding far in the back where the seat cover foreman never inspected, her foot speeding the machine's pedal. For her health, for the bounty of her love, he had walked the pilgrimage—and now this. How had she managed to find him? Softly, through a froth of rosy bubbles, Verdiano praised her name.

"Ana Luz. Who could have done this but you?"

It was like the girl had been electrocuted. She leapt to her feet and broke the fireman's grasp. Flailing her arms, she beat her way through the bystanders, who reeled back from her blows, her scent of curdled sugar. She made it to her car, where a fireman leaned leering against the Buick's door. The girl threw back her head and howled.

Evaristo hoisted himself up and limped over to her. First he got her by the shoulders and gave her a few shakes, then he talked to her. After a while he took the girl's arm like they were crossing a busy street or he was escorting her down the aisle in her soiled Barbie bride dress, and he walked her back to Verdiano.

The girl's face kept changing. Her eyebrows would draw together and apart; from wide and blank her eyes would focus. Finally her shoulders sagged. She wiped her face with her hands, looked down at Verdiano, and her red lips parted like a little slit heart.

Verdiano's brow furrowed the slightest degree, as if he were listening hard. He breathed in, eating the rose bubbles. Then, like someone taking his picture told him to stop goofing around and get serious, c'mon freeze for the camera, he was still. People drew forward, waiting for him to let the breath out, but Verdiano kept it.

The girl's eyes rolled back then, and they had to grab her and hold her for maybe ten more minutes until the cop car, with ambulance trailing, screeched up in a fishtail stop. The doors burst open, and two state cops sprang out. Taking his time, a fireman slid from the back seat and bent over to massage his hamstrings.

⁘

Flashing and whooping ("Aw, man, what *for*," said a fireman), the ambulance sprayed them with grit and pebbles. People kneeled down where Verdiano had lain, picking through the pile of sweatshirts and windbreakers to find their own. Shrinking the world to regular size, oh much better, Evaristo's wife sent a prayer for the *pobrecito*, the little *mojado* dead so young, and set about provoking her husband. "*Bueno,* that dump on Scissors Street, you got your rent back, are you happy?"

Evaristo blew on his hands and rubbed them, rubbed his face, yeah, he was still there. "Hey don't call it that, okay?" His first house. A million adobes he'd laid, a million cinderblocks fit and grouted, miles of scaffolding climbed, saving up for it, his little cornerstone. Yeah, he decided, it was a terrible thing what happened here but not so terrible to have his casita back.

Benny peeled off Catherine's yellow sweatshirt; it was way stretched out. He found his bloody T-shirt in the pile. People who'd carried staffs retrieved them from the ditch and stood by the road, trying to clear their heads before they continued their walk.

Who felt like going seven more miles to Chimayó? Nobody, but were they supposed to turn around and walk back to Santa Fe? With all the world heading the other way? Besides, the day was warming up again. The wind had dropped. The sky was lightening into blue ribbons, and see—there on the wavy piñon hills a little gold was shining. "Poor kid," a fireman crossed himself before jamming on his LOBOS cap. Another one slapped his flat belly and did a few calf stretches. They all ran off, slim muscles prancing. "*Híjole,*" a voice carried back to the last two left, "this damn weather is so crazy."

Catherine lowered herself to the roadside and propped her head on her knees. She needed to sit a while, allow her breath to calm. As she wiped her streaming face with the hem of her T-shirt, she saw the

'Orita on the
Road to Chimayó

muscleman shoot her a glance. He stood in the dusty road shifting his weight, rubbing his forehead. Then he squatted down and, barely meeting her eyes, held out her pink breast. Because his face was so serious, she didn't laugh—though it was funny how he handled the foam rubber. With unease but with respect. Reluctant but wanting something— like Simplicio advancing on the bishop.

When the woman smiled to herself, Benny found her face less weary, her eyelids less scraped, less blue, her wide mouth harmless. In order to stick the breast in her sweatshirt pocket, she had to remove a wad of money. "Oh no," she said, fanning the bills of Verdiano's collection.

An idea struck Benny—it was just that 'orita, he couldn't shape words— could they find Ana Luz? Because the money belonged to Ana Luz, and of all the people there, Verdiano belonged to him and to this woman. She had no breasts. She really had no breasts. Benny was having this crazy sensation of his hand reaching out, simultaneously seeing in his mind how it would be—smooth, sealed, her pink chest. Like it would hurt him to touch it. And what was weird was he didn't flinch, didn't grimace. She was clasping his wrist, whether to slap him back or to keep him with her, Benny couldn't say. He couldn't get out even one word.

It was like he'd been falling, hurtling down headfirst, only to be stopped midair and set down . . . shocked, dizzy, dumbfounded by the rescue.

Everything
Moves

FOR SOME MONTHS after his heart attack, William Shaw had possessed that luminous gaze through which life is unbearably precious. He was near-sighted and deliberate, living in nuance, the world beautiful as a child, and sad, and simple. He was aware he presented a social problem. He enfolded his neighbor Mrs. Archuleta, who asked after his health in a kindly way. He blurted sincerities. Without explanation he withdrew into the spangled texture of a moment. Alone on his patio he wept at the spreading light behind the Sangres when the cottonwoods in the evening chill stood large and black and waiting.

Shaw exercised, reformed his meaty diet, stopped cheating with cigarettes altogether, and at publishers' functions, at book signings and lunches drank club soda with lime. Pursuing his own brand of spiritual rehabilitation (and in case he should become bedridden and die there), he fortified his home with beauty. Into this laid out and visible life came Mike Garcia, who built him a set of willow-front cabinets. The changed Shaw admired him purely, without envy. With advancing degrees and the affirmative-action magic of *Garcia*, Mike had left off the academic climb and returned to New Mexico to learn the profession of his grandfather Celestino. It seemed to Shaw that Mike Garcia—working, singing, cursing in two languages—was the proprietor of his life.

One evening after the cabinets were installed, Mike had gone on drinking Shaw's excellent beer and talking with him. They hit on the subject of fathers. Shaw mentioned that his had never returned from a German prison camp. Mike said he'd been raised in one. In the middle of a story about a rigid, distant father, Mike covered his eyes. This did not embarrass Shaw. His own precariousness made him bold, or natural. He put his arm around the younger man's shoulders, and they sat still and quiet in the dim kitchen. Providing this comfort, Shaw was filled, sustained. He savored the settling blue evening, the red of the peeled willow switches, his own breathing.

He and Mike took a few long walks, talked about Shaw's two extinguished marriages and Mike's problematic one. Mike's wife had lately insisted he go with her to a channeler. The woman spoke with a British accent and claimed a spirit guide named Antelope. She settled herself into a trance, sleepily describing Mike's previous lives as a selfish Arab sheikh (his wife's blue eyes bored into him here) and a Manchurian holyman in a purple hat. As a few raindrops landed on the tin roof— Mike rolled his eyes at Shaw—the entranced woman leapt from the chair and ran outside because her car windows were down.

They laughed. Shaw knew vaguely that he had a spurious supernatural offering to compare with Mike's—what *was* it?—but he was suddenly arrested by Santa Fe's October light—warm, flesh-toned, the color of a young girl's face.

Later on, in the winter, visiting along with his wife, Mike hooted at Shaw's new bedroom walls, plastered with mica chips. *Extremely cosmic, dude!* Shaw finally shrugged, *Extremely, dude*, and laughed with him. But he'd been irate, ready to defend his taste. With a shock he saw that his luminous time, following whatever laws it did, had passed. For a week Shaw tested the flatter air; it did not come back; he was bereft. He felt raw, without the promise of beginnings. But he was also a little relieved. He resumed. He reclaimed his old self-policing, his sarcasm and his small talk, dispensed with benefit of doubt, began to contemplate women. (Mike's wife was a beauty.) And he connected Mike Garcia to the critical moment he descended from gauzy upper regions and slammed into his feet again.

✢

Ten o'clock already, a glorious April day. Shaw sat under a faded pink umbrella outside the Dairy Queen, looking up now and then toward the highway. He shaded his eyes. Pilgrims streamed from the south, in twos and threes, singly and in family knots, walking the side of the highway toward the Nambé road and the turnoff to the village of Chimayó. Half an hour ago, a bearded, work-booted man had trudged by, hefting on his shoulders a two-by-four cross. Down the road a ways, another man slid under the cross and the first dropped back, rubbing his neck and jogging like a boxer. Now two black-haired women in pastel athletic suits passed, their ankles brisk. He shook his head. Amazing.

When Mike asked if he'd like to do a leg of this Good Friday walk, Shaw had hesitated before accepting. Mike misinterpreted his pause. "You're well now? I mean, you can do, say, nine or ten miles all right?"

Shaw assured Mike he could make that distance. And he'd appreciate a chance to see this, even as the outsider he was, the whole medieval spectacle of pilgrimage. Mike was sure he wanted company? This wasn't something he needed to do alone to extract some favor, or—Shaw smiled here—to pay for his sins? He'd asked, keeping it light, in order to monitor Mike's face for any sign of courtesy. But Mike clapped him on the back. "*Jefecito*," he laughed, using the affectionate diminutive, though Shaw had four inches and forty pounds on him, "don't you know by now? My sins have wings."

Shaw laughed with him. His own sins—not a word he used—his blunders, maybe, or the injuries he'd caused others or himself—did not have wings. They remained always available to him.

"*Cómo 'stás*, been waiting long?" Mike came upon him, hugging. How had Shaw missed him? Off balance, he embraced Mike lightly in return; he was the first to pull back. "*Bien*," he said, smiling at his textbook Spanish. "*¿Y tú?* Tired?"

"More than I thought I'd be." Mike took a deep breath, rolled his shoulders. "You're smart to start here."

Typical of Mike's generous nature, Shaw thought, to credit him with foresight instead of caution. "What time did you start?"

"Five-thirty. We've come fourteen miles already."

We? Shaw frowned. Mike stepped back, but Shaw didn't see her until Mike said, "Remember my bookkeeper? Angelena," and she said, "Ahhhh."

Shaw saw the crown of a dime-store panama. The woman was squatting, bouncing a little to stretch her muscles. "I love when he says it like that." She copied Mike, "An-ge-le-na. Like a Spanish angel swooped down to forgive me."

At Mike's cabinet shop he *had* met a bookkeeper, and she'd had a story, too. What was it? A dead lover? A soldier, wasn't it?—Shaw was almost certain, killed in that useless war. The way Mike had spoken, unasked, sideways and mumbling, alerted Shaw. To what exactly? The bookkeeper was forty and looked it, with glasses and gray-streaked hair ineptly pinned, a long skirt. Something about the woman had startled him, though. Her slimness, and a glance she'd narrowed on him before turning to her papers. Shaw extended his hand. The woman grasped it, but not to shake; he caught on and pulled her to her feet. The hat brim tilted.

Shaw found himself looked through. Instead of the usual exchange of glances, he received a swift self-inventory: a big man in his early fifties, whitish hair curling below a baseball cap, crisp windbreaker, expression tentative. He had to marshal himself to focus on her: slim, yes, but not a slight woman. If she'd been a girl of twenty, he'd have predicted lots of lush flesh to come; instead, this woman looked honed down to the sturdy bone. The hat shifted a degree and the light fell differently: my God, not a soft angle to her face, all planes. Cheeks like wedges. Shaw remembered himself and greeted her. "Good to see you . . ."

"Lena. And I'm his *ex*-bookkeeper. Excuse me, what was your first name?" Lena raised her eyebrows at Mike, who jumped in with "Bill," just as Shaw offered "Will." He blinked at the sound of it. Will Shaw had driven away from his first wife in a Volkswagen, in 1965.

Shaw sat while Mike ate two paper platefuls, breakfast burritos followed by donuts and coffee. The place was noisy with walkers, pilgrims; a number of wooden staffs leaned against the vinyl booths. Lena stayed a long time at the counter; Shaw was glad. He asked about Mike's shop.

Mike's eyes lit up, and he drew on a napkin a cabinet door design, shading in the cutouts, the crosses. "Southwestern stuff's red hot right now. San Diego's buying. Dallas. The problem is they don't care if we make it or some monster factory in North Carolina."

"But yours is the real thing, *que no?*"

Mike smiled. "My grandfather used a pattern like this."

"How's your father?"

Mike's smile faded. But for their evening back in the autumn, Shaw would not have asked. Mike had a fine wide face, dark and open, always open, and the primness about his mouth now was so incongruous as to touch Shaw.

Mike gazed over his shoulder toward the highway. Slowly his pained face cleared. A teenage girl and boy walked backward, shaking their fingers at an eager dog, ordering it home. Mike lifted his chin at the pair and turned to Shaw, almost whispering. "It's wonderful, isn't it, that they do this? All these people, walking. Eee, New Mexico."

Shaw smiled. The *Eee* was local diction; you heard it all the time.

Eyes shining, Mike corrected himself. "That *we* do this," he said, with a stroke admitting them both to the day and the ritual. He asked then about Shaw's publishing business.

Shaw described a stunningly photographed Southwestern Styles design book, which he hoped would carry his pet: a study of selected war poets. While he was praising that slim book, Lena slid so quietly into the seat beside Mike that Shaw hardly noticed her. When he did, it was because she drew an inverse attention to herself. She drank water from the paper cup with her eyes slit in a peculiar way and then ate a strawberry sundae intently and in silence. Mike murmured, "Bite?" Lena slipped him a spoon of ice cream and strawberry juice. Mike's interest in the war book had kindled Shaw's enthusiasm. Too bad they weren't alone. Out beyond the highway, the sky was open and endless and clean.

Shaw grabbed his walking stick, ready to go. Mike had one, too, carved as you might expect from a woodworker, but Lena was empty-handed. And poorly rigged out: her dusty jeans worn thready in the knees; too many layers—both a red and a blue shirttail hanging out beneath her yellow sweatshirt. Shaw judged her tennis shoes flimsy and too old.

"How many more miles?" she asked when they were on the dirt shoulder; when Mike told her, she blew out her breath and rubbed her knees. "Dumbo didn't warm up," she said.

Shaw forced a smile. His instinct was right. She would drag them back. She might even give out and strand them. Women like this, he thought; not complaining really, they don't seem to burden but they do. By their very presence. And then she confirmed it.

"*Dime, Miguel, 'mano . . .* if I fall down will you carry me?" She swept off the hat; her hair flagged out. Shaw was unprepared for the beauty in her hard, downcast face.

"Until I fall down, too." Mike's dark eyes were full of pleasure.

Shaw drew back from what he saw as a private conversation; he faced the road. Three young Hispanic men in army green went by, their hooded eyes passing over him silently. Had he made a mistake in coming today?

His self-censure mechanism zeroed in, telling him he was larger, whiter, crisper than the world around him. Well, so what if he was? And yet . . . did she sense it?—Lena had gently tapped his forearm. "I've read a few of your poets," she said. Her husky voice held a different note now, a kind of neutral kindness meant as welcome. He liked that, her brushing his arm, he liked that very much, but to his surprise Shaw resented the neutrality.

And then . . . *your* poets. As though no one else were interested in them. "Have you?" he got out. Why should it bother him now to be included out of politeness, as at a dinner party? They had started off; his strides lengthened so that he had to glance at her over his shoulder. Shaw stumbled on a rock and fought for his balance, which brought his annoyance near the surface.

"Wouldn't think you'd have come across Trakl or Lewis." She might have replied, but Shaw charged on. "I bet you know one we've omit-ted—Seeger and his 'Rendezvous.' Because so much was made of it being John Kennedy's favorite. 'Apple blossoms,' 'flaming town,' 'When spring brings back blue days and fair,' etc. Almost more associated with 1963 than 1918."

Lena was even with him now, her mouth opened. With irritation, Shaw noticed a smear of strawberry glaze at the corner of her lips. She was of an age to recite it, and he hoped she wouldn't go on much past the banal first line: "I have a rendezvous with death," but she stopped, took his hand, and clamped it to her breast. Shaw was stunned. Whether it was the red stain on her mouth or her bright-eyed smile, for one irrational second Shaw thought she might bite him. He stepped back, but she kept his hand, not on her breast really, but in the bony valley of her sternum. She told him, "In here nobody's damn cross is missing," and dropped his hand.

Shaw recognized the line, a misquote of . . . whom? He understood the reproof and flushed. Mike was laughing. "I'm not sure but I think she got you, *Will*," he said.

And Shaw, on automatic, precisely as if his voice box had been pinged with a rubber hammer, asked, "When's Alex going to pick us up? And how is she, by the way?" Alex was Mike's wife, blond, older than Mike (more in Shaw's ballpark, really), handsomely trust-funded, and posses-sive. Something told him Lena would mind the question. Such a dig would have been impossible when his life was tenuous. He felt—what *was* happening to him?—gratified with the result.

For the woman walking beside him in the great sweep of New Mexico grew small and tawdry. Her fists dragged down the sweatshirt pockets. The crease between her eyebrows, habitual, deepened.

Mike hadn't answered him. So, Shaw thought, bingo.

They climbed a little hill, a shortcut away from the highway. Their staffs digging in, Mike and Shaw descended together in the soft pinkish dust and waited. "I'm glad you came, man," Mike said to him, then glanced away.

Shaw cleared his voice of accusation or curiosity. "You needed a chaperone?"

Mike grimaced.

"I thought you and Alex were back on track. A new understanding, new beginning, what was it you said? Had a kind of campaign ring to it."

"Campaign." Mike tipped his finger toward Shaw. "You hit it there."

"So why ask Lena along?"

But then Shaw put it together: *ex*-bookkeeper, she'd said. "She quit, right?" She must have handed him her shop key, gathered her things, say, a photo on the desk, a glasses case, purse, keys. And Mike would be mashing a dust mask, his mouth uncertain. "You just couldn't let her walk. Could you?" Shaw almost crowed; he was truly entertained. The beautiful Alex had pressed too hard, Lena not pressed at all. Irresistible.

He calmed his tone. "If Alex doesn't know already, I'll bet she's a whiz at reading between the lines."

"Lena's car's parked in Chimayó. We don't all go back together."

"*Claro,*" Shaw said, by which he meant *No kidding.*

"Ease the fuck up," Mike growled, and they stared at each other until Mike compressed his lips. "*Oye, jefe,* did I claim to know what I'm doing?"

Lena had topped the hill and was loping down, yelping *Ow ow.* Mike caught her outstretched hand. After a second's hesitation, when he saw it was aimed for him, Shaw caught the other. She blinded him with a smile. Shaw was soothed and exhilarated, discomfited again, turned inside out. The country lane they met was tunneled with trees in sharp April green, and by a stretch of imagination, they might have been hiking in Tuscany.

Everything Moves

The lane led to a bare, brown rise; at the crest stood a tin-roofed church. The place was empty for the moment, and they sat in the back row to rest. The church was light, airy, free of those families of dolls and images often found in the village churches. It had an episcopal look, blond and clean. Lena took the panama off, set it beside her, and shook her hair. She skinned off her red turtleneck and went out to the font. She returned with wet fingers, her thin blue tank-shirt splashed, and knelt, forehead resting on her knuckles. Then she eased herself back, draping her hair over the back of the pew, closing her eyes. Shaw stared. Her nipples had hardened beneath the thin shirt, but her shoulders had none of a woman's rounded slope; they were as compact as a boy's. Here on these polished alder benches she looked wild and out of place.

Then he noticed Mike looking at her. Shaw's own stirring subsided— *Alex won't stand this for a minute, buckaroo.* Mike turned and caught the irony in his face. Mike's glance was flat, and Shaw, with bad grace, grabbed his staff and left them, slipping outside. He'd been going to drink from the water fountain, he was thirsty, but now he could not comfortably return.

When they did not follow, Shaw took off his cap and paced the point overlooking the next leg of the road, wind whipping his hair. He yielded to the image: Mike kneeling between her legs. His strong fingers crooked in the waist of her jeans, the heels of Lena's hands helping him, the muscle ridging her thigh. Then Mike gripping her toward him, his mouth on her, the panama knocked into the aisle—*Why was he doing this?* Shaw pounded the staff on the packed earth, jarring his wrists as it recoiled and bounced. He resented being third party to a mess. He was angry with them for being as they were, angry with himself for minding—why on earth should he mind? He had no great claim on Mike's friendship.

He was angry now, he realized, because he was thirsty and because he'd half expected Mike's presence to work its odd magic on him, to make some large thing happen. Shaw sat down, gouging cornrows in the dirt. When he looked up Mike and Lena, the wind lifting her hair, were walking toward him apart. Between them he was sure he read a set and settled distance. Lena's palm brushed the crown of her head, and she made a face and went back to get the hat.

Mike squatted down by Shaw, saying, "Tell me the funniest joke in the world."

"Wouldn't help."

"You're so wrong."

So Shaw reported a passable joke he'd heard from his printer the week before. As he and Mike hunkered like tribesmen, backs fending off the wind, the joke began to sound funny to both of them. In the easy camaraderie of the moment, Shaw flung back his head. The blue sky held an immense variety of drifting cloud life; above his head a vertebrate streak crossed a white swath as delicately ribbed as picked fish bones or a mimosa fan. They waited until Lena passed them before they got up.

Mike ran, whirled her round, hoisted her. She let herself be slid down the front of him, the blue shirt hiking up her ribs to the crease of a bare breast. *Just opens his arms*, Shaw marveled, *and what he wants comes into them*. Shaw turned and strode away toward the blacktop. He told himself that later, in the sparkling evening of his room, he wouldn't still crave to be touched like that or resent the man who was.

✣

They left Nambé's greening lanes and giant cottonwoods behind. The next stretch was the long road into Chimayó. Hills of scrub piñon, dry sand arroyos, loose dirt, scalding highway and wind. The sky was a baked blue bowl with light slipping off it.

People skirted round them; Lena was limping. They edged back to let a bannered procession pass, maybe twenty members of Saint Therese Little Flower chanting prayers as they walked. *Now and in the our of our death*, Shaw heard. Mike bent over with his hands on his knees. "Hanging in there, dude?" Shaw asked him. Mike shot him the finger.

But as he straightened, he gave Shaw a smile. "You must be cured." His tone warmed Shaw, and they started off again with Shaw in the middle.

"I am." Shaw dug his staff into the dirt. "Hey," he exclaimed, "remember your channeler of the car windows? I've got a bogus story like that." In Naples once, he had been directed to a chapel that housed miraculous relics of San Gennaro, a skull and a phial of blood that was reported to liquefy several times a year, possibly corresponding to the dates of the martyr's trials and death. What these were—a fiery furnace, wild beasts, decapitation—Shaw didn't recall, maybe all three. He'd stood outside in a crowd of people until he tired; the line crept, and those ahead kept admitting others. So a group of people around Shaw, Americans and English, adjourned to a cafe, had a few rounds, and invented the thing. All right, how would the blood animate? Almost imperceptibly, they thought. Voices overrode one another, contributing: a brightening, a sheen, a shimmer so negligible as to be the beholder's own blink.

Shaw, several drinks to the good, had held the opposite view. He argued that pain would remember itself with violence. He'd fiddled with the fountain pen in his breast pocket. Like this . . . a detectable wetting as from a wound, and out of that, all at once, the bubbling of fresh blood! A splash of black appeared on the white of his pocket, glistening, spreading down in a horrible rivulet. "He's ruined his shirt," someone said, while the rest fell silent, shocked despite themselves, mesmerized by the gush of black ink. Shaw smiled at the memory.

"I win," Mike said. "The car windows are way better."

"But which way was it?" Impatient, Lena seemed to think Shaw should know.

"Never found out." Why hadn't he just asked one of the dozens of Neapolitan women for a description of the relic? Shaw knew why: his Italian being less than rudimentary, he foresaw himself a stuttering hulk with a stain on his shirt. Back in his luminous period he wouldn't have minded that, would he? No, then he'd have plunged in. He'd have been pleased enough to watch the woman's white, ringed hands flutter in the dusk.

"Funny," he said, "after the heart attack, I called my daughter at all hours, visited, too. Listened. Tried to show her I loved her. Told her she was a good person, that no, I didn't hate her mother. Warned her babies seem forever but they're only a flash."

He had done this because for that time he lived without precedent; he did not care about preserving the known Bill Shaw. He had done it painfully, but that was the price of reaching her. He stammered and gushed. He sounded like a fool. During each conversation he failed and succeeded by turns, unsure whether he'd done one or the other. Yet—a warmth leapt through Shaw—enough of his awkward attempt at repair remained. "We hadn't been close before; she didn't know what to make of me. I think she liked it."

"How old is her child?" Lena asked.

"She's only twenty, doesn't have one. But . . . I was afraid I wouldn't finish."

"Finish being her father?" Lena leaned in toward him, intent. Shaw shrugged: Yes, finish being her father, why not?

Her fingertips, light in the crook of his elbow, tightened; she looked straight into his face.

Suddenly he wanted very much to tell her about not finishing. Clouds streamed by, dizzying; for steadiness Shaw dug his staff into the hard ground. He coveted Mike Garcia's . . . what? Greed? No, that was too strong. But his believing he had a right to it all . . . could two women be less alike? Alex, statuesque and elegant, with a sunny confidence that came from having known few obstacles; Lena, striking and awkward, at home only with the intimate.

"Do you remember, Mike, my telling you . . ."

Mike nodded. "The prison camp."

Shaw was pleased that his history was remembered. Some teenagers filed by, and Shaw noticed how stiffly Lena moved, how the young ones flowed by her. He took her arm and described to her the manner of his father's death.

"But that's not it. A year or so after the war, a man came to see my mother. She sent me to my room, but I hid on the landing and peered down. Nothing could have stopped me. He'd been in the camp with my father."

All Shaw had clearly seen of his father's friend was his yellow hair, combed in furrows to the forehead where it furled back in a slick wave, and a broad maroon tie. He talked about the meager food, the sickness that swept the camp. "I saved these for you," he said. The man bent forward and gave something into Shaw's mother's hands. Then he stood and walked a few feet away so she was alone with it.

She unfolded two tan squares and studied them. It was hard to hear his mother then; Shaw's cheek gouged into the spindles of the railing. It seemed like she wanted to know if his father had asked his friend to bring these things to her.

"No ma'am, took it on myself."

"You didn't read them?"

He'd been bending to sit, but he snapped upright. He sounded angry

Everything Moves

with her; the boy that was Shaw was frantic lest the friend take away the squares. They were letters from his father, he knew, from his father he would never see again—and maybe one of the letters was for him.

"So scrupulous," his mother said. Shaw ever after marked the word; now he wondered if the man had known it. He understood the next two: "Dutiful. Loyal." The man sat down then, and as if he'd been waiting to say only this, blurted, "He'd a done the same for me."

Shaw did not have to strain to hear what his mother said next; her voice was too high for itself. "'Dear Anne' this reads. My name is Cynthia. My husband meant these for another woman." She thrust the letters back on the visitor, whose forehead had flushed very red. She must have let him out; that, Shaw did not remember. He'd told the story evenly enough but now was short of breath.

Lena asked, "Did you and your mother ever talk about that day?"

"We *forgot* that day." Shaw handed his staff to her. He stretched his fingers; they'd been clenched, as though around a railing. He folded his hands, then spread them, then bent down and snagged a weed, chewed it. He was going to go on talking. He felt like going on, an expansiveness rising in him, but he stifled this; he did not want to usurp the conversation.

"How much better did you do?" he asked Mike and then disliked the jocular phrasing of his own question.

Mike didn't seem to notice. "I told my father I was going back to New Mexico to be a woodworker like his own father. He sent me a manila envelope of canceled checks. All the checks for my books, fees, everything the scholarships didn't pay for. No letter, just a bunch of checks torn in half. That's how much better."

Shaw thought Lena might offer something of her own, but after a few more strides in silence, she sighed, pointed to a pickup and said, "Let's stop." Mike bent over with his hands on his knees and breathed for a while. Shaw, so much fresher, suggested they rest. Mike said they could make it a little farther but then folded where he was; Lena lowered herself beside him.

All along the way people offered free refreshments to the walkers—water, fruit, coffee, cookies. They had passed one truck with a big silver cooler as Shaw told his story; he'd ignored his thirst then. Now he peeled his dry tongue from his palate and licked his lips.

He accepted a Styrofoam cup of cold red stuff, noting with keen pleasure the plump curve of the liquid's surface. Like an ocean attached to the globe of the earth! When he swallowed—Kool-Aid—he tasted the sour-fruit on his lips, his tongue, in his throat, all the way up into taste buds that seemed to be located in his ears. He found his eyes closed, his mouth filled with cold, sharp sweetness; he chewed; he swallowed again and again.

A woman whose face was like the land around him, broad and copper brown, cut with deep creases, poured him a refill and handed it back, saying, "Happy Easter to you." "And to you, señora." Shaw hoisted the Styrofoam cup to her. She giggled, hiding her mouth with one hand, which made Shaw grin and thank her, "*Muchas gracias.*" The woman giggled again, beautifully.

The Kool-Aid restored Shaw's equilibrium—and more; he settled himself on the swell of the hillside, elbows around his knees, content. Though he did not belong to this day, it was fine to sit here in its midst, in the movement of earth and people. The wind pressed him to a place among the endless foldings of sand and rock and the thrust of piñon. Behind him, the Jemez ran smooth and locomotive black, shoved through the earth; before him, the green taper of the Sangre foothills. Far across the way pilgrims crouched before a white cross dressed with a purple sash; the ribbon streamed above their heads. *Everything moves!* Shaw turned to say but was distracted by the sight of Mike on his knees before Lena.

Then he saw her feet. "My God," he exclaimed, "could you have found worse shoes to wear?" Blisters had broken and run, the heel a solid mass just rising again, her toes scraped bloody. She was patching them with Mike's moleskin with care but not delicacy, the way one sticks stamps into an album. One of the patches was already soaked and sliding. She winced, pulling on stiff cotton socks. As soon as her shoes were back on, she passed Mike a squashed pack of Marlboros from her sweatshirt pocket.

Shaw laughed when they lit up. "Now that'll pick up your pace."

Mike squinted at him before angling his face to blow aside the smoke. Shaw, smile fading, gazed off toward the flesh-colored canyons, but Lena's laugh brought him back. "We did fourteen more miles than you did, Will." She didn't bother to turn her face away. Shaw inhaled the smoke and liked it.

Everything Moves

A pickup pulled in beside them and from an aluminum lawn chair in its bed an old man hailed Mike merrily. "*¡Aquí comenzamos!*" He spread his arms. "It's a good place to start, *que no?*" Three women climbed over the tailgate and helped him down.

Mike pushed on his knees, getting up, transferred the cigarette to his mouth, and shook the offered hand. Pleasantries went back and forth. The old man clapped Mike on the back in the friendliest way, nodded to "the señora." He grinned at Shaw, who grinned back, put together a jovial greeting, and held out his hand. "*Hola, primo.*" Hello, cousin.

The old man's face puckered. "Mister, why you call me *primo?* You're not my *primo.*" He pointed at Mike and then crowded Shaw's chest. Shaw caught a whiff of an aftershave he had not smelled for decades. "*Ése,* him I was talkin' to, he din' go and call me that. You don't get to call me that."

Shaw's scorned hand fell to his side; the outline of his body tingled. He expected Mike at least to deflect the remark, but the moment stretched on, the women clucking a mild, incomprehensible protest. He felt refuted to his very core.

Lena said something beginning, "Señor," and having *primo* in it, and the words *ese* and *pardon* and perhaps *big.* She smiled at Shaw, tapping his arm, and ended with a soft but clear-eyed shrug at the old man. He blinked, folded his lips; his chin nodded. Then he turned, throwing off the urging of a woman's hand on his arm, yet following behind her anyway.

Mike met Shaw's eyes briefly, muttering, "Hey, just an old guy, Bill, don't buy into it," then he simply started off again. Buy into it? Of course Mike was right—yet Shaw found he was bearing through the wind, dense, conspicuous, encased, a tightness in the open land. He realized finally that Lena was speaking to him and half turned, "What?"

Behind him, she raised her voice. "I said, 'Did you really call and tell her all that?'"

Shaw had not the first idea what she meant.

He heard her blow out a breath with pretend exasperation. "Your daughter, Will. All those phone calls." Her tone dismissed the old man's slight and focused on the essential matter.

A little hesitantly, Shaw nodded.

Her breath tickled his ear. "Such a fine red heart you have, Grandfather." She laid her hands on his shoulders. It seemed to Shaw that she didn't touch him like a grandfather, no, not at all; she touched him like a man and who he was. Her hands took him in. Shaw swallowed and reached back to Lena's bare waist under the blowing T-shirt. The sun lay across the underside of his arm. The sky broke free of him and revolved again. "Thank you," he said.

To his relief she took her hands away without patting him. He wanted then to give to her, to ask her about her life, the soldier who'd never returned, whatever she would talk about. Mostly he wanted to ask her why she'd come today, why put herself through this trek, this pilgrimage, with a lover she was leaving and who was leaving her. Involuntarily he glanced ahead at Mike. The question flickered in his face, but he gestured toward her feet and asked, "How are you?"

Maybe she guessed it. Maybe she'd expected him to ask all along. "*Aquí no más*," she said.

Here and no more. A stock answer to the question, but not local Spanish. Shaw had heard the phrase in Madrid, a casual reply from a rumpled customer at a bar. And again before a flamenco show at which he'd paid fourteen dollars for two ounces of dry sherry. The guitarist stood next to the black-haired hostess, warming his hands with a Bic lighter. "*Aquí no más*," he'd answered a tourist's greeting, passing his fingers through the flame.

✢

Streams of people solidified on both sides of the road into two ragged columns. Shaw, Mike, and Lena were overtaken by a monk in a rough brown habit and Nikes and three people with windbreakers lettered IN MEMORY OF RAYMOND ULIBARRI. They veered around a pair of feet belonging to a young man asleep, almost in the road. Then they made the bend. Chimayó unfolded below, the brush-tops of trees, tin roofs, silver antennas. A double line of cars and vans headed into and away from the village. Shaw was bumped twice, once by a child with aluminum cans bent to the soles of her shoes, next by a heedless drunken man. The man also knocked into Lena, who would have fallen had Shaw not grabbed her.

She was struggling to stay on her feet while he . . . he was experiencing the enormous surge of energy that comes of certain success. They were almost there. Lena and Mike should separate, Lena had been kind—Shaw was inspired. He touched his knuckles to her dust-streaked, sun-

Everything Moves

31

burned cheek. "I'll carry you," he said. He couldn't keep the eagerness from his voice. He'd cut through the crush of pilgrims, of low riders and vans, pass by the penitents with shoulders bruised from the weight of lumberyard crosses. It couldn't be that much farther, and though she and Mike were exhausted, Shaw was not. He could do this. *For Lena*, he told himself but behind that anticipating her voice warm for him, her hands on him, knowing he could set her down slowly. "Here," he said, "just this last way."

Lena smiled quizzically and slipped her arm around Mike's neck. As though he'd only been waiting for that, Mike seized her waist and they stumbled on, supporting each other. Shaw watched her fingers resettle on Mike's neck and an answer from Mike's arm round her waist, but he refused that. He caught up with them. Their heads were down; they were plodding, making way for faster-walking pilgrims. Voice still light, he struck his breastbone. "Lena, don't break my heart; let me carry you."

Her arm lifted from Mike's neck. As she hobbled toward him, Shaw waited transfixed on the hot road. He waited for her as though for a tenderness suspended just outside himself. Lena thrust her dry lips almost on his. "Eee, Will," she said, "who was it didn't tell you? Our hearts are always breaking."

Her face was dirty and mocking. She let go of him and walked on alone but, through gaps in the crowd, Shaw saw Mike try to gather her in again. She raised a shoulder against him. He persisted; Lena fended his hand off and turned, intending—Shaw could see it—to keep moving and leave him. Mike pulled her round so her body turned against his body and his eyes closed, her hands held his shoulders, her forehead brushed his chest. Only in the halfway point of her slow momentum were they a couple embracing, yet they were. And then Mike stopped her turning.

Shaw raised his staff and strode on ahead, covering distance rapidly. Closer to the shrine, free refreshments gave way to commerce. Children in the yards bordering the road sold donuts, oranges, and pop from rickety card tables. The apple trees were blooming, the dirt yards full of them, their white sprays arching above blue-rimmed screen doors. Then he was there.

People, milling, talking, eating, spilled across the small plaza. They were jubilant, the Chimayó women dressed like Mexican paper flowers, blouses red and blue, blazing yellow. At the center of town stood the brown mud *santuario*, a long line of pilgrims jostling at the entrance. Shaw edged into a little store where he bought a soda from a harried matron and flung himself outside to the *acequia*, the stone channel that cut through the plaza. There over the hubbub he heard his name called.

Alex was waving to him from a bench near the *acequia*. Her short blond hair caught the sunlight; her pale arm gleamed from all the brown. She wore a long rose dress cinched at the waist with a silver concha belt, and she was beaming. Shaw glanced back toward the road.

"You made it!" she said when she hugged him.

"Was there any doubt?" Shaw had always found Mike's wife an attractive woman, but now—her full skirt cascading from the bench, her hands clasped, her smiling face lifted as though she were the center of this carnival jumble—she seemed incandescent. She had on pink lipstick, like a girl, and it suited her.

"Is Mike very far back?" she asked.

"A ways."

"Tired out?"

"Stumbling."

"Well, no wonder, he left in the dead of night. Here's the keys, Bill, the car's over by the cemetery. Go collapse. I've got a cooler with sandwiches and wine, help yourself. I'm going to meet my husband." Shaw was disoriented by her gathering her skirt, as though she were a woman of the last century, or of a dream. He felt a slow panic. Wait, it was in his mind to say. Wait, let's get a drink, no, he had one . . . something to eat . . .

"Alex." Shaw took her hand. "Come sit in the car with me. Catch me up on everything."

"I can do that in a word. Fine. And fixed and all better and just in the goddamn nick, don't you think?" Her eyes shone and she pressed his hand.

"Alex."

But she had started off. "Wait." Shaw blundered behind her, choked with resentment at Lena and Mike for their stupidity, Alex for her blithe authority. She spun, cupped his face with both hands. "Oh no, don't—," Shaw began, but she did, Mike's wife kissed him. The kiss enraged him. It was not meant for him; suddenly he could not think of one thing

Everything Moves

meant for him today except the old man's rebuke. He slashed deeper—
except a square of tan paper that could have had two scribbled words:
My son. Blood burned Shaw's neck and forehead. Hurt surged out of his
chest, quickening into a desire to hurt, so deep, so good that the release
of it overpowered him. "Hurry," he said.

Alex flashed a triumphant smile and whirled away.

His jaw felt loose, his knees unreliable. He managed to lower himself
to the flagstone by the side of the *acequia.* Spring runoff rushed down
the channel, fast and clear. He fumbled off his shoes and socks. As he
plunged his feet into the icy water, the pain struck him, and his exclama-
tion opened into a tormented shout.

Shaw clenched the rough edge of the *acequia.* To change his nature?
Now? He might just as well demand the miracle of the saint's fresh
blood. To find and tend a more easeful man in himself appeared a task
so arduous he could barely credit it, so prodigious he wanted not to see
it. But the image thrust into him like a blade: *an easeful man.* He did see,
he saw that man, and desire surged through him, parting tissue and
bone.

Shaw rocked against the wet stone. He kept his feet submerged until,
little by little, the water grew less cold. Down the *santuario* line, the
people who had heard the big man's cry turned away again. The line was
long and they stood far to the back, sore, dusty, with prayers yet to
make.

✣

Beautiful

MR. POTTER GROUPED US together because the major concepts of science remained outside our brains. He didn't want to stick me or Debbie Perkins or Zulma Díaz with kids who had already thought up great science projects. Besides teaching biology, Mr. Potter coached varsity basketball. He wanted to *win* the science fair. Some teachers are dense enough to think you don't notice when they bunch the hopeless together. The hopeless notice. "But science is everywhere!" he protested when we told him we couldn't think of a project.

We sat, our three desks angled together, our binders opened to blank pages. We didn't have access to cool materials. Craig Schuster's father was a dentist, and Craig and his partner Brad planned to use his X-ray machine to radiate mice. Carolyn Withers was building a model of a walnut shell foundation to show how strong such a construction was. Her father was an architect, and she could use his plaster of Paris and tiny doll people and tiny cars.

Zulma Díaz's parents had emigrated from Cuba, and at home she spoke Spanish. And Zulma, a skinny girl with a caramel complexion and springing hair the color of an old penny, was nervous. If somebody talked to her, her hands flew around, and she shifted her weight from one foot to the other. Like tennis players do, when they want to be ready to run in either direction. She pulled on her fingers, shooting glances at Debbie and me.

Debbie's cheek was flattened against her hand. She and I had an unfortunate history. It dated from a day two years back, when our school was about to become integrated, and our social studies teacher had decided to prepare us for this event by teaching "prejudice." Miss Kratke began her lesson by asking if anyone in our class carried Indian blood. Debbie was Indian, tall and dark—her parents had adopted her from somewhere in New Mexico—but she didn't raise her hand. She looked at Miss Kratke with evil eyes and looked away.

My hand shot up. "My grandfather's Choctaw," I told Miss Kratke.

My grandfather was only part Choctaw, but he was always telling me that ever since I was little. He'd left Oklahoma a few years after a white man had thrown his sister Lillian from a train. The *why* of his story would change—sometimes because Lillian was heading for a car in the train where Indians weren't allowed, sometimes because the man didn't want people to see her with him—but the ending never did. They were arguing out on the landing of the last car, and he pushed her. She might have just tumbled onto the cinders and gravel between the tracks, bruised herself, and dirtied her dress. But Lillian hit her head on the steel rail and broke her neck. My grandfather, a boy then, had dragged a kitchen chair to the bed where they'd laid her out and rocked against its stiff back, willing his sister to open her eyes, to unfold her hands, to get up and walk again.

"Choctaw Indian." Miss Kratke nodded. "Stand up, Patricia."

I jumped up smiling, right into Miss Kratke's trap.

Chatter died off as she paced down the aisle. The class swiveled in their seats as she planted herself a few inches from me and stared me up and down. The muscles around her eyes tightened. "Patricia McNight," she said, "what do you think *you're* doing here with these white kids? Don't you know you'd be better off with your own kind?

"Indians belong on reservations. What are you doing trying to associate with people you have no business with? People who don't care to associate with *you.*"

Miss Kratke stepped to my side, and when my head did not turn with her, she bent to my burning ear. "Your folks drink. They're lazy. They take government handouts. They're stealing from the rest of us.

"Your relatives before that were bloodthirsty savages. Your ancestors. They swooped down and slaughtered innocent children. Murdered harmless women.

"Your relatives were cruel, primitive people," Miss Kratke said. "Better if the U.S. Cavalry had killed every last one of them. Why, class?" Her gaze inched across the room like a prison searchlight. "Why's that?"

Allen Foster muttered, "Because the only good Indian is a dead Indian."

"Exactly!" exclaimed Miss Kratke. Such backward thinking, she'd declared, was pure, old-fashioned prejudice. Did the class see that? We should not judge people by their race or nationality but by their character. Did we understand now how ugly prejudice was, after this demonstration?

I hunched back into a seat that didn't feel like my seat anymore and threw a beaten glance toward Debbie Perkins. I thought she'd have some sympathy.

The blame in her slitted eyes finished the job on me. I guessed that somewhere along the line, Debbie had already had a lesson like this one, and I'd just brought it down on her head again.

Now, with the clock bearing on toward the bell, I appealed to her. "Look, couldn't your mother show us something about cameras?" Debbie's mother ran a professional photography business. She'd taken my little brothers' pictures when they were babies—first Pete's and then Tod's. Mrs. Perkins came to our house with lights on tripods, a velvet backdrop, and rattling toys. I remembered a lot of flashing.

Debbie scratched on her notebook paper in that crabbed, left-handed way she had. "My mother's been kind of sick. Besides, everybody knows about cameras."

"Mike did one on plants once," I offered. "About how they take in water so they grow. He called it 'Green Babies.'"

Zulma brightened. "My father, he always make us a big garden with plants."

Debbie's cheek was still squashed up against her hand. "That's what they're made with," she mumbled, but before Zulma could fully detect the sarcasm here she turned on me. "What grade was Mike in when he did that project?"

"Fifth."

"Oh great," Debbie said.

"Let's meet after school," I said, "that's what they're all doing." *They* being the people who knew what they were doing.

"Have to be after dance." Debbie just stated that like her dance classes would come first, no matter what Zulma and I needed to do. She'd been taking lessons for years and was always starring in some recital.

"Okay, we could meet at my house. My dad's out on strike, so Mom's working. Nobody'll be there. Except my brothers."

"Your brothers," Debbie scowled. One of the older ones, Roy, had liked Debbie, and tried in the bleak style of the McNight brothers to convey his special regard. He tore up her homework. He snagged her skirt, ripping off the yellow rickrack sewn on the hem. After the school photographer had finished Roy's sixth-grade class, Roy spoiled our fourth-grade class picture by sneaking into the back row behind Debbie and leering at her—eyes popped, tongue stuck out—just as the photographer snapped the shot. Mom fanned Roy's butt when she saw the picture. I'd wondered what Mrs. Perkins had to say.

We turned to Zulma, who seemed confused by Debbie's unfriendly reference to my brothers. "Come to your house?" she repeated. Her hands leapt anxiously apart. Debbie and I exchanged a glance.

I tried a joke. "If you come, I'll lock up my brothers. I promise."

Debbie picked up my hand, used it to trace a cross over my heart. I batted her away, protesting, "I said I promised."

This didn't break a lot of ice with Zulma. She said she'd ask her mother.

⁜

We met at my house to demonstrate how plants drink water. I'd dug out the old book the experiment came from. "Roy here?" Debbie craned around my shoulders when I answered the door.

I shook my head. "Track practice."

She stepped in, swinging a white poster board.

Zulma slid out of a two-tone Chevy that let her out at the curb. She watched it rumble off, then slowly turned and walked up the driveway, looking right and left at the neighbors' houses, her arms cradling two bunches of leafy green. She looked like a beauty queen the emcee had just presented with a bouquet, only she was colored and her bouquet was celery. That's what I mean about our materials. Craig Schuster had a state-of-the-art X-ray machine. We had celery.

Zulma was shy, at least at first. She seemed uneasy in our empty house, and, unlike Debbie, smiled when my littlest brothers Pete and Tod ran by, chasing each other.

We laid out six glasses half filled with water on the kitchen table, squeezed drops of red food coloring in each, and stuck in the celery stalks. Three had their original leaves, and three we denuded, per the book's instructions. We each ate a spare celery, and then went in my room, letting the cat in with us but locking the door against Pete and Tod. We started right away on the poster. It didn't occur to us to act scientifically—wait for the results and then illustrate our findings on the posters. We knew from the book what was supposed to happen. All that occurred to us was to get the whole thing over with.

Zulma volunteered to sketch and color the celeries. She had to keep shooing our cat, Smacker, away; he wanted to sprawl over the poster. I noticed she said some Spanish word when she shooed him. He'd side-step and then veer back again, purring like a locomotive. I ate a leftover celery, planning how to stencil our explanation around her pictures when she finished.

My room, about as big as a walk-in closet, had a mirror my mom had hung to give the illusion of space. To fool the eye, she said. It didn't. It was reliable about showing me the baby-fat figure Mom said would rearrange itself any day now. Debbie, in pink ballet slippers and jeans over her dance outfit, stationed herself right in front of the mirror. She practiced turns in it. She bumped the bed and spit out some cuss words my brothers used but I had only uttered in my head.

"It's a really little room," I said, like she couldn't see that.

"It's not the room. It's me. I didn't hold the damn center." Debbie hit her thigh disgustedly. Hard.

I learned that when three people work together, alliances shift. Debbie and I, having known each other since first grade, had the connection. But now Zulma Díaz and I widened our eyes at each other, commenting on Debbie. Why did she act so mad at herself?

She did more turns, which looked perfect to me. Then a series of them where she kept flinging out one leg from the knee and whirling. She bobbled a step as she finished these and cussed herself again. Loud. Zulma flinched over her drawing. Grimly, Debbie planted herself, slippered feet pointed in opposite directions, and made circles with her long arms.

Zulma glanced over her shoulder, as though to see if she were safe. At the sight of Debbie's arms drawing upward, arcing, floating down, she murmured shyly, "It's beautiful."

Beautiful

39

"Yeah right," Debbie growled. Zulma hunkered down again.

If Zulma hadn't used that word *beautiful,* which she meant to refer to the movement, I might not have seen it. But she did. The first in a row of mental dominoes tipped over in my head. This first was that Debbie wasn't pretty, but she was beautiful. The second was that those two could be exclusive categories. The third was that my brother Roy, who had the savvy of a red ant, whose idea of literature was Coach Thompson's playbook, had seen it before I had. Debbie had really long legs and arms, straight and clean and muscled, no bulges except for her breasts mashed smoothly against her black leotard. Her neck was a strong brown stem. Her hair was so black, so shiny, it held white light in it. She'd been letting it grow, and it reached past her shoulders now and, as she tilted her head, cut her cheek with a silky sheen. I watched how Debbie's arms framed the air, carved and told shapes in it. When her long fingers fanned, they were not panicky like Zulma's, but like a sign language speaking beauty.

The last domino to plink over was this one: Debbie didn't see it at all.

"Whoa," I whispered.

"It's wrong?" Zulma jerked back from the poster board like it had gone up in flames.

We bent over and looked. Zulma had drawn a regular green celery, then one bisected so you could see the red color rising through the stalk's blood vessels, the xylems. She'd basically copied the book. But there was something off. I cleaned my glasses with the tail of my shirt and examined the celeries again.

They weren't straight; they gave the impression of bending, swaying. They were both correct, really, but unscientific. They had personality. To me the regular celery looked like a happy old grandmother opening leaf arms to enfold her grandchildren; the curvy red-striped one looked like a sexy celery dressed to do ballroom. We studied the poster for so long Zulma's shoulders contracted.

Finally Debbie's mouth opened. I had my own opinion, but I steeled myself for hers.

She said, "Wow."

"Yeah?" Relief flew onto Zulma's face.

"Yeah," I agreed.

I paused a while, considering. "It's kind of *us.*"

In the River Province

Zulma seemed uncertain, but Debbie smiled. This was the first time since Miss Kratke's demonstration that she'd given me any kind of approval. She liked that I'd said that. I liked that I'd said that. It was just one of those unintentional things you say that shines a gleam. This poster was *us*. We weren't unscientific because we were hopeless. We were unscientific because we belonged to some different category: me, I liked language, English or otherwise; Debbie liked moving; we didn't know what Zulma liked, but it wasn't science. Darwin and Audubon wouldn't draw vegetables like Zulma Díaz did.

"Okay," Zulma said, clasping her hands.

Debbie wasn't one to make a moment of anything. She nudged Zulma, saying, "Hey, let's go check on the experiment" and flipped the lock on the door. We headed for the kitchen. Debbie had a potato peeler to scrape off the side of one celery so we could demonstrate the red food color rising in the arteries. That would be our exhibit. I'd do the text, the lettering, and voilà, a fait accompli.

Debbie threw the potato peeler to the floor. Alarmed, I hurried around her. The peanut butter lid lay tossed on the table with a smeared knife. There stood Pete and Tod, midcontest, each with three stalks of celery crammed in his mouth. Pete had the nude ones; Tod had the trees, the leaves trembling as he chomped.

"You little shits," I cried. "This was our whole grade in science."

Debbie strode over on her long legs and slapped Tod on the back of the head. He coughed out the leafy ones. She headed for Pete, her slapping hand out.

They took off running. Pete tossed his half-celeries behind him. Debbie picked up the celeries and dropped them. They were chewed up, useless. I tried to apologize, but Debbie, enraged, kept pacing past me.

"We could do it one more time," Zulma dared to suggest.

"No," Debbie snarled. "I've had it with celery."

Zulma looked crestfallen.

"Not the poster," I told her. "The poster was good. Really."

We were so easily defeated. It was like our moment of confidence was over, and we were hopeless again. We trailed outside to the steps to wait for Zulma's ride. After a long silent while, Smacker launched himself out of nowhere onto Zulma's nervous fingers, scaring her so she jumped back yelping, "Ay!" Debbie stomped at him; undeterred, he pounced on her foot. She wiggled a finger over his head and jerked out of range when he went for it. Smacker, the dumb cat, kept jumping and swiping.

I said, "Look, Smacker's left-handed like you are."

I was just trying, lamely, to find something to be friendly about. But Debbie snorted, like I'd said left-handed people were lower on the evolutionary scale.

"Jeez, Debbie, I just meant he's trying to get you with his left paw."

She played with him some more. "This cat *is* left-handed." Her head tipped. She looked at us sideways. Zulma and I looked back. "Is this the only cat you have?" she asked.

"Yeah." I was behind here, but Zulma grinned. "We got cats. Our neighbors got cats. Their neighbors got pitbulls."

"No dogs," Debbie said, after she explained the idea. We would only use cats, to keep control.

I nodded, heartened. "Okay. Hey, science is everywhere."

✤

That was our second idea: were cats right- or left-handed like people? We loved this idea. It did not come from a book; we thought of it ourselves. It was original. It restored our confidence. We met at Zulma's since she had our materials, cats. We also had pieces of string and a pencil and a sheet of notebook paper to record our data on.

And this thing happened almost right away. Zulma's cousin was out in the driveway changing the oil in his Impala. He was under the car when we walked by. All he could have seen was her feet in those scuffed, pink ballet slippers, her angry ankles. A man in love pushed himself out from under that engine so fast he knocked over the old pan with the dirty oil in it. His eyes followed the ankles up Debbie's long legs, cocked hip, long slim waist, leotard-smoothed breasts to her canted chin and planed cheekbones.

"*Dios es mi salvador,*" he said. "Blind, I could still see *esta mujer.*"

"*Cállate,* Rafi, *por favor,*" Zulma pleaded. "This is my science partners."

Rafi sat there with his head tilted back and his mouth open, his face lit up. Debbie had one of her feet out, arched, toes pointed like she might flick him away. Zulma raised her eyebrows and shrugged at me.

"What'd he say?" Debbie demanded.

I didn't tell her. Oil wound its way down the driveway. I tried to get the others to notice, but their attention was elsewhere. What a shining trail the oil formed, gorgeous, a black rainbow. It made me sad. Mr. Potter said science is everywhere? Let me tell you. Beauty is everywhere.

"Rafael—we call him Rafi—he says Hi," Zulma said.

"Oh," Debbie said, "hi." She spun away from Rafael. "There's one," she said.

"That's Diablo. He's a tomcat. Spam and Mimi, they sleeping inside."

"Here Diablo Diablo Diablo," Debbie yelled. She strode forward snapping her fingers and making sucking noises with her tongue.

"She don' know cats, does she?" Zulma murmured.

I shook my head. Diablo had leapt to his feet, black fur ridged on his spine. Tail fuzzed to maximum volume, he hissed at Debbie, then slinked rapidly away.

She complained to Zulma. "Don't they know their names?"

"Debbie. Take it easy. They don't like it when you holler at them," I said.

Rafi was right up to Debbie's ear. "You want that cat?"

Debbie retreated a step. "Yeah, we could use him." Rafi jammed next to her again, and she stepped back again, and he said, "I get him for you, okay?"

"Yeah, okay." She cut her eyes toward me, made a face. Rafi dodged a spindly rose bush and high-stepped around the corner.

We went up the cement porch past several metal lawn chairs, those nice old round-backed ones that you can rock, and inside the house. Now it was my and Debbie's turn to be shy. We were the strangers. Mrs. Díaz, much shorter than Zulma and wearing an apron, was all smiles. She offered a tray of little fried breads with jam in them; they looked like scalloped shells. We had to eat before we could do science. I thought Debbie would get impatient at this. Live and learn. She loved the shells, wolfed them down, and she followed Mrs. Díaz around with her eyes. Mrs. Díaz gave us all paper party napkins. I sat on a stuffed green chair covered with eight million doilies under a picture of a pasty Jesus wearing his bloody heart on the outside of his chest. Zulma brought her sister from a back room—a skinny, dark girl with teased hair. The sister had a baby, about six or seven months old, not crawling but sitting up wide-eyed. She wore a pink dress, little gold earrings, and a gold bracelet. Zulma's sister kept circling the baby's wrist for her, trying to get her to say Hi or Bye-bye.

More people were in the kitchen—cousins and a brother. Zulma called to them, and they came in and met us, too. Even though she was watching us to see how we took her house, Zulma was different here; her hands weren't flighty. When the baby started waving on her own, Zulma and her sister broke into happy Spanish.

It was easy for me to play with the baby—I'd always wanted a sister. Always. I'd cried rivers when my mother had stuck us with Tod, another boy. I got down cross-legged in front of her. I adored talking foreign languages. I'd had three years of Spanish and learned German from *Hogan's Heroes* on TV and French from my mother's chipped Edith Piaf record. I used what foreign words I knew and left English in the blanks. And everybody, no matter what language their brains speak, speaks baby.

"*Mira*, baybee," I said.

"*Bebé*," Zulma corrected me.

"Oh, right right right. *Mira, bebé, mira aquí. Así es como los* Munchkins wave *adiós a* Dorothy." I waved my hand side to side widely in the air. I talked in a helium-drunk Munchkin voice. "Good-bye!" I said. "Good-bye, Dorothy, good-bye!"

Mrs. Díaz's eyes had sprung open with pleasure at the Spanish words, but now she looked lost. Zulma and her sister laughed. The baby seemed startled at first, but as I kept it up, suddenly she grinned open-mouthed. Mrs. Díaz slapped her thighs and shouted in Spanish. A cousin with the tiny waist of her white T-shirt tied in a knot ambled in, and another, a young guy with a buzz cut, like he might be just out of the army. There were a bunch of people smiling and talking at the baby, in Spanish, English, and Spanish-Munchkin. "*¡Adiós*, Dorothy, *adiós!*"

Debbie looked dizzy. It made me wonder what her house was like.

A gray cat wandered in, and Zulma, remembering our sworn purpose, gathered it up. We started, me with the data paper and pencil, Debbie with the string. Mimi was a southpaw too: seven left swipes, three right. We moved on to Spam, a right-handed tabby. Rafi had not yet appeared with the traumatized Diablo, so Zulma led us next door to the Perezes', an old couple who seemed to be waiting for us like they already knew about our experiment. They had blocked off their kitchen with cardboard boxes to corral Gato and Gatito, two big tiger cats who turned out right-handed. Old Mr. Perez actually squatted down to egg on his pets, as though he were assisting the cause of science. We walked down the street after that. People lounged on the steps, sat on porches. They watched us coming. We skipped houses where dogs yapped on ropes in the yard, knocked on the doors of cat owners. One lady was suspicious at first, but once she found out what we wanted, she invited us in. She said loaning us her cat was no skin off her nose. We tested Snowball, Flipper, Kiki, Possum, and Fat Boy, and then we stopped in front of a house Zulma said "I don' know" about.

"No cats here?" Debbie asked. "My arm's getting tired." She had a few scratches on her hand from swipers she'd underestimated.

"Lotta cats here. Mr. Johnson's nice but . . ." she trailed off. "His son Murray he espit on me one time."

A black boy came out on the porch and stood sentry over his territory. "'Lo, Zulma," he said, not saying it Sool-ma like her family but Zull-ma to rhyme with *dull*. "What y'all want?" By how he talked, you knew he was a regular American colored boy, not a Spanish-speaking one. He looked hard at me and Zulma and kind of smirked. When his gaze fell on Debbie, it tenderized, it brightened, it straightened itself up. He grew two inches taller and developed a set of chest muscles. Debbie was examining a scratch on her knuckles.

Zulma became flighty again, doing her tennis step, but she explained about the experiment. Murray's chin lowered. "Y'all tryin' a see if cats be right- or left-handed?" he repeated blankly.

"That's right," Debbie said.

"Well now . . ." He bit his lip, considering the idea, but I knew like I knew lightning brings thunder that if it had been Zulma or I who'd spoken, he'd have had some scornful retort.

"Let 'em on in, boy," called a voice from behind a dark screen door. Zulma tilted her neck. "Hello, Mr. Johnson."

"*Buen-as días*, girl."

Murray stepped aside and held open the door. I was glad when Debbie passed him without a glance.

No doilies in the Johnsons' house. They had a rollaway couch with a worn blanket thrown over it and pictures from *Life* magazine tacked on the walls. A whole bunch of old black-and-white ones with soldiers on a beach and a new color one of Dr. Martin Luther King, Jr. They had a

Jesus, too, pale and white-robed but with his heart still buried in his chest. Mr. Johnson sat in a wheelchair with his hands folded around a big, scar-headed tiger cat with chewed-up ears. "How y'all?" he said.

We said we were fine. "That's good," he said. "Studyin' cats, huh? They mysterious beings all right." Mr. Johnson didn't look old, but he had white in his hair, and one of his feet pigeon-toed in. He nodded toward the cat in his lap. "Y'all cain't have Percy cause he a man need his sleep but go on and stir up the rest of 'em. They out back having supper."

Murray led us through the kitchen where two dirty plates sat on a table with an oilcloth on it. We went out the back door and stopped on the weathered wooden ramp. "There they be," he said. "You ladies knock youselves out."

I said, "It's a herd."

"Yeah, Daddy," Murray said, inching near Debbie, "he's kinda a cat Samaritan."

Cats of every color and pattern known to cat genetics were gathered underneath a chinaberry tree, lapping fish heads off some spread newspapers. The gusto they were eating with let you know this meal was breakfast, lunch, and dinner. We had to wait till they finished, but that didn't take too long. Mr. Johnson wheeled himself and the sleeping Percy out on the ramp to watch about the time we waded in.

Debbie picked a smoke gray one to test. "What's its name?" I asked Murray. "I have to write it down for our record." I tried to show him the data paper, but his eyes tracked Debbie, the way she lifted her pink ballet slippers over the cats, the way her arms flowed as she turned and bent. Absently he said, "That's uh . . . Mojo." I wrote it down, and the next two, too, Black Magic and Jack Daniels. He was just making these names up so he could stay next to Debbie.

We were about to test an anemic kitten Murray called Heavyweight when Rafael appeared around the corner of the yard, out of breath like he'd been running. He headed straight for Debbie, a struggling Diablo clamped under his arm. What happened next was a phenomenon exclusive to the animal kingdom. Celeries don't do this; neither do rocks. Over the lovely bent back of Debbie, futilely trying to engage Heavyweight with the piece of string, Murray beheld Rafael. Rafael beheld Murray. Eyes narrowed, nostrils flared, muscles swelled, antlers locked, thunderbolts were hurled. "Brought you Diablo," Rafael said to Debbie, but with one eye nailed on Murray.

Murray scoffed. "What she need that one for? She already got a world of cats at my house."

Dropping Diablo, Rafael said, "You finish here you comin' back to Zulma's, no?" When Debbie nodded yes, he scalded Murray with a glance. "See you then," he said and walked off much slower than he needed to, his arms held stiffly out from his supple body, showing space.

Meanwhile, Diablo was sniffing or seeing or, with his tomcat neurons, divining Percy, and that process must have been mutual because Percy's eyes flicked open, and he streaked like a line drive toward Diablo. They met in the air right in front of me. The two cats became a blur. Pieces of fuzz drifted out from the blur. It took me a second to realize I was seeing a metaphor come alive. The fuzz was their fur. And the fur flew. I reached out to snag a piece wafting around them, and Zulma knocked my arm warning, "Patricia! They bite you to pieces!" and somehow I dropped the data paper. It fell into the blur. With a graceful lunge, Debbie dived after it and jumped back yelping, clutching her hand. Murray ran off and came back with a broom and whacked the two cats. Zulma went down on her knees to pick up the paper then.

"Oh no," she said, low in her throat, as if she were reliving the ruined celeries, her wasted poster. She held up the paper. It was torn down part of one side. The side with the hash marks that counted left and right swipes.

But when we smoothed it out, we saw the marks were still intact. It was okay. You just had to fit the paper together to read them. I sagged, I was so grateful our project wasn't messed up again.

Murray laughed at my stricken posture. From the ramp Mr. Johnson called out, "That's this girls' education, son. You don't laugh at nobody's losing their education, you hear me?"

"But Daddy"—Murray screwed up his face—"they tryin' a see if cats be right-handed or left-handed. But see what I'm thinkin' is, then what?" He addressed us. "Look here, what y'all gone do with this big information? Cats don't write nothin', don't use no fork and spoon, no heavy equipment, see what I mean?"

Then what? We hadn't thought any further than our testing. What good did it do science to know that cats were right-handed? What principle did it discover? What disease could it cure? Why hadn't *we* thought of that? We looked at each other, crushed.

Appreciating that his point had hit home, Murray reached out for Debbie's hand. "Old Percy got you good, girl. Let's us go in find you a band-aid, fix that fine brown hand right up."

Blood from a deep slash dripped down between her fingers. Debbie wasn't about to cry. You would not catch Debbie Perkins crying. She snatched her hand away from him. "I'm okay," she snapped, "and I'm not colored, I'm Indian."

Murray's lips parted. "Somebody ask you?" He blinked, as though against a light wind. Slowly, his chin drew back into his neck. He said, "You In-dian, huh. I see. What tribe you belong to?"

He was needling, not expecting an answer. But to my surprise Debbie acted like she owed him one. Like she was supposed to know what tribe she belonged to, and she didn't, and now he'd found out this awful fault against her. "I don't know for sure," she blurted, "I was adopted."

"Well, baby, let me clue you in. You more in her tribe"—Murray pointed at Zulma and then jerked his thumb toward me—"than hers."

He meant to shame Debbie—he succeeded; her regal height collapsed—but he wounded me, too. Murray saw only that I was a white girl and not an interesting one, either. He couldn't see a trace of my grandfather or Lillian, which somehow took a real part of who I was right away from me.

Zulma had frozen when Debbie snapped *I'm not colored*, but she was moving now. We didn't go through Mr. Johnson's house but around it, and Zulma walked far in front. I was working hard to keep tears balanced in the rims of my eyes. I felt robbed of myself. I was mortified about Zulma and furious at Debbie. But it's complicated being jealous of someone who's so unjealous of herself. The whole way she studied the ground. Her black hair curtained her face. Debbie said nothing except for this: "Know what people used to do when I was little? All the time, they'd stop my mother and point at me and ask, 'Where'd you get her?'"

When we got back to Zulma's house, where Rafael was waiting behind the screen door, Zulma ducked her head and ran in, shoving him back with her.

That was it. I avoided Debbie; Zulma avoided both me and Debbie. In science class we gazed through each other. When Mr. Potter asked Zulma how our project was going, her hands flew around. "Is fine," she said. We said "Fine," too.

A couple of days after that class, Debbie said I should come over, and we would take a picture or something with an old camera her mother had. Do something about the history of cameras. Or how they worked. Something fast and easy. The project was due Friday.

I felt bitter. "That's what I wanted to do in the first place. But you didn't—"

"Ask Zulma, will you?" she said. "I can't."

I stepped back. "Not a chance."

"Look, I can't do it."

"No way, Debbie."

She stomped the floor. When she saw I didn't mean to give in, she grabbed my sleeve and dragged me along with her long stride. Debbie wasn't words. Debbie was motion.

We caught up to Zulma at the cafeteria. She listened with a glaze over her eyes while Debbie rushed through the photography stuff, and afterward she just stood there. "Maybe I do the celery," she said. "By myself."

Debbie made a pleading face.

"No. It's better." Zulma started to turn away.

Debbie seized hold of her wrist. I could see her effort not to be rough when she wanted to be rough. I could see she wanted to fling Zulma, to whirl them both into space, spinning until she'd whirled the hurt out of Zulma. All her energy, her desire to make amends, to have another chance, she channeled into her hand clamping Zulma's wrist. Why couldn't she just say she was sorry? Say Please?

Zulma's eyebrows drew together, her brow wrinkled, she shook her head lightly. "Maybe. That's all I say right now." She tugged her wrist away from Debbie.

✥

Zulma showed up at Debbie's house, but she brought her sister's baby. She kept her distance from us, touring the beige-carpeted living room to examine the many photographs of Debbie, on the walls, in silver frames on the polished end tables and on the piano. Debbie as a fat, slit-eyed baby. Debbie as a fierce little girl with short bangs, Debbie about the time Miss Kratke gave us the lesson. Zulma told us she had to baby-sit, but I thought the kid was insulation against us. The baby was so sweet she'd make the sour air around her sweet, and Zulma knew that. She was family; she was Zulma's house that Zulma carried with her. Zulma Díaz was no dummy.

And I was no dummy—that's what we were trying to believe anyway; that's what this project was supposed to prove, wasn't it?—and when Mrs. Perkins made her way into the living room, both of us understood something. Zulma glanced at me over the baby's head, and despite herself a shade of our complicity returned. Just like we'd done with Rafi and Murray, we looked at Debbie to see if she knew. Poor Debbie.

Mrs. Perkins leaned on a cane. She was much older than she should have been, given the few years that had passed since she'd photographed Tod. Her braided hair was silver. She was smiling at us out of a face so pale and clear I could only think of light shining through white organdy or a sheet of ice or the moon. That was closest: her face was like moon-light. Her eyelids were large, pearlish crescents. Her hand on the head of the cane seemed huge, fixed to an arm too delicate to support it.

She said she was glad we'd come. She showed us into her darkroom, with the strange light and the baths of chemicals and sharp smells. There she talked of the dramatic qualities of sepia prints, which were a special fascination of hers, of the developing process, fixing, and toning. Then, murmuring, "Get the light, will you, dear?"—Debbie pulled an overhead chain—she led us back and told us we should feel free to examine the camera she'd had Debbie set up. It was old but not frail—I winced at that word—if we were careful we wouldn't hurt it at all. "Go on," she ordered, and I remembered how when she'd taken Tod's picture, she'd placed us so quickly, so efficiently, and without pleases or thank-yous ordered us to hold still. With one practiced shake of a rattle, she'd gotten squirming Tod to smile for her flash.

So we examined it, standing there on its three legs, with its old-fashioned bellows. Given our previous project attempts, I couldn't fore-stall a dismal thought: we were supposed to be doing science here, ad-vanced things, future things. Classmates were radiating mice, building experimental houses. We were plunging backward. This was the oldest camera I'd ever seen. It was like from the Civil War. Older. God had owned this camera. As we poked at it, Zulma jouncing the placid baby on her hip, Mrs. Perkins lowered herself slowly into a chair. Her voice began to float around us, telling us how photography had begun. It had been called "sun-writing" at first, she said, because the sun wrote images on a surface. "Photography" meant "light-writing." Certain chemical substances were necessary to prepare the old plates: salts of silver, chloride of gold, vapors of mercury, oil of lavender. Her almost lazy voice continued to explain negatives and positives, light and shadow, acids and sodas, the use of rainwater, residue of a cinnamon color. She dwelt on color, explaining how it appeared on a prepared silver plate, that if you looked closely you saw light then dark yellow, red, coppery red, violet, blue, and green. She made it sound like science. She made it sound like alchemy.

She told me how to squeeze the bulb, how long to wait. Stand right there, she told Debbie, in front of the window. She wanted to catch the natural light in a certain way. Like a soldier with the saddest face, Debbie obeyed. "Dear, bring that darling baby and sit over here by me," she told Zulma. "Now. Ready?"

"Ready," I said. To my surprise Debbie was captured upside down in the camera, small, framed in the window light. She wore a sleeveless black leotard, and she drew herself up very tall. At intervals, her black hair lifted in the breeze from the window. Gauzy white curtains wafted around her.

My hand was poised around the bulb, but Mrs. Perkins didn't say Go. I pulled back to look at her. She was studying Debbie, the window, maybe the cloudy light. Suddenly she said, "Come get the baby, Debbie. Let's take you with the baby."

Reluctantly Debbie obeyed, but in front of Zulma her arms hung at her sides. She didn't take for granted Zulma would just hand over the baby.

"Don't squizz her," Zulma said. "Put your arms under her. No, round so she fit in them. No, not like that. Round. You don' understand? Like when you dance."

"Oh." Debbie curved her arms in that way she had. "You mean like this?"

"Yeah, that's good."

Debbie exhaled in relief. We waited, the light changing as clouds floated across the sun. Debbie stood there, and her mother made us wait like we had all the time in the world. Then the baby whimpered, and Debbie, the breeze lifting her black hair, lofting the white curtains, gazed down into the baby's face and rocked her. The baby calmed, and that seemed to calm Debbie. She pulled herself up, raising the baby in the curve of her arms. The sun burst free of a cloud.

"Now," Mrs. Perkins commanded.

I took the picture. Mrs. Perkins and Debbie would develop it, and Debbie would give it to Zulma. I'd write the process on a poster and give that to Zulma. Zulma would stick the picture on another poster, give it a nice magic marker border, glue some sticks on the two of them so they'd stand up. Done. We were finally done. Nothing was ruined, nothing torn up. Nobody's feelings were hurt.

Except for, maybe, Mrs. Perkins's—her feelings were alive on her face. Her eyes in those half-moon lids, silvery with thinness, remained fixed on her daughter. She was looking toward Debbie and the baby as though she could hold them inside herself like an image not on film or plates, a light-writing she could take with her wherever she was eventually going.

⁕

The science fair began on Friday night. We just had to show up and stand with our project while the judges prowled past, wait for their decisions, and then go home. We sure didn't have to worry about winning anything. An arm had broken off my glasses that morning, and I was fiddling with them when Zulma came up, her hands nervous. "Uh oh," I said, "you did get the posters framed and braced, right?"

She nodded. After a second, she asked, "Patricia, you see the picture?"

"No, Debbie had it in that envelope."

"She talk to you about it?"

"Just said here was the millionth and one picture her mother'd made of her."

"She didn't say nothing about—"

"I'm just down on my knees we're finished. I don't care what the thing looks like."

"But Patricia," Zulma persisted, "this picture it's not . . . regular."

I closed my eyes and saw orange. "What do you mean? It's like blurred or bad or something?"

"No, it's . . . I can't tell you right. Patricia, people been coming to my house to see it."

I couldn't get the glasses' arm to snap in. The frames were hideous anyway. Tortoiseshell, gross. But Dad, rabid about money these days, would rant about how much new ones cost. He wouldn't believe these had just *pop* fallen apart; I'd never broken any before. I said to Zulma, "Well then, the picture must be okay. Huh?"

She nodded faintly.

⁜

I got to school late. I waded my way through all the milling parents and teachers, all the tables. The gym was a hubbub of voices, a maze of kids and posters and demonstrations: diagrams of atoms and photosynthesis, models of dams, drawings of internal combustion engines, geodesic domes formed with glued toothpicks. Every school in town was represented: us and Travis and St. Anne's and what was left of Booker T, those students who hadn't yet been distributed into the white schools. Keeping an eye out for Debbie or Zulma, I skirted the corner of Booker T's section. The last guy in the row had a poster with stenciled print and some diagrams. Its title read "The Wonder of Hydroponics"; his display was roses, red and white, stuffed in huge glass jars like restaurant mayonnaise comes in. I glanced at him in passing. I was a white girl. He was a boy and black. But he happened to have glasses like mine, and I mean just like mine, tortoiseshell plastic, one arm taped at the joint with black electrical tape. I had on an uncool plaid dress. He had on an uncool plaid shirt. He looked at me, and I looked at him, and our eyes clung a fraction of a second in weird recognition—*flash*—we were negative and positive of the same picture. Like when you're blinded by a lightning strike, and it does something to your eye so you see inside out: the lightning is black and the sky white. I mumbled, "Hi."

"How's it going," he mumbled back. Then we blinked—*flash*—and we were different again.

I passed Carolyn's "The Walnut Shell Foundation," a cinch to be decked with a blue ribbon, and Craig's radioactive mice corpses, and I saw Mrs. Díaz, all dressed up, wearing a hat and short white gloves. She stood by a man in a blue suit who must have been Zulma's father. Then I saw Rafael with his hair slicked down, and Zulma's sister with the baby, and the cousin who'd tied the T-shirt over her flat, smooth midriff. I saw the next door neighbors, the old couple whose cats we'd tested, and I had time to think that it was sort of strange but nice how they'd all come to support Zulma's project, and then, beyond a straight back I knew was Debbie's, I saw the poster.

It didn't have the magic marker border we'd planned. It was bordered in molding painted gold and glued at intervals with red silk roses. The photograph, an eight-by-ten in sepia tones, was fixed precisely in the middle. And I swear, until I'd stared at it for some minutes, I did not know who it was a picture of.

It wasn't Debbie Perkins. It wasn't a girl. This was someone else.

These people standing around—Zulma's kin and neighbors and others who'd passed by and stopped, one who was hustling a friend back to see—saw it. Zulma had seen it. She'd built us a shrine, not a science exhibit. I saw it, too: a madonna with child. This madonna wasn't the Virgin Mary, though, the soft, pretty vessel draped in blue and ivory. This one was sepia. This one called your eyes to her bare, defined arms, long, spread fingers, the breadth of her shoulders. This mother's gentle arms were strong. Her face was gentle in its strong bones. And her face was brown, her arms were brown, her child was brown.

Weightless curtains fluttered like wings behind the madonna's shoulders, below the straight black hair and around the graceful form of her body ringed with light. She didn't appear to be framed by light—she appeared to be the source of it. Light leapt out from her, energy made visible, like lightning, like love made visible, a leaping blaze that would warm without burning you. In the picture was a mother whose arms cradled her prized child against all the bitter winds of the world. If your skin was dark, if your heart was afraid, your voice weak, your eyes disappointed or blind with anger, if you were alone and lost from your people—she was your mother. She loved you for all these things. She loved you so that you could give that love to your own skin, your heart, to your voice, your eyes, your name. She was the very image of that love you needed to fold into yourself.

Kids from other schools began to block the aisle, mostly Booker T, black kids, and some kids from St. Anne's who looked Mexican. One of them slipped off his baseball cap, murmuring to Zulma, *"Es la Reina del Cielo. La Morenita."*

Debbie elbowed Zulma, frowned at her.

Zulma hesitated. "He say she's beautiful."

Beautiful was a meager word to put to her. "Oh, Zulma, just tell her." I turned to Debbie. "He said she's the Queen of Heaven. The dark queen of heaven."

Debbie kept staring at people's expressions, people who'd gaze toward the picture, cast an awed glance toward her, and turn excitedly back to the poster again. Debbie turned back, too, and squinted for the longest time. She must have found the right focus finally, whatever that was, maybe the familiarity of her own features hazed away, leaving for an instant only the woman in the picture. Her eyes widened. She wrapped her long arms around herself. She'd seen it—how beautiful she was.

I edged back. This mother hadn't come here tonight for me. I knew that. She'd come for the Booker T kids and their teachers, the St. Anne's kids, she'd come for Murray who wasn't even here to see her, she'd come for Zulma and for Debbie. I threaded through our aisle and sat down against the gym wall while those gathered around craning, black kids, brown kids, tan kids, got a better look. The slick floor was dusty from people's shoes; it was hard and cold. I couldn't get settled. The gym's noise dinned in my ears. The plaid boy paced beside his roses, and Carolyn Withers chewed her thumbnail. Judges were zeroing in with clipboards and blue and red and purple ribbons.

In front of our posters kids stood intent, one boy in a letter jacket with his hands shoved in his pockets and his chin resting on the shoulder of another. People behind exchanged places, hopped to get a better view. The swelling crowd jostled elbow to elbow. Questioners surrounded my science partners, who turned from this one to that. Our project was a little fair within the big one, and I wanted to join it. "Okay, okay," I whispered to the disturbance in my muscles and my bones, to the hunger in my middle. I just quit resisting her. Sitting up straight by the railroad track, raking gravel from her palms and cinders from her hair, my great-aunt Lillian was set on that mother's light. So I picked myself up and walked us back there.

⁕

The Career
of
Saint Librada

SHORTLY AFTER the king of Portugal betrothed his beloved daughter to
the son of the king of Spain, this daughter, Librada, lost interest and
direction. She slept badly. She drank cups of coffee, sitting on the portal, and when her vision vibrated with caffeine, she walked down to the
public library. Fastidiously bypassing those reeking snorers the librar-
ians called Lifelong Learners, she wandered through the stacks. Librada's
reading was eclectic. Poems, self-employment strategies. She found a
book on anatomy and studied the mysterious framing, channels, coils,
and circuitry of the body, paying special attention to the color illustrations. In the Southwest Room, she had the librarian remove from a
locked case a book describing the New World and a seventeenth-cen-
tury Spanish nun who flew to New Mexico several times a day to pros-
elytize to the Indians. Librada sat down at a library table lit by a dim
green lamp. How wonderful: the woman would be in her convent in
Spain one second, the next she would walk out of the New Mexican
hills, her rosy lips chapping in the dry air, her heart bent on conversion.
Librada was skeptical of the nun's motive but drawn to such travels. She
skimmed the book cover to cover but there were only a few mentions of
the nun and in the back notes a nasty condemnation by a nineteenth-
century translator convinced of the woman's blatant insanity.

"That's what *you* say," Librada remarked to the translator.

Tonight was the engagement party.

Librada walked home in the autumn afternoon. The perpetual brimstone odor of their house was overlaid by a school-starting smell of
sharpened pencils and new Bic pens, of ruled notebook paper and plas-

tic binders, crumbly erasers, and Elmer's glue. A smell of training for the future. Librada wanted to train: write compositions of compare and contrast, explicate the poems of Pablo Neruda, draw and label the chalky bones of a skeleton, attend lectures on the history of Manifest Destiny and the Westward Expansion. Without a shred of irony, her mother scoffed: What good would knowing about expansion do Librada once she married the king of Spain's son?

Librada wore a lavender dress to the engagement party and flanked the future groom. He talked a lot, telling guests about his job at the IRS, where he audited cheaters' tax returns, a position of godlike power. Librada excused herself. In the back yard, she plopped into a folding chair next to her friend Arlene, who was squeezed into some orange culottes for the occasion. Arlene, unmarried, hefty, opinionated, sporter of a number of scraggly chin hairs, was often in disfavor with her family.

"Why don't your parents marry you off, Arlene?" Librada asked her.

Arlene smiled knowingly and twined a chin hair in her thick finger. "They gave up on all that business with me. Eee, they shoulda got you somebody better than that poor example *por allá*, though—have you seen that prince from Nogales?"

Yes, Librada had seen the prince from Nogales. Long hair, wide shoulders, a voice you could listen to for forty years.

"I heard he saw you and . . . aw, listen, they're proposing the toast." Arlene raised her beer and clinked it to Librada's.

"Tough luck, *'jita*," she said.

"It's not over till it's over, Arlene."

"Listen at her grammar. Ain't over," Arlene corrected.

After the guests left, Librada collected all the cups and paper plates and beer cans. She scrubbed the pots and the serving bowls, dried and put them away. All this time Arlene's voice pinched her ear: *Ain't over*. She dumped ashtrays and scoured them, dusted end tables clean of cigarette ash. She sprayed a can of Glade to mask the stale, seeping odor of brimstone. When her mother entered the immaculate kitchen to top off her rum and coke, Librada blurted, "I don't want to marry the king of Spain's son."

The queen whapped Librada's forehead with the back of a hand. "You've got a fever."

Wincing away from her mother, Librada mentioned Arlene's opinion of the prince of Nogales.

"Arlene! That lisbon."

"Lisbon?" Librada narrowed her eyes. "Are you speaking of the capital of Portugal?"

"You know damn well what I'm speaking," the queen snapped. And reported to the king when he sauntered in, his tie untied, the last foam from the keg in his cup: "Now she says she's not marrying the prince." The queen flung herself down into a chair.

In a dangerously quiet tone, the king said, "Call him over here."

The prince of Spain ambled back over from next door, a fresh beer in his hand and a story in his mouth of the audit he had performed that day on a city councilman. The councilman was begging him to forget line 33 of his 1040. In return he could zip through a building permit for the son of the king of Spain that would allow him to build anything he wanted, screw the Historical Styles Committee. The councilman would veto the protests of any neighbors outraged over losing their view.

Through gritted teeth, Librada reminded the prince: "You told that one at the party."

"See?" crowed the king of Portugal. "A big house, all yours, Librada. Our properties united in perpetuity." His eyes shone: *All mine.*

Librada reeled away, her hand clamped over her mouth. What could she do? How could she convince them? Librada clutched her mother's sideboard, over which hung a rectangular mirror framed in gilt peonies. A tall young woman—black hair, brown eyes with strong eyebrows, desolate, angry heart. Librada gazed at her face until her eyes rolled backward and she saw nothing at all, a blackness, a purposeful falling. The palm of her clammy hand slipped to her chin. She turned around.

The king and queen and prince blinked, cocked their heads. Little by little a distinct horror contorted their features.

The girl before them resembled a young conquistador. Oñate perhaps, sweating in his armor under the hot sun of the Española Valley, carving his name into a boulder. Perhaps Peralta with lance and metal stirrups, pondering names for his new realm—meeting for the first time the blood-red gaze of the Sangres.

Librada wore a beard. A silky dark beard.

The Career
of Saint Librada

59

The son of the king of Spain rushed over and pulled it, yanking forward Librada's formerly beautiful chin. He snatched the promise ring from Librada's finger and, suddenly remembering the obeisances due the king of Portugal, backed out of their house.

Once the king of Portugal had recovered his breath, he paced, roaring. His cherished dream of a doubled kingdom—denied. In ruins. He commanded, threatened, shook his daughter. When these tactics dislodged neither Librada's resolve nor the grotesque beard from her chin, his fury blinded him. He ordered Librada to her room, ran to the garage where he seized a hammer and a coffee can of sixteen-penny nails. With the queen tearfully assisting, he began to nail Librada to the wall of her room. Her father thrust the first nail through her right palm, the second through her left. With an addled idea of sparing her daughter, the queen placed one foot across the other so the king of Portugal would drive only one sharp nail through the two.

Librada, the pain.

The pain was not humanly bearable, nor was it comprehensible in any immediate way. Librada's body rejected comprehension. It was as if that process were a city misted far in a distance and unattainable by present routes, as if it were, say, Jerusalem. How could Librada even begin to approach such a city? Instead, in a deft substitution, she was presented with a mirage: the anatomy book she had studied in the public library, specifically pages 102–107 and pages 248–254, color diagrams of the extremities. Librada viewed brilliant, searing, jumbled pictures of the palmar interossei, the dorsal interossei, the median and ulnar nerves, the flexor superficialis and the flexor profundus, the extensors of the metacarpophalangeal joints, the peripheral nerve supply from C8 and T1, distal phalanges, fibers, fibers. Having bitten through the tip of her tongue, her lower teeth awash in a rising sluice of blood, she saw shimmering before her the foot's tibia, the talus, the navicular, the metatarsal, the plantar ligaments, the tendon of flexor hallucis longus and brevis, the lumbricals, the abductor digiti minimi.

The abductor, the abductor, the abductor.

Librada, trusting daughter, you never expected this. And yet, the whiff of brimstone in your household hinted at such outcomes, no?

Librada passed out. Her mother mopped up the blood and tended the wounds so that they scabbed and healed. The hands and feet continued to breathe and flow around the nails like a tree grows around a stake pounded into heartwood. The queen fed Librada, saw to her sanitary needs. The king put about that his daughter had become an invalid—in no small part due to cruelties inflicted by the son of the king of Spain, whose citizens were no longer welcome in Portugal.

This story Librada believed herself. Nevertheless, restless, she felt it was time to strike out on her own. With some strange twisting and tugging, as though struggling out of a too-tight dress, she managed to slip away from the wall. Her packing was nocturnal and haphazard; she knew she was forgetting things, this or that, she wasn't quite sure. She fled the old house with a Lucite suitcase and moved into a newer neighborhood. She swept and windexed, chloroxed lace curtains whose hems fell short of the windowsills, positioned an armchair over a galactic splat on the carpet.

In time, odd rumors reached the queen of Portugal's ears. Her daughter seen here. Seen there. Librada was said to be much diminished, fallen off in weight and pale as water, her eyes with a humbled and luminous gloss.

✢

Paula was running from her husband, who had already reddened her eye, which would later darken to a lustrous, velvety purple. She ran to the end of the street. Paula whipped her head from one side to the other. Right? Left? Which house should she try? She couldn't stand here all day figuring it out. By incandescent chance, by the chance from which careers are born, Paula chose Librada's door to knock on. Librada groaned and got out of bed without the least premonition, squinting while Paula babbled her story. Librada let her in where she hid behind the door.

The young husband soon arrived, not having bothered to comb his rooster hair. His cheek was scored with tiny red crescents, fingernail moons, although he was pretending it wasn't.

He jutted his chin at Librada. "My wife come in here?"

Paula trembled. She was barefoot, in a print nightgown with morning glories, the edge of it visible through the crack in the door.

"I haven't seen her."

Librada was natural, saying this. Paula in the flowered nightgown felt it, too, felt sheltered; she sensed an authority in Librada. This she communicated with a grateful tightening of the lips. In return, Librada felt an increased oxygenation, a sluggish blue enriching to a primary red; she felt a seed of fascination take root in herself.

"Come on," the husband said. "Give her out here." He clumped around the side of the house to peer in through a window. On Librada's table sat a white china vase with a curving fall of morning glories, velvety purple. The husband came back to warn her, "You know you can go to hell for lying."

Librada carried it off with style: she flung open the door. The young husband stepped in suspiciously, off balance now in her territory. He looked all around the room and down the hall. At the end of the hall the back door stood wide open. He could see out onto the buffalo grass backyard and the morning sky. Against it a lavender dress strode on a clothesline, as if it were taking a walk from which it would not, this time, return.

✢

In a few days, Librada received an unsigned postcard. *Thank you, Librada,* it read. She was thrilled. She was as enamored of her tiny liberation as of a child she had given birth to, and as in awe of it. At this point she did not think of what the child might someday become, only of the blind exhilaration of cradling it to her, which, incidentally, obscured from her any lingering pain in the recurrent arteries.

"No," she said to Paula. "Thank *you.*"

Librada had discovered her career. Or, rather, it had run up and knocked on her door.

✢

"Librada," whispered Paula to Stacy. Stacy, who had a clinging boy-friend she wanted to shed, petitioned; shortly thereafter, the boyfriend received a job offer in El Paso. Librada, wrote Stacy in a letter to her depressed aunt Iris, who had a husband guilty of serial infidelities she pretended to ignore. One night late when the husband came home, he found two suitcases and a garment bag with all his clothing packed, his hunting rifle minus ammunition, the second-best television, and last year's venison in freezer bags, thawing on the porch. His key no longer fit the lock. When he beat on the door, Iris, weeping, broke off two Marlboro filters and stuffed them into her ears. "Librada," Iris sighed to her friend Filomena, Filomena to Laurie, Laurie to Angie, Angie to Joette, Joette to Lucy, Lucy to Gretchen, Gretchen to Rainbow, Rainbow to her sad friend Julia . . . in this way, as years passed, the word was spread and multiplied.

Librada.

Freedom.

Librada worked and worked. The mundane repetition of the stories she heard—mumbled, wept, confided, begged—didn't tire her; she only fell more in love with her baby deeds. Dedication to her craft settled within her; she could no longer distinguish its will from hers. She approached each case as though it were her first, with grateful anticipation and a hunger for what would happen. She was patient. Librada had a talent for patience. She took pride in this talent, for it seemed to her a capacity essential to her career. She did her best for each petitioner, no matter how long it took. For those who craved a harsh strength, she summoned it—summoned diplomacy or insults or clarity, police or social workers, a scream or the mildest of final words, whatever was required.

She was surprised that in the course of her work, she began to pity the men she freed her clients from. That was an odd product indeed. She lost ill will, lost her impulse to judge. Both, she found, subtracted from the energy she needed to perform her work. Librada spread herself like a transparent garment the men passed through; some felt the brush of that prismed garment and some did not, and that was not her affair. She was a servant, a conduit, a north wind that cut clean against any cheek turned to it.

And yet in time, as she became practiced, she felt stirrings of discomfort, painful twinges in the ulnar nerves, the distal phalanges. These, she identified as ambition. Surely there were other forms of freedom than that of women from men? She might have conducted research in the library, but as it turned out this exertion was unnecessary.

"Librada," Julia advised Silvina.

"You mean her connected to bad husbands and boyfriends? I thought she wasted away years ago. Librada?"

"Yeah, her, from the old neighborhood."

"Okay if you say so. I'm desperate, I tell you." Silvina closed her eyes, said, "*Ayúdame*, Librada." She opened her eyes again. "That feels stupid," she said.

"Yeah?" said Julia. "How's jail gonna feel?"

*The Career
of Saint Librada*

Silvina had written some checks from the back of her boss's checkbook. Two, so quickly filled in and signed. Now she sat in city court with a hundred speeders, red-light runners, peepers, scufflers, and dope-doers—humiliated and freezing with goosebumps.

The judge wore a lot of mascara. She was asking an old lady in a cardigan sweater: "So were there any pedestrians on the sidewalk when you drove up on it?" She amused herself by answering her own question: "I guess not when they saw you coming."

"What are you doing in my courtroom again, Aaron?" the judge demanded of a young man in jeans so baggy the crotch hung around his knees.

Silvina pictured herself down in Los Lunas in an orange jumpsuit. Her heart sank toward her stomach, lodging just above the cesarean scar. "Ay, Librada," she whispered. "Even if I don't deserve your help."

The judge shuffled some papers in front of her, knocked them on their edges to straighten them, and read. "You told the officer, I am going to f—ing kill you. That's what you told him? Speak up, Aaron, that's what you said? Pretty bad words." She studied the papers again. "You were in the tree then?"

His head bobbed.

"How were you going to kill him? Says here you had no weapon. Were you going to fall on him, Aaron?"

Librada slid into the folding chair beside Silvina. "What are you here for?" she asked.

Silvina recognized her. Skinnier than she used to be, but that was her all right. "Checks I shouldn't have wrote," she told Librada.

A stop-sign runner was up. He had a diagram and a Polaroid picture. The judge rolled her mascaraed eyes.

"What did you buy with the money?" Librada asked. Silvina told her.

"I know that stop sign." The judge tossed back the Polaroid picture. "It's about fifty feet tall."

Speeders and more speeders. Fines, fines, fines. The bailiff called Silvina's name. As she walked to the bench, her kneecaps wobbled loosely inside her pantyhose.

"Embezzlement," the judge stated. Silvina had told herself borrowing, but by now she knew this other construction of what she had done, this other name; by now she knew that very deeply.

"You wrote these checks?" The judge fanned them, two blue checks with her boss's name printed on top.

"Tell her why," Librada said.

Silvina flinched. Surely Librada should not be up here with her, but the bailiff had not ordered her to sit down. Silvina began to talk but her breath stuck in her chest.

"Speak up," the judge said. "I don't have all day."

Librada whacked Silvina on the back so that she coughed out her story: the two checks, delirious impulse provisions for Simon, her son. Silvina had in her purse a photograph of her son and his prom date, posed in her living room. That man, the stop-sign runner, had shown a photograph. Silvina inched hers onto the bench.

The judge glanced at the photograph. "What does this have to do with the charge?"

Surely she could see. "The tuxedo . . ." Silvina began. Couldn't she see? In the white tuxedo jacket and black satin cummerbund Simon looked like a movie star. And the girl wore a white orchid corsage freckled with burgundy, dripping with silk ribbons.

The judge said, "You embezzled from your employer to rent a tuxedo and buy a fancy corsage?"

Silvina read the accusation in the judge's tone: frivolous, to steal for luxuries. She couldn't deny it. They were not hungry. They were not sick. She looked to Librada. What could she say?

Librada had a flash and instantly followed it, an inspiration that would expand her original mission. She whispered in Silvina's ear.

Silvina tilted back her head, her forehead screwed with wrinkles. Even to her this explanation sounded weak and ridiculous, but she spat it out.

"Your Honor, I bought the occasion you see here in this picture."

The judge tapped the photograph against the bench. She laid her head on one hand and gazed at it. "Nice-looking kids," she said. "Well let's see, no priors. Restitution to be negotiated by both parties . . ."

Liquid with relief, Silvina took her place in line with the other criminals waiting to pay court costs. She had stolen, wronged her boss. She would have to slave to pay him back, and, harder than that: she would have to rehabilitate herself in her own eyes. A good enough woman

The Career
of Saint Librada

become a thief trying to become a good enough woman again.

Some weeks later, as she scrubbed Mrs. Crane's downstairs powder room, Silvina experienced the delayed dispensation Librada had improvised in the courtroom. This dispensation came, as Librada had planned, when Silvina wasn't even thinking about it. When it was the farthest thing from her mind. Silvina suddenly saw, as if projected onto the peach tile of the powder room, the photograph. Simon and the girl. There they were, their two faces brilliant with innocence but, even better, shining with the gravity of accomplishment, for they had made it this far, to the senior prom.

Silvina pressed her temples. You bought a night. That's what you bought. One whole turn of the earth. One white voyage of the moon across the sky so wide and dark. You did that. Who can say you didn't get your money's worth?

Silvina then loved her discounted self a little more.

Librada understood this: All true careers are love.

⁘

So when she was called by Patty, hunched in the kitchen after hitting her son so hard she raised a blue lump on the inside of his already bruised arm, Librada went. She went when Russell snarled at a man seeking a job, "Wetbacks ain't welcome here," and the man didn't bristle but looked into Russell's eyes, touched his hat, and walked off down the gravel road. She went when Trisha got so weary of faking people into filling out her job applications, telling people her right wrist was sprained, avoiding telephone books and menus, that she managed to approach a librarian with a pencil poked behind her ear and ask: "Who can teach me to read one of these books?" She went when Brian had touched his stepson and wanting to again, and not wanting to, instead stuck a needle into his arm. If they did not call her, she could not go; that was the way of it. But if they called her by name or by a lurch of the heart, she went into any place.

There were failures. As some reimprisoned themselves with jealous new partners, other petitioners reclaimed their homey cages of drink, ignorance, fear. There were always failures, but Librada termed these future reengagements. She waited for them to call again. She revisited Brian when he told a seemingly casual story about a reformed child molester to his neighbor, to see if the neighbor, that day his self-appointed judge, could believe in redemption for such a person. She directed the neighbor to see through the story, experience pity, say, *People can change.* Was there a lack of conviction in the neighbor's eyes? Had Librada not summoned a sufficient response? A month later, she watched from a corner of Brian's unmade bed as he filled a hypodermic with Drano. Librada stayed, mastering jerky contractions of the flexor profundus, cupping the back of his neck through convulsion and hemorrhage. Afterward she told herself freedom is everywhere, even in a last few seconds. But here she felt doubt: that was not really her mission, was it? She wanted them to be free and live. That was the meaning of her particular career. Wasn't it?

Librada had missed a large point: she did not lead her career. It led her.

⁜

Who had called her? Who had said her name? Librada skirted a green Buick parked haphazardly in the road. Its right fender was dented, right headlight jaggedly smashed; a hole was broken through its back window. She surveyed a group of people all clumped together. Pilgrims on their way to Chimayó: a thin Anglo woman folded over a boy lying on the ground, a muscular young man whose pulsing aura revealed angry confusion, a woman in a sunhat, pink ribbons blowing, assorted others including some busy young men, each with a scent about him reminiscent of brimstone—ah, firemen. And a girl dressed in white like a bride, stunned, cowering—her, surely it was her. Librada brushed her lace shoulder; the girl stared without seeing.

Not her then. Who?

She passed through the pilgrims, a riffle of north wind. "What happened here?" she murmured to the back of the woman in the sunhat, who didn't bother to take her attention from the form on the ground.

"That girl in the white dress, she did a hit and run on him. But those firemen rocked her window. They chased her down. She's in big trouble now, the drunk little *puta.*"

Again Librada approached the girl. "Listen, did you call me?" she asked, but the girl's eyes, two glazed mirrors of guilt, did not hold Librada's reflection.

"All right," she said, moving on. Librada made her way to the center of these pilgrims. She peered down. On the ground lay a Mexican boy,

*The Career
of Saint Librada*

67

injured, a bloody handkerchief pressed tight by the Anglo woman to his splintered pelvis bones and sawed arteries.

"Is it you?" she asked, perplexed.

The boy's pearled lids remained shut. Behind them his eyes searched, as if scanning the landscape of a dream, to find her. Then they stilled. "*Sí,*" he said.

"*¿Por qué me llamates?*"

The boy tried to gesture but his hands no longer belonged to him.

Librada, beset by a weighty numbness of her own, shook herself to divert the pain. "What's your name? What do you want from me?"

"They call me Verdiano. *Dos cosas.* Two things, please. I have a *novia* in Juarez, Ana Luz. She's alone in the world. Except for me. She'll be very angry. I need you to free Ana Luz from anger and grief. Can you do that?"

"If she calls me."

"Can't you call her?"

"It's not done that way."

Verdiano was silent. There was an anxious stir within the group of pilgrims as the Anglo woman discarded her handkerchief, saturated with blood, and cast about for something absorbent to stanch the flow. Resourceful, she reached beneath her T-shirt and extracted a foam prosthesis from her brassiere, handed it to her helper, the muscular young man, who gaped at the squeezable intimacy in his hand. She took out her other prosthesis and pressed it to the wound.

Librada studied this woman's face, stretched a little tight across the cheekbones, lined at the eyes: There is one, she thought, who doesn't need me.

"Could you do it that way one time?"

"What?" Librada looked away from the woman to the boy's brown face, paled to the shade of *café con leche, mucha leche.*

"I said, could you call Ana Luz, just this one time?"

Librada considered his unprecedented request. She harbored no professional pique at the breastless woman tending the boy's wound; she did not feel threatened. She felt . . . wistful, to come upon the object of her vocation, freedom, in its natural state. A surge of admiration caused Librada to answer recklessly.

"*No te lo prometo nada a ti*—I can't promise you anything. But I will bring my suitcase of experience and try. Against all convention. One time."

"*Muchas gracias.*" A pulse struggled in Verdiano's throat. She pondered that living place. "What, Verdiano," she said. "*Dime.*"

"Excuse me, Librada, they say you have a beard but I don't see one."

"That's what you want, to see my beard?"

Librada turned away, looked past the little dirt road, past the hills, into the far face of the Sangres. She turned round again. His lids peeled back to reveal liquid brown eyes widened in pleasure, like a child at Christmas who has unwrapped the one toy he asked for.

"Ay, you look like Cortez. When he had taken all of Mexico."

So. She was no longer the novice conquistador but the seasoned one, the one who has traveled the wilds, fought, negotiated, persuaded, betrayed. The last word startled her. Whom had she betrayed? She had attended with care to each case. At every call, she had gone.

"Thank you, Librada. I just wanted to see the famous beard they talk about. But I like it better when you look like a woman."

"*De nada.*" Librada took away the beard, noting with a grimace a tremor in the ulnar nerves. Eee, this job was beginning to take a toll. But she was here. All she could do was pay the toll and continue. And look at him, her petitioner. In the corner of the boy's chalky lips, a pink froth, budding with each breath.

"Juarez," she said softly, "that's where Ana Luz is?"

"She sews Ford seat covers."

"Okay. I'll find her." She touched his cheek, once the color of *leche quemado* and now of *leche puro*, pure milk. She began to walk away.

"Wait, Librada, I said two things."

Librada turned. "But I answered two things. Ana Luz and the manifestation of the beard."

"Ah, I forgot. Pardon me but the beard was extra." The froth at his mouth expanded into a dome of rosy bubbles.

"What, Verdiano?"

"Take me with you."

Librada stood with absolute stillness looking down at her petitioner. The breastless woman sent prayers silently, but to Librada they weren't silent, they were noisy. They broke into her frequency and disturbed her exchange with Verdiano; they rattled her concentration.

The Career
of Saint Librada

69

"I don't do that. Call someone else."

"I want you to take me."

"Oh Verdiano, what you ask." Librada crumpled at his feet, at a pair of tan boots with worn-down Chihuahua heels.

Verdiano ignored this posture of resistance. "Talking makes you so tired," he said. "*Momentito.* I need to catch my breath." The boy closed his eyes and inhaled. He took in a deliberate, calming, preparing, ready-to-travel breath.

Librada, kneeling at his feet, conducted a furious debate with herself. Don't try it, she said. Make him send for someone with qualifications. Make him call another name. No, no, she countered that position, don't think about it. *No sirve por nada,* just do. Go through what you don't know. So what if you're not Saint Joseph or Saint Michael. Neither are they Librada. She drew her own preparatory breath. Told herself, Jump.

Librada reached out and seized Verdiano's hands, pulled him to a sitting position. She stood, braced herself, and hauled him up. They stumbled badly as she scooped up his white cowboy hat, but she caught the ground to keep them from falling. She set the hat on his black hair. He was heavy, leaning against her, stumping with his one good leg, dragging the shattered one. Together they struggled over the uneven ground past clumps of piñon, away from the group of pilgrims, now bending strangely, like willows in a land of water. They struggled away from the narrow dirt road. It took all Librada's strength to support him toward the red hills, in this direction she had not gone before. She didn't know how far she would have to go, nor did she try to calculate such a distance; it seemed best to disengage her faculties. She didn't speak. She lugged him, gripping the white shirt over his ribs. She half carried him, and she didn't look where she was going. When did it happen? That she did not know either, for she was in a place without hours, without seam or marking, longitude or equator or pole.

He ceased to lean on her. He straightened and bore his own weight. Oh, he said. He adjusted his hat. Found his stride and walked on ahead. Left Librada behind, disoriented, panting with exertion, sore, missing the heft of his body.

✥

She could no longer ignore her increasing disability. Librada was frequently now crippled by cramps, made clumsy by jerking spasms. Nevertheless she packed her suitcase, tossing into it a number of pleasing liberations, some new, some vintage. She even, at the last minute, folded in her escorting of Verdiano. Librada, Intercessor for the Dying, another turn in her sinuous career.

She latched the suitcase and sat down on her bed. How could one be so long in a career and still have things to learn? Become famous without becoming triumphant? It seemed to her that triumph was a beginner's trinket, relegated to the beginning of her career when each liberation contained a boost of pride and pleasure. That first postcard—*Thank you, Librada*—seemed her sweetest triumph now. Her heart, like a giddy clerk, answering, No, thank *you*.

I'm just tired, she thought. A little under the weather. She hefted her suitcase and caught a bus for Juarez. On the way, the driver played Carlos Santana tunes, and Librada slept fitfully against a window, dreaming of lurid diagrams of the extremities.

She found Ana Luz in the evening on El Calle de las Novias. Not at her machine at the seat cover factory but slouching on the steps behind her tiny rented room. The girl fumbled in her skirt pocket for matches and lit a cigarette. Look at her, eyes like coals, a chin sharp with disappointment, her feet pigeon-toed in unbuckled plastic shoes. Here goes, Librada said to herself, trying this new approach. "Ana Luz," she called softly. The girl squinted. "Ana Luz," Librada said, louder, "Ana Luz." She felt the girl's heart, a pyre from which she had to draw back. The girl shook her head like bees were in her hair and stomped back up the steps, the straps of her plastic shoes flapping.

For two nights Librada tried. She tried in the days at the Ford factory, navigating her way down the narrow aisles between the sewing Mexican women to where the girl hunched over her machine, coughing and whipping the seams around. No welcome. No response. *Nada.* Librada was not used to being ignored. She was not used to being the petitioner. It rankled, this feeling of helplessness, of rejection. She addressed Verdiano. "Listen," she said as she waited for Ana Luz to come sit on the concrete steps facing the alley. To light up her Delicado, let the ashes sift down, litter her faded tank top. "Listen, I told you this was not the way. I did what you asked. I didn't promise success."

Librada waited while, on the other side of the building, people passed, gossiped, gnawed roasted meat and salted mangoes on sticks, complimented lace dresses in the Street of the Brides. At ten past eight, Ana Luz let the door slam behind her and slapped down the steps with a paper shopping bag of garbage.

"Ana Luz," Librada said hoarsely.

Just then the bag's bottom soggily collapsed and rancid crusts and dripping soda cans scattered down the steps. A little tan mutt materialized and nosed at a crust. Ana Luz wrenched the morsel from its teeth, scowling. She gathered the rest of the garbage. She tipped the bag up so it could not spill any more, clutched it out in front of her chest, and strode across the alley to dump it in an enclosure.

Librada tried a commanding tone. "Ana Luz!"

The girl plunged soiled hands in her hair, dislodging the clip that fastened it to her head, the pointy tail like a defeated black feather. She whirled around, her face twisted with fury. "You got a lot of nerve pitying me," she said. "*Déjame, mujer. Vete.* Go back to El Norte. Go save your ownself, Librada, you fakey saint."

Dismissed, Librada left the alley and wandered down the Street of the Brides. The street where Ana Luz might have selected a dress for her coming wedding, once Verdiano had sent back the money orders. Librada boarded the Greyhound and took a seat. The bus pulled onto the narrow streets headed for the bridge and El Paso, farting diesel fumes. The tape deck struck up a merry *conjunto.* They were hardly past the bridge, their destiny I-25, when Librada, disconcerted by a warm, crawling sensation, saw the blood. At first a seeping she unobtrusively smeared away on her gray cloth seat. Seepage increased to fat red plops. Her seatmate lowered her magazine featuring the glamorous stars of the *telenovelas.* She saw Librada without even trying, like Librada was an ordinary person. "Should I tell the driver to drive to a hospital?" she exclaimed.

"No, no, don't do that."

The woman nodded shrewdly. "Ay, you don't wanna see *la migra.* Did your man cut you? Do you have a disease?"

Librada could only rock herself. How does one hold one's own hands?—that was her question. She was emitting whimpers. The woman, alarmed, called out for anyone on the bus who might have some medical knowledge. A curious voice in the front called back, "*¿Qué pasa?* Is someone having a baby?" The floor beneath Librada became slippery with blood. A young man lurched back with the bus's first aid kit. "Here you go, lady," he said, extending the green metal case gingerly so as not to come in contact with the blood. Librada looped gauze in awkward configurations, secured it with butterfly clamps. Some people's faces showed distaste; they moved away to other seats. Their repugnance was a further humiliation to Librada, she so accustomed to being greeted with relief, with respect and gratitude. Help me, she said to the long years of her career, the infinite patience and labor. It could not. She could not control the arterial flow, the spasms.

The seatmate, Elisaida, patted Librada's gauze. "Cry, *mujer*," she said. "It'll be better tomorrow." Librada burst into tears, sobbed hacking sobs, the kind that make people wince and turn away, relieved it's not them who've been stripped of all dignity, whose nose is pouring with snot. Everyone on the bus could hear her, and according to their temperaments titter or pity, make up for themselves stories that accounted for the spectacle. Everyone was a witness. The bus rolled along to Librada's noise. She wept past Hatch and Los Lunas, past Elephant Butte and the Bosque. Elisaida got out at Albuquerque. She touched Librada before she took down her suitcase. "*Oye*," she said, "everybody falls apart sometime. Take care of yourself now, *entiendes?*"

Take care of yourself.

Save your ownself, you fakey saint.

Free yourself, Librada.

⁜

Librada trudged home from the bus station, unwound the gauze, and lay in a bathtub filled with ice. After some long time, she felt better, sufficiently numbed. She shuddered remembering her public humiliation on the bus. When that image loomed, she pictured large mammals. She favored elephants, stereotyping them as kindly and intelligent, tribeloyal, fond parents; whales were also large enough to block a view. She imagined one surfacing and diving near Chimayó, its bifurcated tail descending behind the crest of the red hills. She worked hard for another year. Then, during a routine liberation, as she approached a woman out cold on the floor, she heard the husband say, "Over here." Still moving toward the woman, she threw a glance at the man with his head in his hands.

"It's me," he said. "I'm the one that called you."

She squatted down beside him. "It's you?"

*The Career
of Saint Librada*

He hammered his temple with his fist—"Me, me, me. Don't you get it, Librada?"

She inserted her dwindling force between the man and his blows. Me, she echoed.

⁕

Scorched by the energy of rage, Librada ripped down her shorty curtains, ripped bubbled wallpaper from the bathroom walls and dented blinds from the bathroom window, ripped up the stained and beaten living room carpet, ripped browned crocus heads from green stalks. When she couldn't find another second of ripping to do, she hauled plates, cups and saucers, gravy boat, and salt and pepper shakers to the bathroom and broke them singly against the tile floor. She crunched through the debris and set out swiftly for the old neighborhood. The king and queen of Portugal were long dead; her sisters had moved to California and Las Vegas. But the house remained.

A latticework of vine had overgrown the portal. Librada beat through the vine and produced a rusty key. She fumbled it into the lock, dropped it, knelt down, and picked it up again. Despite the month—April—and the walk, she was cold, as if she had swallowed a stone dressed in frost. The lock clicked. Names spilled from her: Guadalupe the brown virgin, her robe strewn with roses; Saint John the Baptist striding into clean water; Gabriel the communicator and bright Rafael, protector of innocence, his muscular wings spread over all the wounds of the children of men. Cesar Chavez, Sojourner Truth, Abraham Lincoln, a private citizen, she didn't care, whoever would hear. "*Ayúdame*," Librada pleaded. She walked down the hall toward her old room and stopped short in the doorway.

Dirty windows filtered a forest green light. From outside, the nonchalance of birds.

"So you've finally returned," said a voice from the wall. "Hello, Librada. Long time no see."

Librada peered—one glimpse—at her whom she'd abandoned. Her whom career had buried as springing flesh and red muscle, organ and vein bury bone, as blossom hides seed. She reeled from the impact of memory. Brown eyes alight, strong eyebrows, olive skin and high cheekbones, the piquant curve of adolescent lips, hips, and breasts.

"You thought I would get old like you? How did you manage this career you have? You're so slow, Librada. There's a hammer in the corner."

Librada buckled into the doorway, banging hard against it. "I'm here," she said. "Don't ask me to hold one more drop of sorrow."

"Don't ask *you*? You left me here, Librada. Look at *my* face. No one has looked at it in such a long time. I got lonely."

Librada looked again: a girl's face, still molded with a faint trust it crushed her to remember.

She stumbled around to each corner in turn before she found the hammer. She gripped its dusty wooden handle and began the grisly task of reclamation. With the claw of the hammer, she pried out the sixteen-penny nails. She drew them through flesh long attached to them, flesh that had accommodated but not forgotten their piercing metal shafts. She freed the feet first, then the right hand then the left. Breathed in its fetid sigh *Ahhhh* as she caught the slumping body. Wrestled her weight under its shoulder blades and knees to carry it. Laid it down on the musty bed, arranged the splayed limbs, and sat with it. She brushed back hair from its forehead, brushed the matted strands and braided them. She tore away the brittle clothing and washed the body, face and neck, breasts, belly, taking care with the sex, the creases of the thighs, washed the legs and the soles of the feet, the marbeled scar tissue. All the while she salved its lonely ears with endearments. Finally she took the face directly to her and kissed its lips. She helped her body to its feet when the personage arrived, creaking the old floorboards. She kept her eyes fixed on those oaken floorboards; she did not look to see who it was. "Thank you," Librada murmured, handing over her naked body, "thank you for coming to me."

⊹

The April sunlight felt hard-edged; she herself sinewy, bursting through. She took some time off to get used to this reconstituted self, a kind of training. She wobbled in a circle on the shoots of the buffalo grass in her yard, ended by spinning, entering her balance as she went. She jogged down her dirt street. Jumped drooping barbed wire and ran the bank of an arroyo as a spring rainstorm transformed the barren dryness of sand into rivulets, the rivulets into a single stream.

When she finally resumed her career, she was pulled here and there, heeding a pile of messages. She clambered into a slow ambulance to ride along as 80-year-old Georgia took her mother, Eppie, 101, away from the machines to her own familiar bed. "I've been calling you," Eppie complained, "since last Monday."

The Career
of Saint Librada

"I'm sorry, there was some business."

"*I'm* your business, honey. Don't forget who you are."

Librada gave the *anciana* a wry smile and wiped her mouth. "Nice if they'd flash the lights and scream the siren"—she made conversation to calm her—"isn't that the fun of ambulances?"

"Oh, Librada, don't rush me," Eppie whispered. "Not even one minute."

Librada straightened a kink in the IV tube and rocked along in the languid ambulance.

Her intuition coupled with her shrewdest calculation told her she would never see Ana Luz again. But who could say? Some day she *might* see Ana Luz. Trudging toward a spot off the side of the road, on one of the shortcuts to Chimayó. Headachey and rumpled from an all-night bus ride. Her shiny mocha lipstick would be worn off and the skin beneath her eyes puffy. She would have a limp bunch of Safeway flowers, daisies and carnations dyed unnatural colors, and these she would scatter on the ground. She would sit for a while under the brilliant sky of New Mexico, as round as a turquoise bowl. El Norte, to her a place it seemed traitorous to find the sun and the moon. She would say exactly what seemed best to her to say; as to the composition of her speech, she would not have asked one person's advice. She would have come without Librada. She would be annoyed to meet her there. They would engage in a marathon staring contest, a woman with industrial sewing scars and a minor saint incorporated by the supplications of women. Librada would win. Because by then she could stand there without regard for hunger or thirst, for weakness in the knees, for a fly on the nose. She could stand there—who but a saint could do this?—without the superfluous imposition of patience. With readiness that ran in her like a river—a river runs because it runs, because it is a river.

"Back off and give me some room, *mujer*," Ana Luz would say at last. Grudgingly. Ana Luz was a hardhead. A lifelong learner. One of those ones who find their own way in their own good time.

✣

Another
Exciting Day
in Santa Fe

ANDY C'DE BACA'S disgusted at his new neighbors; the husband's crushed their common mailbox. Banged-up and booted, it lies facedown on the concrete porch, a pathetic little testament. Not that Andy doesn't recognize the impulse that caused this wreckage, but when he wrecks things, they're his own. He squats down to the mangled tin and wrestles out his light bill and a circular from JCPenney. He jams them into his jacket pocket and raps on the neighbors' door.

A young woman with a bump in her middle and hair like mahogany opens the door. When Andy points to the mailbox corpse, she whispers, "You hopeless asshole."

"Hey, look—," Andy starts.

But her head slumps, propelling ribbons of deep auburn hair across her forearms. "I'll buy us another one." The woman gestures toward the mailbox.

He could swear he's seen her before, back when he was still a cop patrolling the plaza. She sat cross-legged by the defaced side of the obelisk, where some revisionist soul had chiseled off the SAVAGE that preceded INDIANS. A woman with hair like hers, deep mahogany. Then Ramiro had pointed and said that the mayor never fixed the obelisk like he promised, and Andy had said since the obelisk was Santa Fe history, now the chiseling was history, too, and they ought to leave it, and Ramiro said that was the most dumb thing he'd ever heard, and they got into it for a minute, two bored cops bristling on the plaza. When Andy looked around, the brilliant-haired woman was gone. As, in his experience, women go.

His neighbor is holding out her hand. "Sorry, I'm Kate," she says. He shakes her hand. "Some days I'm sorry I'm Andy, too," he says. The corners of her mouth crimp up a little.

They chat a while about how much she's paying, how she beat out other prospective tenants for the house. "You want a place, send out a pregnant woman," she laughs. If you want a house, you could get one yourself, Andy thinks, but doesn't say that; instead, he describes the landlord's peculiarities. There's an attentiveness in how she listens that reluctantly charms him. Kate's young, pregnant, and sticking with a bad marriage, which fact Andy has already divined as neighbors do; he's heard the yelling from his own house, a crash or two, heard their doors slam. There's no car parked in their space. He's seen her walk to work, her middle obscured by a three-quarter coat, head ducked, plowing past the construction dogs remodeling the house across the street. "Hey, baby!" they holler, "looking good!" and whistle at her.

He heads down the path but turns back on a whim. Eyes Kate's waist-length hair and luminous complexion (a mystery: for nine months her skin will turn to pearl), her bump of a belly, and says, "Looking good anyway." Kate, unpleasantly startled, discerns the irony in his smile and smiles back, sort of.

✢

One summer night cars converge on the little pink house in front of Andy's. They block his truck in. He's mad when, at six A.M., he sees this; almost misses his cup of instant when he pours in the hot water.

A knock at his door, to which Andy grudgingly responds. What he sees doesn't make him any happier. It's a hippie. Long blond hair half unplaited, red-rimmed blue eyes, from loads of pot, Andy judges. He's wrong there. The man has asked for marijuana, actually, but Kate and her husband don't use. Neither do they have on hand cigarettes or even coffee, Kate being careful with her pregnancy. The man's been up for thirty hours, Kate his last call.

"You Andy?" he asks without preamble or greeting—without courtesy, as far as Andy's concerned. Andy nods stiffly.

"I'm Dr. Keeler."

Doctor? Andy thinks. You're shitting me.

"Could you come stay with the woman next door? We've got to take her baby to the hospital. We need one of the parents there, and she's lost too much blood." The guy is practically swaying on his feet. "Just for a while," he says. "Midwife'll be back."

Midwife? These back-to-the-earth Anglos, why don't they go to the hospital in the first place? His sisters got spinals even. But Andy sets down his coffee and follows the doctor next door.

He pulls up a chair to the bed, instantly wishing himself back in his house with his coffee. Her shoulders are naked, and there's blood all over the sheets. Kate doesn't even look like Kate. Her formerly brilliant hair is tangled into rats, snarled and frizzed; her face is overspread with an ugly red rash. There's a pail with something horrible in it; Andy nudges it under the bed with his toe.

"They couldn't get him pink," Kate says. "And he's got a cleft lip and a hole in the roof of his mouth." Her eyes beg him to say this defect isn't the end of the world, which it seems at this raw moment it might be.

"That's not the end of the world," Andy says. He gestures with someone else's hand. He feels like someone else is talking. "They fix that all the time. My cousin Yolanda's baby had one. Little girl looks good now."

"She does? Promise? Can she talk all right?"

"Oh yeah," Andy assures her. He's making it all up. "There's lots worse things."

She's agreeing with him even before he's finished. "Lots worse. Lots. He's alive." She tells him about the doctor and midwife both working over the baby, though her breathy speech increases Andy's anxiety; he thinks she probably shouldn't talk. What if something goes wrong? He was a medic once, but that was ten years ago, and childbirth was never the emergency he encountered. You're way out of your league, he warns himself. The sun's flooding through her east window; the smell of blood in the room is beginning to stifle his nose. She has girlfriends; he's seen them sit together on the back step. Kate calls him over and introduces them, waggles her eyebrows at him, a matchmaker. He can't dredge up a single name now. "I could call somebody for you," he offers. That's how it should be. There should be women here; there should be family. These people that move all over and leave their families far away, look what that gets them.

"I need to get ready to go," she says.

"No." Andy throws out his hands. "Lie back till that midwife gets back here."

Another Exciting Day
in Santa Fe

But she is pulling herself to a sitting position, maneuvering herself to the side of the bed. Andy flinches when the sheet drags back revealing a flash of her naked, blood-stained crotch and streaked legs, her big slack belly with the brown line going down it. Kate clutches the edge of the sheet over her breasts. Her head stays down. Her feet poke over the bedside then dangle. "Will you bring me that dress over the chair there?"

Andy springs up, retrieves the tenty dress she's worn for the last few weeks. He gives it to her and then sees with chagrin he will have to help her put it on. Kate raises one arm then the other, not letting go of the sheet until the dress has covered her. "There," she says. Her face is so splotchy he can't tell if she's blushing, but she's not. It seems she's not even thinking of Andy. "He's gotta be okay," she says. "Please." Blood is smeared on the sole of one foot. She wipes her eyes and her nose and pushes back her hair, her fingertips meeting the knots. "Do you see my hairbrush?" she asks.

Andy spots it on the dresser. He'd felt obliged to say, "He'll be okay," when he has no idea if that's true or not, so he's relieved to shut his mouth and go fetch the brush. He hands it to her. Kate's panting; her lifted hand shakes. She has so little strength that she merely scrapes the brush across the surface of her hair, catching all the knots. "Ow," she says softly. Here it comes, he's sure of it, she'll bust out crying now, and what will he do? But she raises her face to him. Her ugly, rashed face. Her voice trembles. "Andy," she says. "I have a baby."

He nods twice. He takes the brush from her. With a reluctance so vast it feels like the force of gravity, Andy sets the brush to the crown of her head. It's the last thing he wants to do. He's embarrassed, as embarrassed as he's ever been in his life, but for her, or else he's pitying her; it's too hard to figure out. He feels sorry about the harelip, but even more about his presence there, that a neighbor she doesn't know all that well, a man, should tend to her body in this intimate state. Embarrassment turns to dismay: Andy realizes he has never touched a woman in this way. Even if this had been Teresa in the bed, the girl he should have married, he would not be brushing her hair. Teresa's mother would be. Her sister. He can hardly believe he is standing in a bloody sunlit room with the hair of a woman who doesn't belong to him caught between his fingers.

✣

The usual rushed afternoon: Kate's dropped off Charlie at a friend's house, is standing in the busy office of Crippled Children's Services with her eligibility renewal form. She hands the paper and the paycheck stubs to Bill, the social worker, a sweetheart who's always kneeling with a clipboard at the feet of women with variously lamed children. He rushes around, a frail, blue-eyed dynamo, scribbling on his clipboard, recording bad nights, ear infections, spiky fevers, stutters. Kate takes the crimp in Bill's long-lashed eyes as concern for her, which it is, because that is how Bill is. She hogs him, asking questions just to hear Bill's unpitiful answers, sincere and flippant at the same time.

"Fabulous," Bill says now, "you still qualify. And, hey, stay for the cleft palate meeting."

Kate smiles guiltily. They don't have to know about Andy's shop, about any of the extra jobs. She glances at her watch, slides into a seat by the door in case it goes on too long. These group sessions are Bill's brainchild, his baby: attend to more than the physical wounds.

A chunky, middle-aged Indian woman with the scar and the horse-shoe-mouth clings to the podium and lisps her story. A yellow school bus arrived on the rez and hauled off all the kids who needed surgery to a distant Albuquerque hospital. She was eight or nine, her little brother only three. At the hospital, they wrenched his hand from hers, dragged him whimpering down a long hall. She worried about him because he was so scared and so little and their parents couldn't visit. The children hurt, and they were in those rooms alone except for other frightened children. No faces that loved them when they saw them came. That's how they did it in the '50s, the woman says.

What a barbarity, Kate thinks. But after a while her own problems steal over her: this morning her anal employer, a realtor, has literally taught her how to erase. That's only disheartening, really: last week she found slits all along the upholstered back of the couch. Moths? She ran her fingers over the rough cuts, not quite believing the evidence, as when she was robbed once and stared for ten minutes at the vacant spot where her TV had been. Gently, covering her fear, she asked, "Did you do this, Charlie?"

It's not Charlie's way to deny what he's done, to make up a lie. His lips pursed, his repaired lips that are now barely scarred; his eyes reflected misery. Kate knows her son hates being singled out of the class to go see the speech therapist; his teacher has told her that. But the real problem is that his father and new girlfriend have left for Europe for an indefinite stay.

"Your dad's not going because he doesn't love you," Kate told him. "You know he loves you. You know he'll come back." Charlie's face had clouded further, but he let her hug him.

Kate's eyes squeeze shut. Had she been right to have him? Pregnant and with a botched marriage, but she did it, she had him anyway, she wanted him. Kate thinks maybe she had not had a heart before Charlie. Maybe, even, that's why she had him: so she could have a heart. How selfish is that?

An eighteen-year-old girl walks to the podium but doesn't stand behind it. She stands out in the open. The bridge of her nose lifts only slightly from the dish of her face. The girl says she's excited because she's decided what she wants to do with her life: teach music to children. She clasps her hands and sings a song in a tuneful, nasal soprano. Everyone applauds when she finishes. She beams. The audience beams with her, Kate too; she can't help it. The girl says she's had ten operations. She describes the early ones. She tells how her mom and dad encouraged her when kids made fun of how she looked and talked. The doctors want her to have another operation on her nose but she has told them, No. She likes how she looks now. "Besides," the girl says, "it isn't how you look on the outside." She doesn't define "it," whose antecedent is clearly some good and attainable height she knows about by education and by experience. "It's how you are on the inside," she says. "And my inside is pretty."

As the girl talks, Kate's head drifts forward and her chin skews sideways. Admiration glows from her face.

✣

Andy is suffering one of his occasional spells. His heartbeat accelerates, and a heaviness seeps into his stomach. It will be seven years before he checks all the Yes boxes on the VA's Post-Traumatic Stress form—now Andy just attributes these spells to life. Yesterday he ran into Phil Martinez out buying an anniversary ring with a different stone for each kid. This morning he was ambushed by a little, square, eighth-grade picture of Teresa turning up behind a can of stain stuck to a shelf—

when had he stashed it there? The heaviness mixes with some musty drops of shame and hopelessness, of fear, alchemizes darkly into a mishap at work. If he ever had an accident in the shop, he figures, that would be it. There's the woodworkers' legend, a radial arm saw blade snapping free, biting straight through the breastbone, splitting a man vertically, blood geysers, blood lake lapping the sawdust floor. Okay, Andy doesn't own a radial arm saw. But a slip of the wrist, metal teeth, severed veins—that could happen. No one to slap on a rag, apply pressure. No telephone in the shop to ring unanswered. No one would know; no one would come. Maybe his brother Ralph after a couple of days, maybe a salesman from Woodworker's Supply. He doesn't remember he's asked Kate to work; he pays her infrequently to stain or sand when he's under the gun. If there's no rush he does it himself. Always. Andy C'de Baca runs a one-man show. The heaviness develops a temperature. A chill climbs his spine, knob by knob, branches into his ribs, spreads in his chest. He feels a rapid thump: no one, no one, no one.

He was running boards through the table saw. Has one left. But he doesn't feel like cutting now. Andy picks up a calming chisel. He'll carve a while, this will pass.

Kate enters the woodshop shoring up her attitude. She and Andy will talk a little as they work. They're not neighbors anymore, but they are friends, ears for each other, commiserating about what boring, worker-bee lives they live. She'd never weep to Andy about the stabbed couch, the absentee father. That's not their way. Their friendship has funny, silent bounds; Kate's not sure why it's endured. She knows why it's kept its platonic nature, at least on her side—Andy's not a Charlie fan. Needy kids make him nervous. Kate tolerates an on-again, off-again boyfriend allergic to marriage. Andy entertains serial crushes on hot, inaccessible damsels and a woman who flies in from Phoenix every few months. Kate has not missed the distancing properties inherent in their respective m.o.'s, but in place of self-reflection, she has Charlie.

She just *likes* Andy. He's usually so low key cheerful. "Another exciting day in Santa Fe": his stock response to "How are you?" A new dirty joke fastidiously told, something with bananas or talking rabbits, the precision, the Spanish rhythm almost taking the dirt out of it. Kate understands she's counting on that.

She scans the shop. Table saw, planer, jointer, clamps on the wall, girly calendars, the family tree chart Andy's uncle Ernesto has penciled for him, his brother Ralph's beginner *retablos*, piles of chair parts like pine bones, work table, uncapped jug of glue, freshly oiled *ropero*. No Andy, wiry black ponytail, white undershirt, concave belly, bulging biceps. Has she mistaken the day?

A strange sound, somewhere between a grunt and a sigh. Kate steps forward. There, leaning against a wall, a chisel twined in the hands hugged to his breast. His eyes are shut, his face contorted. Such a private pose. She looks off, looks back, there he is, anguish in the slope of his shoulders. Kate swings her toe forward, kicks the work table. Tactfully she pronounces, "Ouch."

Andy's eyes flicker open. He does a double take at Kate, unhuddles himself from the wall. He sniffs deeply, blows out his breath, flicks at an eye with his thumb. He walks over to the table. "Forgot you were coming," he says.

"You all right?"

"Oh yeah." He knows she must have seen him leaning there, but she doesn't ask what's wrong. Andy's disappointed; from time to time she has mother-henned him. He could use some clucking today.

After a beat, after she just stands there, he shows her what he needs her to do: sand the chair parts and then the finish on the *ropero*.

"I know. You told me on the phone."

"Oh." He smiles faintly. "I did." He nods like that is settled. "Now where did that chisel go?"

"You're holding it."

They look at each other bleakly.

Kate pushes back her hair, the mahogany hair that now reaches only to her shoulders; her hand stays on her forehead. "Are we in despair?" she finally says.

This is why Andy likes Kate: she is the only person he knows who would say such a thing. When it comes to women, Andy favors small, shiny girls who chatter so he doesn't have to talk much, so it doesn't come down to much that's real. Kate's tall, solid, and prone to silences. Still, he finds himself angry with her now because she's right about the despair, because why is it her who can do this, because her voice is so soft, because that is as far as she will go, he knows it. She reads his heart and then she leaves him alone with it.

In the River Province

"We're in despair," Andy agrees. He scowls and sets down the chisel, picks up the last board he needs to run through the table saw, sets that down, too. He wanders over to a pile and takes a spindle for the unfinished *trastero*.

Kate slumps, her expectation of some light, distracting work with Andy ruined. She steps into the woodworker's apron, pulling up the elastic behind her knees, ducks her head under the loop, ties the strings behind her back. She applies fresh paper to the sander, reaches for the chair leg, hits the switch. She puts her head down and sands. One hundred grit, then on to 120, the miller's daughter, spinning pine to gold for six dollars an hour. The sander noise is irritating at first, but as she works it becomes almost lulling. She finishes a chair and reaches for a leg of the next, but her hand fails to close on it.

Andy's back is bowed. He is wiping excess glue from the spindles with an idiot tenderness. In the beginning, when she was still trying to make up something to him, to herself, she had wiped Charlie's scar like that.

Kate skirts the table. Hesitates. Such a contrast to his weathered face and neck, that creamy white shoulder, a working man's, unsunned. She lays her hand on Andy's shoulder.

His chin sinks. He stares at her hand. She had to go and touch him. Andy grimaces, sucks in his breath and shrugs out of her grasp, stumbles off into the bathroom, tiny as a trailer's.

The flimsy door shuts. Kate hears the toilet seat hit the bowl.

So much for her humanitarian gesture. It's not the gesture he needs, she knows that. He needs some enfolding, some patting and murmuring. She picks up the chisel, dangerously sharp as always, and stands there fidgeting, surrounded by the still machines. By the calendar with the bare-breasted router girl, nipples rouged, cutoffs scalloping her crotch; the calendar with a princesa Azteca, all color and no fire, fleshy lips simpering "*Sí*, señor"; the butcher paper family tree that incites Andy's Spanish *orgullo*, that you under no circumstances make light of, C'de Bacas stretching back from the Sangre de Cristos to the shores of Spain; the gallery of starter saints, not even that is fair game for comment, although Andy's mouth twists in consternation as he studies them—his brother Ralph's first efforts at painting *retablos*. Santiago's sword meets only the tips of his sausagey fingers, as though attached with superglue.

Another Exciting Day
in Santa Fe

85

Saint Guadalupe's fiery rays drip rather than spring. Saint Anthony, Andy's favorite, appears to be dressed in a sheep. Saint Jude wears an unintelligible hat, maybe a sous chef's, maybe the beret of a debauched scholar, one side punched in, the other bulging. With their pupils pinpointed in great white eyes, the saints look horrified, as if they are facing their trials with no more equanimity than the rest of us.

A lose-lose. Kate's afraid that if she asks him what's the matter, she'll be butting in, or, worse, she'll offer up a comfort that showcases the limits to her tenderness. If she doesn't ask him, she's callous. She clears her throat. Wills herself to say, "Can I help in any way?"

No answer.

She sighs, goes over and puts her cheek to the door. "Andy. I'll leave you alone." She starts to walk away, but turns back with a disorienting sense of déjà vu. "Want me to call anybody?"

Andy's strained voice. "Who?"

Who? He has nine brothers and sisters, innumerable nieces and nephews, and a mother. Even though when his father died, she'd put Andy and a couple of the other kids in an orphanage for some years. Some long years—Andy had grown up there. God, that must have been awful, Kate had thought when she'd heard that, and she feels it again. Andy hadn't made much of his orphanhood, but the fact that he'd told her said something. Imagine a child's panic, no, Andy's—a nun snaring him like a trap, him struggling and wailing after his mother as she walks away away away and gone down some desperate linoleum hall. Kate sees the Indian children left in the hospital. Then Charlie, so frightened of losing his father he has murdered their couch. It's suffocating, that child panic, total. She braces herself against the door jamb, commanding: Stop, stop.

Kate forces herself back to her friend Andy here behind the door. He has a buddy in the cabinetmaking business, Mike Garcia, who stops by with a six-pack, literally talks shop. Who else? Kate's never met any of the women Andy talks about.

"I could call Mike."

"What would he do?"

Kate gives up and heads away from the door. It cracks open. Andy passes her, a strand of his black hair flopping from the rubber band as though he'd been pulling it. He leans against the work table to regroup his ponytail.

"Just taking a piss," he says.

He doesn't make eye contact, since they both know how silly this lie is. You can hear every drop, splash, and fart behind the bathroom door. Kate, self-conscious, always pees before she shows up at Andy's.

"Sure, okay," she says, but she doesn't mean it. She's not helping Andy, she's not helping Charlie; her head aches.

Andy straightens his shoulders. He hates appearing weak in front of Kate. That's not how they are together; that's not the rules. He remembers the time he saw her, right before she got divorced, what, maybe three or four years back, in the Safeway with big black sunglasses on. She'd pretended not to see him. He'd rolled his basket over anyway to say a word, then squinted at her lumped cheek, her ugly left eye. *Shit* was the word he'd said.

Kate pivots, retrieves a ball of steel wool from a shelf, begins to sand the finish on the *ropero*. Steel wool is quiet. You can't talk over a sander's whine. It's stupid, she's decided, a friendship from two separate corners. "Look, Andy." Kate plants her feet. "Tell me what's going on."

Her sacrificial stance piques him. Andy runs his fingers over the spindles. "Don't want to."

Kate, exasperated, thinks: Well, you started it. To avoid snapping at him, she glares straight ahead at Ralph's rejects, Santiago's fat fingertips magneted to the sword hilt, moves past him to lost cause, last ditch Jude, ranges on to the family tree, generation after generation of C'de Bacas drawn out on ever-widening branches. "Then just talk while I sand this, okay?"

Andy has followed her glance. He makes a pained face at Ralph's *retablos*, as he would to see a joint fastened with nails instead of mortise and tenon. He clamps the head pieces of the spindle panel, thoughtfully tightens the clamps. He finds his spokeshave so he can shape the seat of the last chair, the one that isn't ready for sanding.

He hooks his head at the chart on the wall. "See the first one there? His father was a soldier. He had to leave Spain because of his wife. Something she did, nobody really knows. Uncle Ernesto's story is the wife was royalty or even a nun maybe, but she fell in love with this soldier and ran away with him. Took something valuable with her and sailed to the New World where nobody could find them."

"What did she take? Like jewels?"

*Another Exciting Day
in Santa Fe*

"Are you asking me did I inherit the family jewels? I did okay in that department."

Kate looks over at him. He doesn't look up at her, but he smiles a better smile.

For sure she knows no rubies and emeralds filtered down to Andy. Half the time he lives on MasterCard. There's no telephone in the shop. That's to save money but also because the credit card people call him up from New Jersey. Ay, tradition, try and eat it, Andy says.

"Story is it was a book. Ernesto thinks it could have been one of those that monks spent all their lives painting. A book like a cathedral. Whatever it was, it's her son Juan María that's the first on the chart there, that my uncle worked back to."

"And that's the story?"

"No, Kate, that's not the story. The story is the Indians stole her youngest boy and rode off with him. She and her husband went to the governor in Santa Fe and asked for help. He wasn't a helpful man. Children were cheap. She could always make some more. She showed him her book and told him she would pay, and for the book he agreed to search for the boy. But she was too smart to give her book to him. She tore out just one page as a bribe. The governor took it, but he didn't do anything to find her son.

"Later on there was another governor who was a lot like that one. As a punishment to Indians who didn't work hard enough, he would lash them with a rawhide whip until sometimes they died. The woman was afraid her son would be one of them. She took the book and went to buy him off."

The spokeshave whispers on wood. Andy rocks with it. The woman saw the Indians in chains. She looked at their brown skin and their flat noses and then she looked into their eyes and she couldn't turn away. She opened her book and tore out three pages for the governor. She bought three unbloodied backs, none of those her son's. The next time she heard, she bought more backs. Brown backs. She kept going whenever she heard, even if the prisoners were from distant pueblos. Page by page the governor dismantled her cathedral and took it for himself.

"Wait. I know this story," Kate exclaims. "It's like O. Henry's, isn't it?" Or maybe not O. Henry but one like that, a magi story, she read it years ago.

Andy glances up, annoyed. "You can't know this story. I just told it to you."

Kate thinks: Uncle Ernesto, plagiarist historian. "Right," she says to Andy. "But . . . did she get her son back?"

Andy shakes his head. "No, she never got him back."

"So it was a lost cause," Kate says, disappointed.

Andy frowns. He continues to pull the spokeshave evenly. After a while he says, "You're *cabesuda*, Kate."

"What does that mean?"

"It means if that's how you look at it, every cause is lost."

Kate slouches. Her hand clenched on the steel wool stops sanding.

"What happened is when the Pueblo Revolt broke out, the Indians killed all those priests, and they killed Spanish people but not that family. That's how come I'm standing here."

When she doesn't comment, Andy sucks his tongue. He finishes the seat, wipes away dust with a rag. He picks up the one board he still needs to cut and goes to flip on the table saw. Instead, he turns his head to the *ropero*. Kate's behind it like a big quiet mouse. Andy goes over to peer at her.

She sits on a five-gallon bucket, her hands still. "I missed that."

Andy looks around. "Missed what?"

"That it wasn't a lost cause. What the woman did," she says. "'*Cabesuda*' means dense, huh?"

It doesn't, exactly. What Andy means is that Kate has stubbornly clung to one tree while refusing the forest of his story. But why hassle?

True or not, Andy's story pleases Kate: the persistent mother stumbling into a larger good she had not intended or foreseen, one with lasting consequences. Kate feels like she's been wearing a clamp on her head, and now it's looser. Her tunnel vision is widening. "Hey, Spaniard," she says, because she knows he likes being called that, "wanna go get some coffee?"

"Spaniard" perks Andy up, tells him Kate's not insulted. He's Hispanic now, but he's been Spanish, Spanish-American, Chicano; he wouldn't admit it to Kate, but sometimes this naming is hard to keep up with. "Lemme cut this board," he says. "Bert's?"

"Yeah, Bert's is good. I could get a lime coke." Kate has it in mind to tell Andy about her great-grandparents who homesteaded New Mexico.

Another Exciting Day
in Santa Fe

Conquistadors aren't the only ones with history, she chided him once. Andy's comeback: "That's because Anglos overrun everybody else's history when they were just minding their own business." As Kate disentangles herself from the apron, she decides, No, she'll tell Andy about the singer, the girl whose inside is pretty. She surveys the *retablos*, chooses bug-eyed Saint Jude with his mashed hat, petitions him: Make me pretty, okay?

Andy's fired up the table saw; the place is noisy again. He guides the board in.

And the table saw blade hits a knot in the board and kicks it back at him, hurls it into his chest. The blow knocks the air from him. He staggers. Kate shouts but he can't hear what; his knees crumple until he kneels in the sawdust and then totters onto the dusty concrete floor. He clutches his chest. Kate is squatting beside him, her eyes frightened, her lips forming words. The shop dims, blackens; his head lolls downward. He hears his name at varying decibels, Andy Andy An-deee. His heart stops. Or he thinks it stops. The board has hit him on the heart's downbeat or something, arrested its ticking. He sucks in air but can't get any, somehow manages to scoot back until he can sprawl against a wall, eyes closed, absorbing the shocking pain. Kate scrabbles after him, knees and palms in the sawdust. They lean there, Kate a warm, blurry mound hovering at his shoulder. When he finally notices that he is taking shallow breaths again, more than panting, he runs his hands run over his ribs, searching for sharpnesses. Maybe no ribs broke. The shop swims back into focus; forms of jointer and table saw solidify again. The crushing pain levels off, and he makes out distinct words, Kate asking him, can he breathe, is he bleeding, is he all right?

He means to nod but succeeds only in rocking, and that hurts like a bitch.

Kate is pinching up his shirt. "Let's go, Andy," she says.

Andy doesn't want to go anywhere. Doesn't want to move. Ever again. But she's got her hands under his armpits, so he pushes with his feet and they're standing.

They shuffle like elderly Siamese twins to her old car, where the operation becomes complicated. The passenger door is stuck shut; it's an agony to maneuver himself behind the wheel, over the stick shift, into the bucket seat. He can't straighten enough for the seat belt, couldn't stand its binding anyway. In the emergency room, Kate takes on the check-in desk, fills out the forms, penning his grunted answers. They finally call Andy C'de Baca. The nurse, a portly man who stands on the backs of his heels like Colonel Sanders, swishes shut a blue curtain, saying, "Chair for you, Mrs." Kate doesn't correct the title but she can't help darting a glance at Andy. Maybe he didn't hear.

Andy's grimacing as the nurse helps him up onto a gurney. His eyes are shut. But he extends a hand toward her. Kate laces her fingers through his; for a moment their palms squeeze together. Then he releases her hand and jokes with the nurse about how he's keeping his pants on. No hospital gowns for him, so don't even try.

After the doctor completes his exam, maybe one rib cracked, and Andy waves off the confirming X ray since he has no insurance, Kate finds the payphone to call Charlie at his friend's house. He begs for a new action figure like Jeremy's got, the Emperor, the one you have to send off for. "We'll send off," Kate says, thrilled to hear Charlie's delight. When she comes back, with the lightest step, Andy's already bartered his follow-up treatment at the doctor's office. He'll trade the guy an end table with a carved drawer face, a rosette. "Oh yeah, all by hand," he says in that flat, craftsman's voice in which confidence is measured by the lack of inflection.

"Deal," the doctor says, flicking his pen. "Take it easy now." He bypasses the nurse who's steering in a wheelchair.

Kate mouths *Whew* and wipes her forehead. Andy smiles.

The accident happened, and they've handled it. They feel released, in control, lightheaded with clear purpose and action. As Andy gingerly slides off the gurney, the car keys in Kate's hand jingle. The dolefulness of the day has vanished. The world is upright. It is yellow and blue, and Kate and Andy are out sailing its waters, having an adventure, as they imagine other people with exciting lives have every day.

✤

One day, a Valentine's Day, Charlie appears at the breakfast table armed with a red rose in a tube and a poem. He's fifteen then, his thick hair waving to his shoulders. "What do you think?" He hands his mother the poem.

Kate squints to decipher Charlie's tiny handwriting. The poem is full of thees and thous and praise and self-abnegation, its message that It is

Another Exciting Day
in Santa Fe

enough to behold thee, Lady, and thy happiness will serve as mine. "Who wrote this?" she asks.

"I did."

A trick: tears somehow bypass her eyes, still clear, and leap right onto her cheeks. It's a sonnet, it's beautiful, and the poet has stationed himself afar. How much of this back-in-the-shadows stance is his mother's influence, his mother who has suitors but not a husband? Kate looks up at him fiercely. "Someone will love you, Charlie. They will love you so much."

She's his mom; she is bound to say this stuff. Still, he likes to hear it. He's a little awed with the tears his poem induced. To shift the focus away from him—and his mother totally embarrassing herself there—Charlie dips his head to sniff the Safeway rose. Faint rosy smell, fridge smell. The girl he plans to gift with the rose owns awesome breasts. But the rest of her—her milky arms, her knees are so collapsibly thin she reminds him of a little colt he could just scoop up.

⁑

The VA counselor says Andy is just who his program is looking for. He tucks the questionnaire Andy completed into a folder. Why hasn't he come before? "You don't come to what you don't know about," Andy says. The counselor holds out another form, one with lots of blank, duplicate pages. Andy's to fill it out, write in his own words, describe his service in Vietnam and his life afterward.

Andy takes the form home, drops it on the kitchen table. It bothers him there, so he sets it on the counter, on the far side of his wayward toaster, which lately has taken to flinging up the toast so it lands down in a crack between two cabinets. After the fat form lies there a few days, gathering crumbs, he shakes it off and moves it to his night table. For two weeks he has bad dreams, and then one day after work, still itchy with sawdust, Andy sits on his low bed, puts his gooseneck lamp and his alarm clock on the floor and uses the night table as a desk to write his story. Once he gets past the halting first page, he writes on until he's used seven more. Take a boy not long out of a Catholic orphanage, with its strict rules, its rows of noisy kids and nuns around all the time, with its exact hours and promises. Make him a medic. Don't give him a gun. Send him off in choppers, his hand on chests, necks, bones, holes, seeping, pumping, still, his fatigues stiffening and stinking with blood. One chopper goes down. Andy thinks how to describe this. "Fast" is all he comes up with. The chopper goes down fast. As he writes it, he experiences about half a jag of big black terror before some kind of shut-off valve engages *click* and he feels exactly nothing. His hand cramps up but he keeps writing. The liquor later, he quit; Teresa, the high school girlfriend who died; the other women he scared, drove away; the spells he's suffering more frequently now, he writes it all down. He turns it in to the counselor, who tears off the white copies, says the determination process takes time, but Andy has a good case. He hands Andy the pink pages.

What does he do with them?

They end up in his friend Kate's hands, in a restaurant parking lot, Andy leaning on a Land Rover, arms crossed, as she reads. Several pages in, she raises her head. "All these years . . . ," she starts but bites it off. She lowers herself to a curb, props her head on outstretched fingers, and reads through to the last line. Kate doesn't ask how she could know him seventeen years and not know this; she doesn't express the emotions rippling across her features. She says only, "I am so sorry, Andy," looking up at him as she refolds the pink pages. The heel of her hand becomes a fist as she presses them flat.

"Now you know more about me than my mother does," Andy says. Now he can put them away.

⁜

It really is a tunnel, that corridor Charlie's heading for, lit with the soft false yellow of electric light. He will walk out at LaGuardia, bound for college in this state far, far away. Kate is forty-three years old, standing in the Albuquerque airport just as dawn sheets the runways with a thin yellow light. How did they get here? How much did she hurt him? What did she give him? Is it enough? Her heart is in her stretched smile, in the two fingers she holds up in the V sign for victory, for peaceful love.

Charlie looks back, lifts one hand. He gives her the brink of a smile, his eyebrows tentatively raised. And he's gone.

Kate comes home to find a message on her machine—Andy says the reporter who interviewed him brought a camera so he's pretty sure he'll make page one of the *Journal North*.

Andy has taken on the governor, by extension, but his principal opponent is the Museum Foundation of the state of New Mexico, which has chosen to license (read: sell off) traditional Spanish furniture de-

Another Exciting Day
in Santa Fe

signs to the North Carolina Furniture Mart. Outrage to Andy—the museum is stealing work from local craftsmen, betraying a heritage it was chartered to preserve. He's circulated a petition, stirred up the guild.

Kate has a vicarious stake in this. She was typist to his unilateral rebellion, editor to the proclamation all Santa Fe read on the Commentary page. She managed to reword some of the more incendiary phrases, for this reason, Andy: If you call people names, they won't hear you. Reluctantly Andy agreed to that compromise, but anything further was distasteful, reeking of cowardice.

"Right," Kate said. Her next idea was to corner them with the press, but Andy had already thought of that tactic.

"Yeah, I'm on it," he said. "Lotta *chingada* phone tag."

The guild will meet with the museum people in a downtown office suite with a T. C. Cannon painting on its earth-toned walls. They will be gracious but wary, the museum people, recognizing the blond reporter Andy brings with him. He will count on Emilio Gutierrez for fireworks—the man has four daughters and no sons to take over his shop—and sure enough, after twenty minutes of ball-less verbiage, Emilio will come through. "My grandfather lives through me," he will break out hoarsely, raising his emotion like a sword before every craftsman in the room. "To do this thing," Emilio refuses to name the scurrilous outsider company, "is to finish our grandfathers. To murder the work of our hands. Why would you do this?"

Kate, fresh from the airport farewell, triumphant and bereft and shaky still, imagines, accurately as it turns out, the photo of Andy—truculent expression for the camera, arms militantly crossed, a genuine *Santiago y a ellos* pose. The ninth-century Spanish battle cry: *Saint James and at them!* Nothing dies here in this crazy state, Kate thinks, nothing is forgotten. Like you could forget the children of your body or of your hands. Here the past is blood and red muscle that bursts into passionate speech.

⁘

Petitions, charters, contracts, letters, records: with busy pens, they document everything. Don Juan de Oñate, official governor, bidden by the king to "attract the natives with peace, friendship, and good treatment" forges up from Mexico. He rides on a saddle trimmed with ocelot, leads a train four miles long—cattle, goats, horses, mules, sheep, settlers,

Franciscans, and soldiers. On the last day of April 1598, Oñate calls a halt by a grove of cottonwoods. He claims for God and King Philip II all the eye can return to him. By early the next year, as retribution for the killing of his nephew, Oñate has ordered one foot cut off every man in the village of Acoma over the age of twenty-five, after which they shall serve twenty years as slaves; women too are seized into slavery. Oñate's tenure as governor is fraught with barbarity, dissent, frustrations, and failure to discover even one golden city.

The Acoma also document: lips to ears to lips.

Plans for the annual Oñate festival are gearing up, this one commemorating the *cuarto centenario,* four hundred years of settlement. Though the committee has knowledgeable members, many an average citizen could place Oñate only as a street name, a decorative statue. Some miles past Pojoaque Pueblo's lucrative Cities of Gold Casino lies the village of Alcalde. Its Visitors' Center features such a heroic statue—mounted, helmeted, plumed, armored, caped, and spurred. There, on a frigid January night in the dark of the moon, an Indian committee fires up an electric saw and patiently saws off Oñate's bronze foot.

Andy and Kate read about it in the newspaper.

They have remained friends year after year. *"Dime,* Kate," he'd said once, two or three years back. Lacing his hands: "Why was it we never got together?" He only half meant it, knew he'd always been turned to mush by tiny, talkative women, and Kate, look at her there, half a head taller, drug store specs crowning her short hair, the woman wasn't gonna say a damn thing. Kate shrugged. She wouldn't go there. She'd caught an unfamiliar softening in the familiar brown eyes; she'd heard the other half—the half that said, Why didn't you love me? They were friends because they didn't love each other. Because whatever tenderness passed between them didn't cost what they'd paid before. It was almost free. They'd loved each other how they loved each other, and Andy was *cabesudo* if he didn't know that.

Today they sit at Kate's kitchen table, alternately laughing and gazing respectfully at the newspaper's grainy photo: the revised Oñate, greeting the New World *pie cortado,* his bronze foot missing. The paper says the furious sculptor is already designing a new booted foot, but, as Andy could tell him, the weld will show.

Another Exciting Day
in Santa Fe

Night
Class

MCGEE DISAPPEARS in windy April, Phil Turner's first semester teaching, just about the time Phil's begun to know that when he makes a spectacle of himself he will not die, nor cause his students to be dead, walls will not collapse, floors will not buckle. He'd had big, bona fide doubts about teaching. He stuffed these. He was sick of working Santa Fe's restaurants with the other overeducated, sick of climbing ladders at cold construction sites. The big 3-0 loomed, the pressure to *be something*. So he took this job. He met himself here. And might have fled the meeting if not for his officemate McGee—if she hadn't slapped on the crazy glue when he needed it.

His first classes were agony. They had crawled on hands and knees, the silence so stark he imagined he could hear seconds tick off the soundless wall clock. Eyes, mirroring his misery, stared back at him. His ability to gather sufficient self to speak to them in a choked voice and to get through the enormous minutes until he could decently let them go was so tenuous Phil could actually see it in his peripheral vision—taut, pale gray strings. For the last quarter hour of his second class, he had slid a grammar lesson onto the plate of the overhead. He switched on the machine. Nothing happened. He'd twisted its knobs to the left, to the right, tapped it, the gray strings jerked, and panic poured into him. He'd snatched up the sheet, muttered, "Be right back," and hit the workroom on a dead run to copy it. When he returned to the classroom with the copies, prodded through the door by a gun muzzle at his jugular, an incriminating square of light glowed on the blackboard. Someone had plugged in the overhead. With a sweaty trickle icing his ribs,

Phil saw the huge loop of cord protruding from the side of the overhead's cart. No one spoke.

Then he had done it. Plunked the paper on the overhead, sped through the lesson in that uncanny silence, like the silence before an earthquake, scribbled their homework assignment on the board, and, brutally relieved the class was over, smoked the chalk. He'd leaned against the blackboard for support and out of blind habit stuck the white stick in his mouth. They began to laugh. Brays, cascades of giggles. After a few seconds in which he palmed the chalk and hot blood slammed into his face, Phil had laughed, too. Who wouldn't? But he had run it again on the drive down the hill. The tall, drooped figure that was, alas, himself, propped up by a blackboard, a stick of chalk between his lips. Seeing nothing but the yellow line and his fists on the wheel, he thought desperately about signing up for nursing school.

They had come back for the next class. They had, all of them. Their presence seemed to Phil so heartrendingly generous that he blurted to McGee he was quitting so he might, for their sakes, be replaced by a real teacher. He felt like he had nothing to teach them, nothing to give them. Soon enough they would see the nothing, and he would see them see it, and that would be that, wouldn't it?

McGee snorted and barked, "Phil!"

"What?" He wheeled.

She'd drawn herself up from her short waist and walked her chair toward his. Then pointed like an oracle. Except no one looked less oracular than little McGee, scudding toward him in an upholstered office chair. "You're gonna do great, Phil."

His knees sagged with gratitude.

"Everybody goes through this."

"Not you."

"Sure me. Back in the Ice Ages. I came into class with my skirt caught up in my pantyhose. Butt in the breeze."

"You did that?"

"I still cringe." And she did.

Phil measured this against his debacle with the overhead, the chalk. It was up there. "Thanks for that picture," he said, and he meant it.

"No problem. The terror was getting a little thick in here."

"So what's the secret, McGee?" He couldn't look at her as he said this, but he meant it, too.

Her voice was matter-of-fact. "Try not to hate them," she said. "It's bad for your stomach." McGee had risen and looped the strap of her old-fashioned book bag over her head. "God you're tall," she'd said. She'd reached up and thumped his stooped shoulder blades. "Stand up straight, boy. Go get 'em."

Girded, Phil continued to enter their rooms. He did not take compliance for granted and so remained in a state of lock-kneed tension. Occasionally laughter would drift in from next door or a rowdy burst of voices. He couldn't imagine either sound in a classroom of his. Ever. What did it matter if none of the students spoke? For all he knew, they could be invisibly learning in their own private air spaces. But it did matter. As a sign that their interest might have been engaged. It mattered because it was so lonely to stand up there in front of them, knowing that his was the only voice he could expect to hear.

One February day in his two o'clock class, a bunch of sullen eighteen-year-olds, a girl named Rita raised her hand to ask a question. This was unprecedented. She'd seemed, like the rest, satisfied with gazing. Phil locked in on her to listen and saw *how? in what?* Rita's own nervousness, her desire to succeed and her fear of failing. On the day she raised her hand, he felt somehow accompanied; he'd managed not to pall them into torpor with his rictus face. Some time later, a young guy in a hairnet lingered after class to offer his take on an assigned story. Phil took the responses personally, though he knew well enough they were not personal, because he needed to. He claimed from them a bit of heart. He stored them up, found that heart was cumulative. One evening in March, the cold steel muzzle at his neck did not force him into the room. Phil walked in, gunless, under his own power, whatever that was. That night, as he drove home down the hill, he saw the mesas fall away as they always had, grandly into sheer air, the bluish moon hanging over the full range of the Sangres, the sky behind like an unlimited expanse of breath, free and blue. He had gripped the wheel, navigating the plunging curves, chanting, *Thank you, thank you, thank you.*

✢

Phil sits down in McGee's chair, scooting it back, and pulls out the slim middle drawer of her desk as far as it will go. Takes out the papers, sets the pile on his lap, sifts through them. Nothing helpful there: notices from Admin, last semester's upgrade instructions from Computer Services, some quizzes stapled together, apparently ungraded. Left in the drawer is a litter of pennies, paper clips, pushpins, a highlighter, an opened box of Tampax. Hunched over, Phil thumps the very back of the drawer, as though he might find a spring that will shoot open to reveal a secret compartment there.

He wants to discover an itinerary, a Post-it from McGee to herself in that flowing hand, those large, second-grade letters she forms so well, a destination, some name and number that will turn out to be a distant friend's. He doesn't. But then, that's the kind of thing you take with you, isn't it? Phil jams the papers back and reads the notations on her desk calendar. Some Saturday seminar she's teaching *Jesus McGee when do you sleep?* student appointments for two weeks ahead of the Thursday he saw her last. By now she's missed half of those.

The police have declined to pay the school a visit, much to the VP, Joan's, disgust. McGee is an adult, and "It's a big world," as a detective informed McGee's mother, and her mother wrathfully informed Joan. A missing person is not a crime.

Unless, Phil thinks, you know that round, brusque, contradictory person. Unless she sits right behind you. Phil peels back the pages of the big desk calendar to see if there's anything written in May, June, the rest of the year. Shakes it for hidden scraps of paper.

"You're all snooping in her desk."

The voice snaps him around. Craning through the doorway, a sturdy girl with spirals of gelled black hair. Her eyes are sly within their crust of mascara; her double-rimmed lips, a brownish outline painted in with maroon, pursed. "I would of done that, too."

"Yeah?" Phil sighs, repositions the calendar, stands and tucks in his tent of a shirt. "What's up, Carmen?" Sitting down in his own chair, he mimes dignity.

"Yeah, since the cops hadn't got off their big fat asses. How would you like it if nobody went looking for you?"

She advances frowning, her arms dragged down as she sheds the backpack she's carrying. Phil thinks she means no one would be screaming into the phone for an APB on Carmen Tapia, should she disappear. She's from Chimayó, that lovely village famous for pilgrims and holy dirt and heroin traffickers. One brother in the pen, another dead from AIDS. A mother who, with clockwork tears and lamentation, cannot manage to love her daughter more than she loves the stuff.

Carmen is McGee's student; usually she strides into the office and flings herself down by McGee's chair, back to the wall. Now, she looks that way but does not approach the chair. Instead she slouches heavily against the new file cabinet, which, since it's still empty, rocks and skids into the wall. Carmen pitches backward with a squeal, one arm windmilling. Phil's halfway out of his chair, reaching to grab her, but she's already wresting in the arm, sinking down, pivoting. Her knee automatically begins a mean jab upward before she stops herself and freezes, face-to-face with the black file cabinet.

Phil winces, hand to his groin. At the beginning of the semester, before he got used to her, Carmen's tirades had shunted Phil into a sealed-off and cushiony part of himself. This used to happen when he was sixteen and his father ran other drivers off the road. His mother would be crying, and his sister curled in crash position, head between her knees, and Phil would be there in the back seat, tranced, joints loose, palms on his lap.

Carmen turns back from the file cabinet slowly, scowling to cover her blush. "Listen, Mr. Turner, why I . . . why—" Her forehead wrinkles painfully. "Listen, I saw her."

"What?" Phil's head thrusts forward. "When?" he exclaims.

"Last night," she whispers.

She tosses her long hair off her shoulder, bores in on Phil, a test. When he waits, quiet, she says, "Okay," and blows out her breath.

"She was walking down a street by the ocean. The street was boards, all nailed smooth, you know? There were some palm trees and a harbor that ships were sailing into. Maybe San Diego or like Baja, I don't know what that looks like. She was giving out fliers to people she passed. She gave me one, but I couldn't read it. She had on red high heels, like patent leather maybe, shiny. Can you see McGee in *puta* shoes like that?"

After a bitter slash of disappointment at this account—he should have seen it coming, he thinks—Phil sits back. No, he can't feature McGee in *puta* shoes. She wears Nikes, boxy, techno-design white and silver things her nyloned legs sprout out of.

"And then I was there and not there, you know how it is. Like I was a camera. But McGee could see me. She turned her head and looked straight at me in slow motion. She pointed to the ships. They had all these white sails. The water was all sparkly. She kept pointing." Carmen's eyes close as she pictures it again. "She was like all happy, Mr. Turner." Her tilted face is mystical. Carmen believes in dreams, in signs that reveal the shimmer of a brighter universe. Her eyes open, intense, hopeful. "She ditched."

Phil recruits enough energy to lift his eyebrows.

"She's burnt! She needs some rest, that's what the dream means. Don't you believe she could be down in Baja soaking up rays?"

Phil does indeed believe McGee could be burnt and, if not in Baja, somewhere.

"Will she get in trouble for ditching her classes?"

Considering Joan, Phil says, "Dr. Schafer's human."

Carmen's mystical mood vanishes. "Dr. Schafer," she growls. "How would that cow know how it is? She makes 50K a year, and McGee she drives around like a *rata* hunting her tail."

True. McGee commutes to teach high school in the valley and picks up night classes here. She's told Phil that Carmen needs to face facts and get on with it, but he's overheard her awkwardly coating this advice with sugar: *You know your mother loves you. Some people just can't act on their love,* etc. Phil thinks Carmen comes for the sugar.

He nods at her. She makes him still. This is because Carmen siphons anger from anyone around her, draws it like charged ions from the wind. Around Carmen, Phil is relieved of the anger he carries, could not find it if, armed with a scalpel, he vivisected himself.

Not until he's hiked out to his car in the parking lot that night does it occur to him to wonder if she has the same effect on McGee.

⁂

Four-thirty, Paulie Martinez is out in the small quadrangle's cement planter, what a surprise, smoking. A jut of his chin invites Phil to join him. Hugging his jacket around his ribs, Phil leans against the planter so he won't crush the unidentified green shoots. Paulie, crushing, perches in it cross-legged.

Paulie says, did Phil hear somebody saw McGee that Thursday, around midnight, sitting in her car at Lasso Nights? "Lasso Nights, Cowgirls Free." Paulie's top lip contorts with distaste.

Thursday, the last time Phil saw her. Phil's head jerks up. He hasn't heard that. Why hasn't Joan passed on that information, if she has it? Paulie would have looked knowing there, behind the smoke of his Basic, but his dark eyes don't always point in the same direction.

His mouth looks knowing. "Additionally . . ." he says, flipping ash to the wind. Additionally the word is somebody saw McGee downtown by the plaza and even gave her a "Hey, how's it going?"—on the Monday after.

"Monday?" The day McGee didn't show up. Eight days ago. "They're sure it was McGee?"

Paulie inclines his head. "What they say."

"Who's 'they'?"

Paulie shrugs. He never reveals sources. "She's booked, dude. MIA."

That's the rumor sweeping the school—McGee's taken off somewhere. Phil would lay odds Carmen has spread her dream around.

Paulie's thin cheeks suck in. With a stylish flick of thumb and forefinger, he launches the butt into the air and scrambles out of the planter. "Gotta go save the lab. That Ketterman"—the school's computer specialist—"dink's so lame." Trotting away, he calls back to Phil, "Don't go smoking any chalk now. Stuff'll kill you."

Phil's accelerated, on-the-job training has been provided by cigarettes.

One by one students approached him, usually the older ones, the non-trads. At first they squatted down beside him, asked for a light. Later they offered their packs to him, even the emergency singles they had stashed behind an ear. Paulie was the first. Slid down the concrete wall and bogarted his cigarette. "You're a teacher, right? Hey, where you from?" Phil told him. Soon learned that Paulie's the best in the world at some computer game. He engages and kills opponents internationally. The implements of his trade—elaborate blades, poisons, predatory lures and spells—are secondary to his true weapons, cunning and contacts. Paulie has groupies. They appear not as panting young babes with ripped fishnets but as awed type on his computer screen.

Jason Spoletti's bipolar, with the tangled ringlets of a Medici prince. He's aggrieved he can't get SSI like this guy he knows but proud he makes his own living detailing cars. Bipolar's a dance, he tells Phil, you got to have the timing. When his meds are firing, Jason's got it. He blows on his fingertips and polishes them on the shoulder of his torn jean jacket.

Night Class

Adelina's husband left her for another lady. She's got three kids, *here let me show you their pictures*. Jeremy, who lurks in the back of the class glaring out through a screen of hair, was raped in jail. He wrote that in an essay. He creased the essay in thirds like a letter, handed it in.

It amazed Phil, what they'd tell him. Anything, everything. He carried it home with him, this amazement, to his roommates who call him Professor then diss his paycheck, to the bar where he's doing his shy, earnest best to romance the sexy Irish bartender. It dogged him. Took Phil weeks to understand that the elusive property amazing him was courage.

Each of his confidantes seems to clutch the belief that by going to school they are working their will in the world, playing their hands to the limit of their nerves, changing their lives. Now when he hears a story—Anna's ex-boyfriend hasn't come once to see the baby, *he's crawling now I'm so tired after putting him to sleep I can hardly see to do my homework*— it gets him to the quick. What also gets Phil, a tender mystery he can't fathom, is they seem to feel it's something special to talk to him, their teacher, while they smoke their cigarettes. Or maybe he's just a novelty. Maybe they find him as much of a cipher as he found them at first. He doesn't ask himself why the unburdened don't squat down or slide beside him on the bench. He doesn't find that mysterious.

Human touch. They bring their faces close to his, flicking their lighters. They sometimes steady his match hand with their own warm hands.

❖

Phil stalks over to Admin, tilts into Joan's office, catches her vengefully whacking the space bar. Computer Services has just upgraded, and everybody's in learner mode again. Joan, a harried woman in her fifties with a taste for pricey manicures and a way of cutting the rug out from under Phil, hates upgrades.

No, Joan says, no official word. Maybe she'll try the police later; they've certainly not called her. She takes off her glasses to rub her eyes.

"What?" Phil says.

"Just . . ." She slides on the glasses. "I had to talk with her mother, and I got tired of hearing what a good girl McGee is for doing her mother's will. Permit me one second to be pissed as hell."

"Well, mothers—"

"I'm angry at McGee, Phil. It's dangerous to be a forty-two-year-old good girl."

In the River Province

This is a confidential remark for Joan, extremely un-Admin. She taps the desk with coral nails filed straight across at their tips. "Look, Phil, as long as you're here . . . the sub covering for McGee's come up with a fulltime slot, and I'm stuck. If we moved both 101 classes down to 205, could you cover till I locate someone else?"

"Sure."

She exhales loudly. "One brick off. Thank you."

Phil hesitates. "She could be just, you know, cooling out somewhere."

Joan's strained face gains a bit of life. "Paris on the Concorde. Champagne all the way."

Baja, Paris. "Everybody's got a destination," he murmurs.

"Oh and Phil," Joan's already clicking the keyboard, "there's no smoking in 205, either."

Next day Phil hears from two eager students more or less the same information Paulie has offered. Stale news by then, he'd already read about it in the *New Mexican* under the headline: MISSING TEACHER SEEN IN SANTA FE. Sightings. McGee is being sighted. Student consensus has solidified: she's done the Big Run, what every frazzled student and teacher dreams about. She's bailed. She's blazed. She is out-a-here, boys and girls, moving into myth.

Why not? Last year a teacher from Albuquerque stumbled out of her junior high classroom and drove her Honda sixteen hours right up to the Gulf of Mexico.

Phil tries on a scenario: McGee at some Motel 6 just across the Florida line. Her New Mexico license plate obscured with patted mud. The room bought with cash. Card signed with a fictitious name, Emma Bovary or Jane Eyre. Florida jungle breathing through the chain-link around the leaf-strewn pool. Quiet, dark green, moist. McGee in opaque black glasses, square like her face, her plump white body brilliant with Bain de Soleil, an escapee's wicked smile on her lips.

The wicked smile, that's the part he believes.

⁜

Rosa's just buttoning her coat as Phil ambles into the office to snag his video. Not a hangout kind of person, Rosa, she has kids to pick up. That's okay. It's the end of the week. On the short walk over here, he's had the greatest fantasy of what he'll say tonight to Siobhan, the bartender, and what she'll say back, and car keys jingling.

"You off, Rosa?"

She nods. "It's terrible, this wind, huh?" Then she wrinkles her brow, shakes her head. The headshake is not about the wind. It scatters his fantasy, brings Phil down. He's suddenly angry with McGee for taking over too much of his life.

"See you Monday," Rosa sighs. "Have a good one."

"Yeah, you too."

Phil plunges into an exercise on persuasive writing, reads over the students' shoulders, squats at their desks. When that's done, he hands back graded essays. McGee has advised him to give students their grades at the tail end of class "so they don't sulk on you." Phil forgets. He's anticipating his plan to illustrate "persuasion" by showing Henry V's St. Crispin's Day soliloquy: Branagh whispering and roaring to his ragged band. Before he can get to that, though, one boy, crumpling his C- essay, complains about having to take Comp at all. It's stupid and useless. He's Computer Science. After this class he won't ever need to write another essay in his whole life.

The other students perk up at this challenge.

"But this is practice," Phil says. "Did you not understand that?"

The boy's name is Randy. Phil slides into the vacant seat next to him. His cupped palms stretch out across the desk, as though full of something to give.

"You can make a verbal argument the same way you write one." He looks into the boy's face, not one who's sought him out in the quadrangle, not one who will. "Teach to the interested," McGee has lectured him, a veteran's advice. Phil has forgotten this, too.

"Won't there come a day when you need to persuade someone? When you need to make a case?"

"Not to a computer." Randy's pout draws a laugh.

"Well, to a boss, then. Maybe you'll need a raise."

"Yeah, Randy's gonna need a raise from minimum," someone snickers. Randy jerks around.

"How about to a friend you're about to lose? To a girl you want to love you? Maybe to your father?"

Randy's eyes flicker.

"You better hope that day comes," Phil says. "You better hope that a lot. What will you be without it?"

The dead silence in the class finally brings Phil to himself. He unwinds his tall frame from the desk, passes around Henry V's speech, explains the antique words. He shoves in the tape. Leans against the wall, absently pulling the skin over his Adam's apple, monitoring their responses. Some seem interested as Branagh vaults onto the scene; some fiddle. Jason Spoletti, car detailer deluxe, the guy with timing, watches wide-eyed, fingers hooked over the edge of his desk. Phil slouches in the dark. Kicks himself for overreacting to Randy's common complaint.

When Phil met himself, he encountered not only the gray strings and the ancient backseat trance tripped by Carmen Tapia. He met a part of himself that is *always* and *never,* that feels *how it feels!* like a torrent, a river, and it gleams like a sword. It embarrasses the shit out of him. He stewed over these fragmented parts to McGee once, over jasmine tea he brought in from the Red Dragon. She'd listened, her plain face impassive, loading her tea with packets of sugar.

"Oh honey if you mean crazy, that's not even twenty percent. Could be worse. *Believe me.*" Like many of McGee's opinions, this one had simultaneously comforted and unsettled him.

It is a couple minutes to the end of class; Branagh is inciting cheers from his muddy men. Feet are shuffling. All over the room backpacks are zipping. Somebody whines, "Can we go now?" Deflated, Phil waves them on. Randy is first out the door. As the room empties, he stops the tape, walks over to turn on the lights.

Jason remains, facedown at his desk, chestnut ringlets splayed and dripping over the edge. He'd thought Jason at least had been enjoying the film. Deal with it, Phil orders himself. This might be his life, temporarily anyway, but it is, as Randy has so forcefully expressed, only a stupid Comp class.

"Wake up, Jason." Phil taps his shoulder. "Show's over."

Jason shrugs off his hand. Phil doesn't know what else to do but stand there. When Jason finally raises his head, Phil sees he is weeping. Jason hoists his arm, smears his wet eyes against the shoulder of his MEN ARE GOOD T-shirt. Motions toward the black television screen. "Saw God, Phil," he says. "Would you leave?"

Phil closes the door gently behind him.

Back in the office, he lays his head down, like Jason, on his right arm, which rests on his own appointmentless desk calendar. What is he supposed to make of a class like that? He's tired, he's bewildered, and he has exactly twenty-eight dollars to last him the five days until his paycheck appears in his workroom box. A fair amount of that will go for four-dollar beers at the bar. He keeps on setting himself in front of Siobhan, with her glorious mane of clipped-up, falling-down hair, though she slags him for being too serious. Maybe because he's repeated his students' stories. Maybe because her accent transfixes him. When she speaks, shamrocks tumble from her lips. His eyes drift closed, and he is there on the tall stool at the bar, Siobhan's busy white hands wet and sparkling.

Phil's eyes flick open, focus on the new file cabinet, burnished black. "Shoes," he says aloud. He realizes that, drifting, Carmen's dream has intruded, the sparkling water, the ships.

Can you imagine McGee in puta shoes like that?

No, he hadn't been able to, had pictured McGee's unfetching Nikes.

But she had had a pair of shoes around, an extra pair, kind of sandally items. Not very high, but Phil supposes they'd qualify as high heels. Some pastel color. Pinkish, almost flesh-colored. "Makes your legs look longer," she'd said that and glanced wryly down at her short legs, "yeah, right." He sits up straight, remembering now. Sometime during his first, stage-frightened, disjointed days on the job. She'd packed them away in the gray file cabinet by her desk.

Phil shoots up, hustles over, slides open the top cabinet drawer. Files. Manila folder after manila folder, dog-eared. In the second drawer, exam bluebooks, rubber-banded by section. But these are pushed back to allow a space in front. The bottom two files are full.

No pink shoes.

The eerie thrill of his discovery subsides. She might have taken them out of the cabinet months ago, for all he knows. And what does it prove to know McGee had once filed a pair of pretty shoes? Phil falls back into his chair again. Imagines eagerly displaying the space in the drawer to some jaded detective. Good thing the cops stayed home.

⁜

He'd left her eating chocolate. Orange-filled chocolate pretzels. She had stopped on her way in that evening to buy a bagful. Phil had declined when McGee offered him one.

"Oh, come on." She hovered by his chair with her book bag and the chocolate in a white paper sack. Made a show of sniffing, wrinkling her un-made-up nose. "All those disgusting cigarettes," shaking her head mournfully, "and he won't take one little piece of chocolate." Even with Phil sitting down, McGee wasn't a lot taller than he was. "Let's see, how much am I gonna sue you for when I get second-hand cancer?"

"How about fifty bucks?" Phil's grudging response. He didn't like this game.

"Oh not hardly enough. I'll have the chemo bills and the radiation bills and the oxygen canisters and then the wig. Have to get a wig. What do you think about black and spiky? Something dramatic to set off the gaunt cheeks."

McGee sucked in her cheeks. Her chapped lips puckered. Her sort-of-blond hair, chopped into bangs and at the jaw like she cut it herself with kitchen scissors, had a few strays lofted by static electricity.

"Hot, truly hot," Phil said.

"Seriously, Phil. Quit."

"Seriously, McGee. Chill."

She flapped the sack at him and made her way to her desk. "You know I thought about you when I read this book this week and . . ."

Relieved she'd shut up about his smoking, Phil bent over a composition again.

". . . written by a young woman, a Dutch Jew . . ." He heard the book bag thump, and two clunks, which meant McGee had put her feet up on the desk. He picked his way through an essay as she talked. Standard coworker mode, no need for eye contact.

The woman, McGee said, had ministered to detainees at Westerbork. "Where?"

"Jumping-off place for Auschwitz." A Jewish saint really, Phil should read this book. She had to run here and there to hole up and write. Wrote so vividly about all the people, helping them pack their coats and sweaters, find a plate or a washcloth, holding their sick babies. The deal was, she was so . . . vivid. Incredible. Really alive there on the tracks with the Auschwitz trains huffing. Her letters—

Phil glanced back at this shift in McGee's voice, raw, covetous. Her little paw was crimped into the sack. She was gazing down into it, as though its contents were excruciating. Square jaw line and whacked-straight hair the only angular things about McGee—otherwise, she was as circular as a snow-woman. Little round breasts topped a rounding midriff attached to a bottom rounder yet. She had on what he would call a poofy skirt, and she looked like she was sitting on a pillow. Eating candy with her feet up, envying a concentration camp inmate. Phil's head skewed to the side at the pure weirdness.

"Over and over she writes about how the world is beautiful. She honestly felt that. She had a place, a shelter, for all that suffering around her. Somehow that left her a place for herself. I think it made her free. I know it made her brave. She was . . . impossible."

Without her usual veteran-of-the-trenches expression, McGee looked flattened, dissatisfied. She looked—hard for Phil to credit his eyes here—lost. Not lost like him, sinking, flailing, grabbing on. Lost like she knew where to go but would not strike out for that destination.

"You really admire her," he said slowly. "Don't you?"

"She also wrote," McGee regrouped, flashing a wicked smile, "about how cigarettes pollute the body. I was getting to that."

"Always the punch line, McGee." Phil wanted to zing her back; at the same time, wanted to say something nice to her. Finally he let it go and asked McGee for a pretzel.

"Hah," she said, "he caves. Catch."

She tossed him one. Their camaraderie, such as it was, had been restored. Eventually McGee introduced a new subject: Carmen Tapia's latest tragedy. Her mother had borrowed her car, brought it back with a hole where the CD player had been. They discussed Carmen until it was time for their night classes. He hadn't seen McGee afterward. She hadn't stopped in his doorway, as she often did, to declaim, "And another one bites the dust." She must have used the side door. She must have gone straight to her car.

Sometimes they walked to class together, Phil in 203, McGee in the barnish 205. But that night, McGee was apparently in no hurry. She was still tipped back in her chair, her feet in the white-and-silver Nikes on her desk, crossed at the ankles. One eyebrow arched, she'd blessed Phil on his way. Parodied the sign of the cross with her pretzel, said, "Body of chocolate." Popped it in her mouth.

✢

Phil pushes out the door with his hip, on his way to 205, where both his and McGee's classes will cram the room—some forty-odd students. He balances his books against a fat stack of handouts, grips these tightly against the onslaught of spring wind. He's taken only a few steps into the quadrangle when the double doors to Admin begin to swing open.

His two bosses, usually pulling into their driveways at this time, each pushing a door. Two colleagues who shun each other unless yoked by some official duty—Enrique, the president, his thick black eyebrows lowered, and Joan, her face grim. The doors swing so slowly that to Phil, who's blinking, they open again and again in a kind of crazy replay. Then Enrique and Joan release a door, his door, her door, and at the same time, each catches sight of Phil.

They huddle. Joan, hair blowing, almost imperceptibly shakes her head. They angle toward C Building, where Enrique's office is located, ignoring Phil.

He has been avoided. He should go on to class; he is exactly two minutes late now. But he can't. He cannot do that. He strides over, flapping khakis molded to his thighs, his long shinbones, and plants himself in front of them. He scrutinizes Enrique's face, Joan's.

"The cops called," he says.

"No," Joan corrects him bitterly, "they did not. I happened to call them."

"You know."

They know. Joan allots him one spare and ghastly sentence. Phil jack-knifes, clamping the handouts against his chest. "But what happened?" he cries. "How did that happen?" Joan winces, and the three of them shiver miserably in the wind, staring into one another's eyes.

"Goddamnit." Joan can't take it. She retreats into her professional capacity. Phil *will* cancel class and let the students find out from the ten o'clock news. In their own homes, with their families. This is traumatic. This is *not*—she squints meaningfully at him—a rookie assignment, does he get that? The school has procedures, responsibilities, and he's no counselor. She'll write an all-campus bulletin, have her work-study send it out. No, the work-study left. Joan sags. She'll do that herself—and McGee's mother? "I'll speak to her," Enrique says.

"Look, Phil." Joan shields her creased brow from the hair beating across it. "Cancel the damn class. Take yourself home." They leave him standing there.

Out of the corner of his eye, Phil sees semaphoring. Yells, "Later," shaking off Paulie Martinez.

Night Class

III

He lumbers down the narrow hall for 205. He means to dismiss the class from the doorway, but he does not make it that far. One of the chairs that line the wall catches him as he sinks into it, drops his books and drops the copies, which fan by his feet. A head pokes out of 205, retreats. It returns with more heads.

Call the class, call it. Phil continues to slump in the chair.

Paulie blasts through the side door. He clamps the cigarette in the corner of his mouth between thumb and forefinger as he hunkers down by Phil's knee. "Dude, it's ill," he says, "oh, it's so ill."

Phil fixes on Paulie's independent eyes, black and deep. "Don't feed me any rumors," he warns.

"On my life this time. Aunt's a dispatcher." Details spill out: cops have McGee's car. Blood in the trunk. Blood at the scene, little house southside. Confession. Suspect led police to the body. Arroyo up north. Battered, strangled. Nude.

Phil has flinched repeatedly. It occurs to him he will read these details in a newspaper. Everybody here will read them, and they will all see McGee, as Phil is seeing her, in the last vulnerable, terrified seconds of her life.

"She went with this guy?"

"Looks like it."

"How'd they find him?"

"Ran off at the mouth."

"Jesus." Phil closes his eyes. He needs to get up, cancel the class, and get out of here. But just now he is on his knees in the packed sand of a distant arroyo. He feels space. Dizzying, unsheltered space. Scything wind. He provides a blanket to cover her, wind riffling this soft, unlikely blanket over two small feet bare of nylons and shoes. He touches one foot at its unprotected instep, whispers, *Jesus, McGee, McGee.*

"You okay, man?"

Phil straightens. "Paulie," he tries thickly. Clears his throat and tries again. "Paulie. You could go help Dr. Schafer put out the all-campus bulletin."

"Gone," Paulie says, and he is.

The sentries at the door plunge out first, followed by the rest. A girl darts to scoop up the handouts and deliver them to the safety of Phil's lap. The hall fills, keeps filling. Forty-odd intensely silent people crowd him. Night classes, men and women, mostly eighteen and nineteen, but they are also twenty-five and forty-five and sixty. Apple shampoo, clinging cigarette smoke, sweat, clashing perfumes—the hall is stifling. They are crammed shoulder and elbow, knees pushing into the backs of knees.

Carmen shoves through. Her spiral hair cleaves her face, already beginning to flame. The flush creeps up in blotches, singeing her neck, one steep, heated cheekbone. "Tell us," she says.

Not a rookie assignment. Ten o'clock news.

Phil stands up and tells them. Joan's sentence and, beginning with "It's possible that—," a curt summary from Paulie's details. There is a groan from forty throats, a mass, guttural note. The groan curdles into quiet, as though a collective breath is being drawn, then the corridor bursts with pent-up horror and pity. "No, who would do a thing like that?" "No, it can't be—" "No, why would—" *No, no, no!* and *Why?*—a swell of shrill, girls' voices, male exclamations and growls. Rising then, cutting through the reverberation, is a vicious solo from Carmen Tapia. The murderer is damned, savagely and for all time, McGee absolved, *so what if she went some place she shouldn't have went that's not her fault who did she fucking hurt?*

Phil breathes in the fire of Carmen's breath. He pats her shoulder—it feels like he is smoothing iron—but makes no other effort to tamp the anguish. He's as much a part of the piteous clamor as they are. He expects they will want to disperse and go home as he does, but when no one leaves, when it seems the hall will stay solid with shock and outrage, he gestures toward their room. "Maybe," he raises his voice, says, not knowing if this is true or not, maybe they should all take just a minute?

The crush of people funnels clumsily back into 205. They wrestle paper from their packs and write, as Phil bleakly suggests, whatever they want to write at this moment. Whatever needs to come out. Some fall to at once while others, including the teacher, take longer. Eventually all heads bow. The wall clock sweeps on to their industrious scratching. Twenty-five minutes are gone before pens begin to plink against desktops, thirty-five when the room is sealed in quiet. Some dare to read their compositions aloud, and they are awful, raw things, and good.

✤

I Loved You Then,
I Love You Still

HIS PLAN couldn't have been simpler: walk the Good Friday pilgrimage to Chimayó, make a prayer to Saint Anthony to take away the Syndrome, get a baggie of the *santuario*'s healing dirt, hitch a ride back to his truck.

It wasn't just to save a few miles on his not so springy bones that he took the shortcut. Andy took the shortcut because he loves the noises trees make in the dark, thick time before dawn. Always has. So instead of humping blacktop, he'd cut through this way with the trees rustling around him. He meant to come right out on the Nambé road that winds through the hills and down into the village of Chimayó.

The road kept on not being there. Andy didn't even snap when the two guys ahead of him, one swinging a flashlight, their jackets taped with reflector strips, vanished. Now it's four A.M. and he's sitting under a cottonwood, waiting till he can see his way out of here. This is what he gets for walking the pilgrimage at night so he can come up on Chimayó just as the world is growing light at the edges.

It's the Syndrome's fault he got lost. Periodically, since about December, it seizes control of Andy's facial muscles, causing his eyes to wink and blink, his lips to *ooo* into a fish face. Or maybe the fault is Teresa's—she's barricaded an avenue of Andy's brain for thirty-nine years, keeping out who knows what other bright information or chances. He'd been pondering how to evict her from the private preserve of his memory as he ambled along the shortcut, a *pinche* little foot-worn track that meandered and curled, branching off here and branching off there.

Now he'll miss dawn shining up the hills.

Andy uproots some tasseled weeds and throws them. They blow back on him, *cómo no*, so he knocks them off his pants and uproots some more and holds them in his fist. His back rests against the cottonwood's furrowed hide, his feet are dug into last fall's crackly leaves. The wind is up, teasing his ponytail, tossing the top branches. After a while, he chews the tasseled weed; it tastes like celery.

Thirty-nine years since they were eight years old.

An excitable girl, Teresa, small with lashing black hair. A sparrow-sized girl but not a sparrow. No, if Teresa had been a bird, Andy thinks she'd have been a parrot: mango yellow and lipstick red, blue and neon green. She'd have sung or scolded all day. When she got mad, her family ran for cover—even her stooped *abuelo*, who'd ridden with Pancho Villa and who prowled their yard with a crooked stick to defend the house. *Dime cuando la sangre no está caliente*, he'd say, retreating to his room. Angry women are bad for a soldier's nerves.

But she didn't get mad at Andy. Exasperated, maybe. She dug at him as though with an impatient yellow beak—pried, prodded, tickled, and teased him. What do you want, woman? he'd laugh, though she was barely a woman and he barely a man. Only *el mundo*, Teresa would stare him in the eyes, and a hundred dollars. Give it to me.

In those days Andy didn't have the hundred. As for the world—how could he give her what she already was?

If Teresa would vacate his head, the inside of him would be more spacious and peaceful; Andy could, for one very small instance, go to plays. His nephew Berto was always asking him to come down to the high school, see him act. Just last month Andy put on a jacket, paid two dollars at the door, stumbled over a fat extension cord to the metal folding chairs around the stage. How could anybody see in here? Everything painted flat black. The kids wearing baggy suits and dresses, contorting their mouths into English accents, Berto a detective with shiny hair. A house scene. Slick, too, except for a door that stuck so a girl exited through a window. Then after the first act, some kid stagehands dressed in black began to move the furniture, quietly. Picked up the chairs. Turned the sofa. Quietly, quietly. Brought in a lamp, a rug, smoothed the humps. The neck hairs beneath Andy's ponytail crawled; his heart chilled. He went out and sat on the steps, came in an hour later when he heard the applause, shook Berto's hand. Went home and turned Teresa's photograph facedown.

In the River Province

Ramiro and Sammy, city cops like him, his brother locals keeping him out of the scene. Squeezing him at the door. It was easy; Andy has never weighed more than one hundred thirty pounds in his life. They told him to go home, go back to the station. State cops had it all fixed anyway, had been there first; had, he was sure, the locals were sure, doctored the room to erase any signs of a fight. Left the gun in her hand and picked up the knocked-over stuff, a lamp, bills on the floor, a rack of *Sports Illustrated*, smoothed the twists in the rug. Did that to cover for one of their own, their cop buddy, Teresa's husband.

After that night at Teresa's, Andy turned in the blue uniform. He bought himself a saw and some carving chisels and became a furniture-maker like his father.

Andy cocks his head at the silky tree voices, *sisss sisss crisp sisss*, all around him, boughs swaying. It's chilly, but the wind carries some strong spring in it. The trees shuffle and brush; they love it out here at night. Imagine, Andy thinks, a tree in a house . . . He realizes he hasn't been seriously outside in the night for a long time.

He hasn't walked the pilgrimage since the year Teresa broke up with him and he *fuck her* signed up and went to Nam. Teresa coming into his kitchen asking for her pictures back. Andy knew which ones she meant, the Polaroids of her naked on his bed, her pretty little body curled on the red and blue Indian blanket. But why was she doing this? What had he said wrong?

Nothing! She threw out her hands. Then she drew them back in and whispered, But somewhere in my heart is starving.

He had always accepted that this girl was dramatic. He accepted everything about Teresa—except that his acceptance puzzled and annoyed her. Andy sighs and stirs his hand in the old leaves. He should have built a few roadblocks, given her something to throw herself against. He should have developed some drama himself.

She took the Polaroids. The screen door banged. Andy sat there tingling, his hands and feet shocked cold. He called and called her on the phone, but her mother said some gringo was writing Teresa poems. One night this gringo even slept outside her bedroom window; the boy was obsessed. Her mother said, Let her be a while, Andres, her head is full of cotton candy. Eee, girls, you know how they are.

He guessed he didn't know how they are.

I Loved You Then,
I Love You Still

He signed up a week later and then made the pilgrimage. It wasn't a knife he carried in his heart, more like an anvil in his bowels—he had to drag himself along the road. It was snowing when he started out; Andy let the snow pile up on him. He passed only two other walkers and at the head of the Nambé road an old man tending a *luminaria* for the pilgrims' comfort, stirring the fire around. The old man had some mean-looking boys with him. *Watch your back* occurred to Andy, then *Who cares*, but one boy came forward and invited Andy to warm himself a while.

The pilgrimage worked for him that time. At some point, maybe when he was hunkering by the fire, sweet piñon smoke nestling in his hair and clothes, or maybe when the snow stopped and he was peering upward at an isthmus of stars, Andy knew he would come home untouched.

Vietnam's heat met him like a furnace blast in the face, right there on the steps of the plane. Andy walked down into a mortar attack. People running off the plank across a huge flat field, diving behind a sand-bagged embankment. Andy jumped over, landed on a sergeant who yelled, Get off my ass, you fucker! One little fat Mexican guy behind Andy just running in circles around the field screaming, *Me van a matar! Ay, por Dios! Me van a matar!* Finally crawled underneath a gasoline truck. *Ay, por Dios,* Andy said to himself, the guy is cinders. When the attack stopped, Andy jogged over and got him out from under the truck, talking to him in Spanish, asking him if he was all right. *Sí, estoy bien,* the man said, *Gracias a Dios, Gracias a Dios.*

First day.

Prayers all over the hut on the day they read the assignments—Not in front, Not in a combat unit, Not in front, Please. The sergeant called his name: Andy what-in-the-hell is this name C'de Baca?

Trying to explain it was Spanish from Cabeza de Vaca. The sergeant rolling his eyes, sticking him with *Alphabet.*

Muttering all around him, Please Please. Andy knowing he'd be okay. The sergeant's thick thumb on the clipboard.

Alphabet, Medic.

Medic? Andy's faith wavered: not the most okay job he could think of.

The sergeant again: Naw, you're going to Medical Supply first.

Medical Supply. Far out.

Andy stretches his chin and massages the muscles around his mouth. The neurologist has tried five kinds of pills on him already. They don't work for shit. He says Andy's brain signals are haywire. Misfires. Andy thinks stress. Andy thinks he hasn't been touched in three years, but who tells a doctor that? Either way, the Syndrome could go into spontaneous remission. Any day, gone, just like that.

Ramiro squeezing him at the door to Teresa's house. Go back, get out of here, man. Sammy, get him out of here.

Sammy shoving him into his city cruiser. Two city cars, four state. Sammy's acned face, like he had fifty vaccinations on it, mounds and dents, scared eyes, shaking his head. They were cousins; Andy knew what his aunt Lola spent on Sammy's skin—ointments, pills, blood-purifying herbs.

Sammy whispered, Look, didn't Teresa use to be left-handed?

The back-slanted handwriting. The notes passed to him in civics class. Later, on the pretty envelope delivered to the base hospital, a wedding invitation, he was stunned, like he would come home to see her marry the gringo. Like he would go even if he was back home and his front door opened onto the altar. Andy took his keys and raided surgical supply. He brought back a big-ass saw, femur-grade, held the envelope on edge, and began to saw it into strips. Would saw up the shiny-print invitation, too. A guy up in bed wearing sunglasses in the dark, watching.

The guy asked, Who you amputatin', man?

Andy told him to mind his own fucking p's and q's.

The guy laughed. Man, you must be Alphabet. You Byron Ricks's friend?

Sawing. Paper strips falling around him. I know Ricks, Andy said. Why?

Why you think? Cause you here tonight instead of Ricks. Alphabet, you are one teeny tiny stupid fucker.

I wouldn't talk that way to a man with a great big saw if I was you and couldn't run away.

The guy's sunglasses caught a beam of light from the hallway. Listen, motherfucker. I might just rise up and fly right out of this bed, for all you know.

I guess so, Andy finished sawing the invitation, you don't have no feet.

Deal with it, the guy said, you got to deal with it. The sunglasses were sunk back on the pillow, the guy's chin up in the air. Still hurts,

I Loved You Then,
I Love You Still

don't it, my alphabet man? She is gone and she still hurts you like a son of a bitch. You can still feel her shape, her nice warm skin, her wigglin' little self. You go to touch her, don't you? Now speak with the doctor, Alphabet. You go to touch her, right?

So what you care if I do?

The chin thrust up from the pillow, talking. Man, you go to touch her again and again, and it is just your own weak dreams. Deal with it, you got to deal with that shit. You know your problem?

Andy stopped sweeping up the paper shreds, leaned on the broom. How is it you claim to know so much about my business?

The guy crooning, Ain't nobody need to tell Noah about the flood. So you listenin', Alphabet? Here comes your problem. She is invisible and she is the realest thing you know.

Andy turned his back and mock-sauntered out of the room for a dustpan. But there in the supply closet, as if she'd waited for them to be alone, he heard her laughing voice. Clearly as the clang of the dustpan, which he dropped: *El mundo*—and a hundred dollars. Give it to me.

Andy squints toward the sky through the top branches but gets that strobe effect the Syndrome produces. He could use a cup of coffee. A friend told him some people give it away to the walkers—tastes like brown water but the coffee smell and the caffeine are heaven. Every year those same people park their Airstream on the road, set up a card table, give away donuts and cookies, too. Nobody doing that when he walked last time. Just Andy and his legs going down the road.

Teresa's voice on the phone the last time he talked to her: evening, Andy was putting on his uniform for the eight to six A.M. shift. Her voice gave him a shock, so familiar, like she'd really been always with him, just gone for a while.

She said, I made myself one big giant mistake, Andy. He doesn't want kids, he just wants me. Every breathing minute. It's like living under a boulder you can't push off.

I'm sorry it turned out that way. Andy wasn't sorry, for himself, but her voice, without its bright bird-lift, made him sad for her.

Why didn't you get married? I thought you would.

Didn't happen for me again, Teresa.

Well, I'm going to leave him. Tonight. I'm going to do it tonight.

In the River Province

They sat there a while, Andy thinking his ribs might crack from the pressure of anticipation. Then she said it.

Andy, could you still love me?

He would have laughed but his throat choked. Yeah, I could.

She sighed, then tensed up again. Sure you mean it?

Peeled his tongue off the roof of his mouth. I mean it, I do.

Still love you.

A few hours later Andy was slumped behind the wheel of his own cruiser, numb, not really sure how he got there. Someone crouched in the space of the open car door—Sammy, face like a wound stirred around, poking him. Andy, Andy. Didn't Teresa use to be left-handed?

He nodded, She's left-handed. Cruiser dials lit like a space ship, didn't know what was what anymore.

Sammy looked back over his shoulder toward the four state cars. Eee man, I'm sorry, Andy. The gun's in her right hand.

His head fell forward. Forehead pressed into the metal ridge of the screaming horn, matching his outside to his insides, until Sammy pulled him off it.

Still love you.

Andy pokes a finger in his ringing ear, kills the echo. Considers whether the Syndrome is creeping next into his ears. If it gets into his ears, he'll hear like he sees, like his little niece Bernadette wrenching his truck radio dial back and forth, deafening the middles out of sentences.

Still you.

The sky is graying. Andy should get up, but instead he shifts his head on the trunk and snugs his jacket, wraps his arms around himself. His eyes wink closed, and he lets them stay that way. There've been women since—a neighbor lady, a pretty clerk at Woodworker's Supply, a customer from out of town, a good friend, Kate, whose hair gleams like polished mahogany. But it never clicks, never sticks, he can't explain it.

Andy sees the Polaroids of Teresa again, her body a snowdrift on a field of sky and apache teardrops, her bright eyes that want everything, her sly smile, the Polaroid going clunk on the dresser, and he dives toward the bed but lands on the roof of St. Anne's, lands on a day they were eight and still located in the same geographical world.

Some fantailed pigeons had got loose from a cage and roosted on the

*I Loved You Then,
I Love You Still*

school next to the orphanage. On the roof two stories up. Man offered five dollars to get them down, big money, and Andy the smallest and quickest of the boys. Light. Cartilage for bones. Pretty little waddlers with colored tails, purrrting and gurgling like water whistles.

April day, wind chasing the clouds across the sky, Andy up on the roof with a gunny sack, running and sacking. Four nuns down below praying, then squinting up and screaming, Andy, be careful! Praying again. Andy pretended to slip, windmilled his arms around just to hear them screech. Great. Caught a pigeon, shooed it into the sack, sloping shingles and blue sky, the top half of the world.

Then he saw a girl standing by Sister Fatima. Big, fat, sweet-hearted Fatima, hiding her eyes. Andy gave them the slipping act again, collapsed, grabbed at a shingle. Laughing to himself. A pigeon skittered sideways. Fatima swooning, hooting Andy! Oh Andy! The other nuns black and white semaphores.

Don't look down!

He hears his own faint command to that young Andy, Don't look down there! Look at the bird. He grabbed it, about to shove it into the sack. *Prrrt*, it said, its eye a rainbow, dumb little water whistle.

Andy looked down.

And looks down and looks down the length of his life at the girl beside Fatima, head tilted back, tide of black hair lapping her waist. Heel wedged to the instep of the other foot like a T square. Arms folded. Sun snapped from her eye, shot him a dazzle of prism, zap!

Andy jumps like a trout. His eyes pop open. He's flinched onto the dirt with both hands, banged his head on tree bark. Did he go to sleep? Must have, look, the night's gone. Everything around him woody and bud-green, clean morning shadows sharpening these gossipy trees.

Sissss, Crisp, Teresa, Sisssssss.

Bullshit, even if every *chingada* word is true.

Andy creaks up to his feet brushing off his pants, batting cottonwood fingers out of his hair. He can find his way out of here now. And it's not Teresa goddamnit, he'd take a nice, not-so-pretty, old-as-he-is woman any day of the week, any hour. It's not Teresa. It's what they would have been, him and her together. That was his part, his place, his turn on the wheel. It just never rolled that way again, and what is he supposed to do about that?

In the River Province

It's after seven o'clock; he'll make the *santuario* by ten. The road is right up there, he's pretty sure now. Andy peers ahead.

Specks in the distance hopping up and down like fleas. Some low, some higher. His eyes are acting normal, but Andy puts the heels of his hands to his eyelids anyway and holds them steady. The specks up ahead become bouncing balls with legs. Maybe little heads?

A trailer with white siding, no skirt, pot of stems with a bleached ribbon, a toy lamb, flat. Bouncing balls are children, baby children, one hopping on a card table, the other two kicking up the road. The one on the table probably not three, hand-me-down sweatshirt over stained foot-pajamas. Face like a sunflower zipped into the hood.

"Yay!" they're screaming. "Yay! Yay!" The littlest one claps, stomps baby feet. Waylaid, snatched by chubby hands, Andy's claimed, captured by miniscule businesspeople, towed to shore, their valued customer.

Does he have any change? How much do they want?

"Free ice tea! Free ice tea!" shoots up from both sides of him. One detaches long enough to slosh tobacco-colored water from a pitcher. The little one stomping the card table, pitcher trembling in the quake.

He asks them, "Is the road straight ahead there?"

"Free ice tea!"

Their eyes like quarters as he accepts the Styrofoam cup.

Andy tastes the tea. His eyelids flicker, blinking and winking; he sees plantations of sugar cane shadowed by Hawaiian volcanoes, Himalayas of lump sugar, beaches of extra fine granulated. His teeth twang. He makes a fish face.

The children imitate Andy, even the baby on the table puckers and smacks.

Andy pokes out his chin to ease the crimp in his mouth.

"More? Hey, you want more?"

He holds them off. Tries again, "The road's right out that way, isn't it?"

They shrug, fish-faced, gleaming.

He sets his empty cup down on their table. The little one is squatting, hands on baby knees. "Ummm good," Andy says, "thank you." He waves at them. He walks off but can't help looking back.

Back in December he'd gone and asked Teresa's mother if she minded if he ran the memorial notice.

I don't mind, her mother said. I'm glad somebody remembers Teresita like I do every living day. You know where that rotten bastard is?

I Loved You Then,
I Love You Still

123

Andy didn't have to ask who she meant. I don't wanna know, he said.

Okay, I won't tell you, Andres. You're my real son-in-law, Teresa's mother said, not that *hijo de puta*.

Andy ran the ad on the eighteenth anniversary of the day Teresa's husband put the gun to her head, maybe just to scare her; maybe he screamed too when it went off, who's gonna know now? There in the obits Andy shouldered past the other dead people and in their approving presence—a Schumacher from Chicago, an *abuelita* from Río en Medio, a guy named Freddie in a too fast car—finally said his piece.

I Loved You Then, I Love You Still.

Is that what you wanted to hear, Teresa? Can you hear me now?

Forty-seven years old. This is how it turned out.

This stupid mystery is your life, he marvels, and he skinnies through a barbed wire fence and trucks across a bit of field where a brown horse startles him with a husky neigh like an engine turning over. Then someone's backyard. One house, another. Wind's up again. A cottonwood swipes down with its young, mustard-green knuckles. Andy dodges, and comes upon it.

There past the trees, colors jerking along. A bob of white and blue. There's the road, the world going on all the time right beyond where he could see. A couple with their arms around each other, a yellow dog on a rope. Two women in conversation, one stout in the middle, one with bouncing, wiry hair; some teenagers all in black walking backward to give their leg muscles some variety, punching each other.

Andy crosses a ditch and climbs onto a curve of the road. Does a little two-step on the slippery gravel. The woman in front of him stops to tie her shoe; he's obliged not to step on her. His mouth is okay, but he runs a hand across it. "Morning," he says.

"Hi." Two women answer him back. "Got some miles to go, don't we?" the stout one says. She straightens, using her middle finger to poke back the glasses that are riding her nose.

"Yep." Andy walks around them. "But you'll make it."

He's out of Nambé's trees and into the hills. If he'd been on schedule, he'd have seen the mountains roll gently away and the sun strike the hills amber and rose. So that part of the day is gone, and the hills are rusty red, but he'll still come down to the village where the *acequia* will be gushing and the fields are soaking green, where the apple trees float their white blossoms above the boughs. The priest will have shoveled out the healing dirt into a box on the altar. Pilgrims will rub it on their knees or kidneys, take it to sprinkle in the four corners of their house. That's how it is, and that's how it will be, and if Andy C'de Baca is only a bird-shadow skimming the hills, what a fine light thing to be.

A pain stitches two ribs tight. Who is he kidding?

"*Ya pa qué,*" Andy whispers, a bitterness that seeps into his mouth every so often now—What for, Stop wanting, Give it up. Occasionally he yells that. The worst is just to find himself against a wall in his shop, his eyes stinging.

But this time he bargains. He makes a deal. *If I could have that feeling like after I got home from Nam. Teresa was married, past, I let her go. I went out and sank my feet in my mother's garden, felt the sun on my face. I had my life. I just was. The treetops angled their beams into my empty hands, I thought I would burst from the peace of it. I wanted nothing, belonged to no one but that living day. If you give me sometimes a minute like that one, I'll be satisfied with this damn life, okay? I won't look for more. I promise I won't look for more.*

"Then . . . ," he demands from the bitterness its part of the deal, "just shut up."

"Is he talking to himself?" someone asks.

Heat prickles Andy's neck. He turns to see the two women he passed catching up to him.

"If he is, we might as well talk back to him," the stout woman says. "If you don't mind. Talking helps me not notice how tired I am." She's Irene, and this is her sister . . . Andy doesn't catch the name. Irene laughs, "Let me tell you, my sister and I already know every last word each other could think up to say."

"Andy," Andy says, and as the women smile and nod, he automatically takes the outside next to where the cars pass by.

"So do you walk every year?" Irene asks. She has a good stride for a tired woman.

"Once before. Been a long time."

Irene says, "Yeah? My husband used to walk years ago back in the sixties. When did you come?"

"'Sixty-nine. It snowed."

I Loved You Then,
I Love You Still

125

"Yeah?" She looks at him then, and it's like they know each other a little. "In those days most people forgot about the pilgrimage. They thought it was old-timey stuff, all primitive. Then we get computers and satellite dishes and"—*fff*, she blows out her breath—"here they all are again."

People are strung out in clumps all along the road, before and behind them. One family pushes a stroller with a pink balloon tied to it. Far back a tight group with a banner crests a hill, a human galleon with flag flying the wind. Two guys in headbands and prison tattoos veer around, nodding as they overtake Andy.

Irene describes her husband's diabetes, which needs a lot of attention, and last week he couldn't make out the newspaper anymore, which she won't get into, but it leaves her a load of work to do. She's started seedlings to put out next month, on every windowsill and on the kitchen table she's got her green babies—tomatoes, peppers, squashes. She already set out her onion and garlic, now that's a pretty one growing, some herbs and one other thing . . .

"Marigolds," her sister reminds her. "To keep the bugs off."

"Marigolds, right." Irene's head bobs.

Andy's stuck back on her husband and the blind newspaper, but the mention of flowers jumps him to something he hasn't remembered in almost thirty years—these plants with white flowers by a trail in Vietnam. When he ventured near them, the plants' tiny white faces shrank back from him like frightened people. He tells the women about this curious phenomenon, and it's nice, telling someone something he's remembered, just like that, without storing it up to tell later and then forgetting all about it.

"Did the flowers go back how they were after you scared them?" the sister asks him.

He points his finger. "You know, that's exactly what I tried to see. I think they did."

"That's amazing," she murmurs. "They'd have run away if they could."

"They weren't the only ones," Andy says.

"Yeah but the point is how did they *do* that?" Irene is emphatic. "As a rule, plants just sit there. Some herbs, though, have medicinal properties that—"

Medicinal herbs calls up Andy's aunt Lola and a flash of his cousin Sammy's lumpy, agonized face at the cruiser, but Andy shuts off the picture. Shuts it off. Instead, he listens to Irene. She has a low and easy voice that goes fine with walking; every so often he asks her a question. Of course he knows about osha for colds, who doesn't, but she's telling him about an osha cure for snakebite and her uncle, who poked his head into a rattlesnake hole and got bit six times in the face, and all his teeth fell out, then grew in again.

"You expect me to swallow that *cuento?*" Andy chides her.

"True story!" Irene protests, laughing.

"Would you look at this one," Andy elbows her as a red-haired man jogs past, barking into a cell phone. Irene shakes her head. She says she walked last year in the afternoon when a helicopter kept chopping around overhead to get pictures like the pilgrims were refugees. That's why she's walking early this year.

With a lift of her chin, Irene's sister indicates the red-haired man. "Why bother to walk? E-mail your prayers."

Andy laughs. He can smell summer not too far off in this fresh morning, and he does not want to be any other place than he is right now. The sun spills yellow on the red hills; the clear yellow light falls over him, too. Over Andres C'de Baca, furniture-maker, uncle, friend, kind enough man, lover of trees.

The sister smiles at him in a weary, friendly way, and the smile invites him to notice the lines around her mouth, her eyes, how the springy waves of her hair are threaded through with willful silver. Her skin is the color of honey inside those little plastic bears. Her hands are jammed into her sweatshirt pockets. He can't tell if there's a ring.

But he's looked, hasn't he. To see if she's a free woman.

Andy you son of a bitch you broke the bargain you went and looked.

His lips quiver. His eyes tic. Andy slips the rubber band from his ponytail in order to snap it on tight again, a subterfuge to turn his face aside. Neither woman seems to notice that his heart is a sorrow he carries in his arms, or that on the round hills inside him, light is breaking amber and shadowed violet, or that at first grasp his long hair escapes him, waving out in the wind, whispering that he cannot quit. But who, today, is so different from him? Who's not carrying a sorrow?

I Loved You Then,
I Love You Still

127

Today hills walk into the hills, a procession of scarred green walks down to meet the blossoms on the trees' spread arms; Andy C'de Baca is only one among them. He pops on his rubber band, savoring the perspective that those other days visited by loneliness and regret are the illusion, that this day is the real day.

Irene squeals—she's skidding on the gravel shoulder. He grabs her arm. On the other side, the sister throws out her hands to catch her, and Andy looks.

✤

The Saint
of
Bilocation

FRAY ANTONIO made several false turns in the convent's winding halls
before at last discovering the courtyard. He brushed a dozing yellow cat
off a stone bench, sat down with his book, and gazed around him. He
was home in Spain. See how lovely and clear this April day was, pale
sunlight just washing the treetops, glittering off the blue tiles. He sat
for a long pleasant time overhearing one of the convent's many music
lessons—a *romance* in a minor key accompanied by mandolin. He admired the measured phrasing of the distant female voice. He breathed
easily. A student began the verse and broke off; then the teacher's precise
voice sounded again. As her voice rose, he began to anticipate its point
of resolution. He perceived an inevitability about where her notes would
fall or rather be placed or end; at any rate he was gratified to hear it.

It brought back to him an assertion by the archbishop of Mexico's
secretary, an ink-stained Jesuit: "Mathematics underlies both beauty and
truth." Didn't Fray Antonio agree? Fray Antonio had no opinion. The
Jesuit's remarkably narrow eyes stretched wide. But surely he had an
opinion regarding the new Italian publications on astronomy? The clas-
sical theories were crumbling. The universe had proved to be a construction of twirling spheres! Fray Antonio sat up; he could produce a con-
tribution here: hadn't the Inquisition summoned the author? The secretary
believed so. There was a silence. The secretary sipped from his goblet
and allowed that mission priests labored far from such discoveries and
must encounter strange opinions. "Yes, often," Fray Antonio said and
drank from his own goblet. But he felt he must say something more and
fell into a conversational trap: that of speaking of a matter too close to
the heart to a listener too far removed.

"I have most recently," he'd confided, "heard an old Indian sing, an extraordinary sound that struck in me a need to understand as well as to teach and convert . . . to effect a kind of union . . . as though of two flames, different in nature of course, and the Christian one . . ." He trailed off; the secretary's mouth had twisted, as though Fray Antonio had confirmed some private suspicion. "I can't explain it," Fray Antonio apologized with a small smile. "It's not mathematical, I'm afraid." *Ah!* The Jesuit's inky finger flew up. He could not vouch for the kind of singing Fray Antonio had heard, but *real* music *was* a mathematical accomplishment. At least they could agree there? Fray Antonio had replied cautiously that he considered music a true ornament to the mass, much as seasonal greenery. The secretary's long upper lip had twitched. From then on the Jesuit had discoursed on scales, semitones, octaves, the perfection of fourths and fifths and combinations thereof. Fray Antonio had nodded alertly.

He waved a hand in the April air, dispersing the cloud of that memory, and listened to the mandolin. He thought he could agree to this much—music was beauty made manifest. He wished he had thought to say that. That much he knew. As for truth, he had watched sailors plot a true course by siting on the frail light of stars.

The yellow cat jumped onto the bench and butted him until he scratched its scarred head. "An arrogant person, wasn't he?" Fray Antonio said to the cat. The archbishop's secretary had become a sore point.

It festered, the hesitation about his appointment as interrogator, whispers in the hallway beyond the archbishop's chamber, some sidelong appraisals cast his way. He was sure it was the Jesuit's doing, all because he had no pretty conversation. Well, he *was* after all the muddy mission priest the man had so clearly taken him for, wasn't he? Simple. Mass to him was no spectacle of calculated parts but a ray: God and souls and interposed between these Fray Antonio their priest, faithful servant of the Holy Church. At least he hoped he was a faithful servant. In his last days in the River Province he had not been so certain.

But he would not think of that now. Now he was home. Fray Antonio cocked his head as the student tried the *romance* again. A certain vibrance, yes, but even *his* crude ear perceived the less secure rhythm and therefore—he supposed it was so; the Jesuit would be cringing—the less beautiful.

His calm disturbed, he turned to his book and ran his hand over the fine binding. This was the one he would present to the king, though of course the king had already read it and now—staggering news from the bishop of Viseo—wished to grant him an audience, after his work was finished here. Fray Antonio's hands on the folio trembled. The king wished to meet him, Fray Antonio Jimenez Vera of New Mexico, the priest who had brought the New World so vividly into the Old.

He fled into his prayers, including one for strength and guidance in this present endeavor, his interrogation of the abbess, Sor María, repeated his thanks for arriving safely here in Spain, though the voyage had been mostly tedious. He prayed that His Majesty might be persuaded to dedicate larger funds for the missions and for additional priests, that a great number of heathen peoples might be converted. As for his own audience, he did not take that to God. That was his responsibility, a temporal matter. Noting the tremor in his hands, however, he urged himself—Fray Antonio was very fond of reminders, even to himself— to keep about him the dignity he commonly possessed and not to be rendered dumb by the magnificence of the palace or the court.

After eight years in the wilderness, even this provincial convent seemed magnificent. This cloister was a miniature, lovely and secret as a compartmented jewel box—*civilized* . . . Fray Antonio lingered on the word. The cloister was cleverly walled away from the church; the courtyard with its charming fountain must be entered through a series of tiled arches, past twisting staircases, past niches in which the stiff wood bodies of the saints were dressed in fastidiously detailed finery. By comparison, the New World was, he would say . . . a place without bounds. Earth and heavens folded into one, the land airy, the sky firm. One was startled by the moon floating in a river, the immense blue shredded in the branches of a wintry cottonwood. Fray Antonio occupied, when he was not riding out into successive horizons of brown and savage peoples, a mud dwelling by a raw turn of river with two other priests and a contingent of soldiers as guards.

Fray Antonio opened his book, located a passage the archbishop himself had remarked upon: the day Fray Antonio had converted the Xumanas and they had raised their arms to him, these hundreds of Indians, to signify they wished baptism. He could not help reading it again. He read to himself in a low voice, though he was alone here—

he'd scanned the courtyard to make sure of that—on the stone bench. A tingle diffused through him; it was thrilling to know the world would read his words. He could not have imagined the excited interest that had been kindled by his book. The people of Spain wanted to hear about the New World, and not only they but also the people of France and the Netherlands. The type was being set for these translations.

Fray Antonio did not realize that his voice had risen, for his eyes had closed as he recited. He was almost to the end of his passage when he looked out again, gazing dreamily toward a crook of two olive trees beyond the spouting fountain. At once he stopped speaking. He was shocked and humiliated to be caught so privately, but first he experienced a surge of terror.

For a face peered from the shady place, mocking him. Head and hands lilted along with his phrases, eyebrows contorted mournfully; its expression was a parody of exaltation. When the priest froze, the face mirrored him, clamping shut its little mouth, the lips drawing into a fierce and silly pucker, its eyes bulging. And such a face—small and white, plain as a painted angel's yet as dreadful as a demon's in its wicked mobility.

As soon as he could catch his breath, he huddled his book against himself and lunged forward; the cat tangled his feet. His imitator faded away through the greenery, disappearing into a tiled notch. Running there, Fray Antonio could not discover the hold with which to unlatch what must be a door, certainly was a door—the outline was visible to him now, cleverly tiled to resemble the wall. He pushed in frustration and the door snapped open to a passageway and a slender flight of stairs. Fray Antonio stayed where he was, gaping. "What are you?" he demanded; "what sort of thing?"

Patting his chest, he remembered himself, his dignity, his place, his mission here. His good sense gradually returned to him and his even breath. Had he become so proud he couldn't bear a little mockery? A child probably, evading musical instruction or chapel.

He would return to his cell, he decided, to prepare his questions for his interview of the abbess tomorrow. This sensible resolution was met by a resumption of the music lessons. He smiled at himself then—Fray Antonio Jimenez Vera of the River Province of New Mexico, appointed interrogator of the abbess Sor María de Ágreda, vain author cherishing his own perishable words—and clapped a hand to his ear. He strode away, pursued by a passionate clarion fanfare in every key, wild, inexpert, simply horrible.

⁜

Baptista huddled in one of her lesser places, a stairwell converted into a repository of saints' spare clothing, and stood San Rafael on her knees. She had grabbed him down from his *nicho* for sustenance and for company here in the darkness; everyone said he was her best. Guard me, Rafael, who guards the spirit, Archangel, Minister over all the wounds of the children of men. Guard me, Patron, you who guard the young and the innocent and eyesight and lovers.

How she'd chased the pigeons, collecting real feathers for his wings! She didn't care how insane she'd looked. She'd chased round and round, almost forgetting her purpose in the pleasure of running, the sky spinning, the skittering birds. Purple and sea green she'd dyed the feathers and set them in curved stripes. Stroking them was life. Her hands were clever, everyone said so; she had pleated his yellow undertunic minutely. Just the clear fine yellow the treetops caught early after prime, and she'd given him a blue mantle, draping it so the wind flew through. She tatted the gold lace for his breastplate and hem, glued on his bald head two snippings of her own brown hair and tousled it—the wind again—and tormented Amalia with her pleadings until she got from the smith a flat copper scrap for the crown of her angel's head. "Have him round it now," she begged, "round it perfectly into a halo and don't leave the rim sharp. And will you ask him to polish it?" Baptista stood her ground when Amalia complained. Her Rafael's face was not bored like Saint Michael's as he killed the dragon. With her paints, she'd made him curious; his dark eyes saw everything and his lips smiled, his cheeks flushed pink like the abbess's.

The abbess.

Baptista knocked herself hard on the head, a habit of hers. Why had she mimicked the interrogator? She knew exactly why. She had done it as she did all else, as she chased pigeons—she gave her head another knock—because she had found herself in the luxurious midst of doing it. Now she was afraid to present her diary. He might not believe it or what she could tell him.

She could tell him, Yes I have seen the abbess on her travels. I have seen her grasping a crucifix which did not return with her. I am her servant by the grace of God and her own infinite patience, and as she did not forbid me to do so, I wrote everything down in a book I keep in my cell. I can give you the book with the dates and written below how the abbess behaved and illustrations—oh I loved painting them!—of how she appeared on these occasions. Truly it is my heart that sees and my heart that paints, though my fingers are stained for some days after, and I want you to take this book.

Then they will make her a saint, and she will be remembered forever.

She sat at her desk abstracted with her eyes open and unseeing, and so great was her devotion I could not wake her. Her hands turned and circled in the air, she made the sign of the cross, she spoke words I could not understand. Sometimes she stood in a fall of sunlight and became that sunlight itself, hazed and gold and still, yet moving in a thousand ways. Sometimes she rose in the night and wrapped in her cloak walked until she grew small in the silvery distance. She walked inside the night and then came out again. Thus it seemed to me, and I was not frightened. I had been two years in the convent by then, two years my brothers had forced me here with my meager dowry, and what I saw—only that—allowed me to remain in this world.

I saw stone walls and mountains and oceans were as nothing to her, and one day they were as nothing to me, and as I hid in a stairwell, I sent myself through to the outside. With no transport but my own crude senses, imagination and memory, I flung myself down beneath a wide tree. Above me the blue case shone, and the clouds lived their busy life. Beneath my back the earth breathed its chill, but the grass on top was warm, and I lay there circled by everything wheeling—sky, clouds, swallows, sun, evening stars. Their course ran through my body and filled my poor spirit again.

When I returned, time was not what time was. I had exchanged a measure of sullenness for a measure of peace and did not hide away for some long amount. Then I learned this exchange was not permanent but would have to be repeated, over and over. I ran to the abbess and threw out my hands.

The abbess said, "Learn this, Baptista. This is the nature of our life on earth."

And I said, "I know this life is a dream and a preparation for the life that comes to the good. Because of you, esteemed and beloved mother, now I see it is possible to let my soul give me my life but, misery to me, only part of my soul lives in eternity. The rest of it lives here in my body this minute and also tells me things to do."

"Baptista, you will not harm yourself?"

"You have made me understand that to do so would be to forfeit my home in heaven."

She took her hand from her throat. "Will you hide away from us again?"

"I am sorry, Sor María, but this sin might occur."

She could have locked me away. She could have set the silver cap on my head, with its crown of silver thorns that pierce away all bad thoughts. The disciplinarian often makes me wear it, though it functions precisely as she would not have it do—it fills me with murder, even as the blood trickles into my hair. But no one is like the abbess; she did not do this. Instead, she set her white hand upon my head, and her eyes pierced mine. "*Niñita*," she said, "understand well. From within these walls you may write in your books and work your paints and laugh when it pleases you. Outside you would suffer and die from the strictures of the world."

I had my answer ready: "No, I would walk to Seville and make myself a seamstress."

"The church would find you, for apostasy is a great sin. What do you say to that?"

"I say my face is plain like a thousand other women in Seville, and now I am grateful for what was once a sorrow."

"And what do you say to your brothers, who beg me to keep you out of fear their little sister will become a whore?"

"I say I will not become a whore, but if I did, I say the Church herself teaches that whores may repent and afterward become seamstresses in a lively street while nuns may only repent. I say men are various while, forgive me, Sor María, the hours of a convent are one eternal bowl of pottage and clabber."

She only laughed a little sadly. She said, "Grow into the beauties of this life, Baptista. Others have. Many others, even a few who came as unwillingly as you."

I hung my head.

She begged me never to forget my prayers. She said though she had more complaints about me than the night has stars she still would have me with her. I would remain her servant, and she asked that I work very hard to reconcile myself to this life.

The Saint of Bilocation

"Never," I promised, "I will never forget my prayers. Nor you." And I covered her warm sweet hand with kisses.

Light struck Baptista's eyes; cool air plastered her cheek.

Sister Epifania's voice reported, "Here she is." Footsteps congregated outside the small door to the stairwell; hands reached in. Before she could be seized, Baptista scrambled from her hiding place, still holding to her guardian Rafael. She surrendered him to Amalia, who slouched to the side of Epifania, biting her lip. Rafael looked on curiously, a gust of wind ruffling his brown hair, as Baptista's shirked tasks were sternly recounted to her and her punishment.

Her punishment! Perhaps the visitors caught a glimpse of her at the head of the procession, unveiled, dressed in the shameful white flannel, perhaps not. But Baptista's sidelong glance caught them. The important priest from the New World, the interrogator, the reader, the worried one she so carelessly imitated, was accompanied by a soldier. How tall, how brown the skin of his face. Whitened lines at his eyes.

Prodded ungently from behind, Baptista glared down on the thumbs of her knotted hands and the walk's stone, the familiar threshold of the chapel. "We did wrong to put her in sackcloth!" Carlos, the youngest of her brothers, had cried out. Jorge's and Raimundo's faces had grown pinched at her pleading. But they had carried her back here. Baptista flinched as lozenges of amber, ruby, emerald—the rare light of the chapel—settled onto her white flannel shoulders. A wall away lived springtime and trees dressed in the tenderest of greens and sunlight plain and clear as tears.

✢

The abbess's confessor, an old priest named Fray Luis, had arrived again to conduct them to her room. Politely Fray Antonio invited him to wait outside the door.

Fray Antonio passed a finger before his lips. Then he cautioned his guard on many expeditions—his friend, truly—the soldier Juan de Vaca, that he was to be silent during the interviews. There must be no more exclamations. Did he understand? Juan nodded. Quietly and with much grimacing, Fray Antonio continued to remind Juan of all that he knew very well.

"The archbishop has charged me with this task, that the infant Church of the New World not be damaged by a fraud or by an insane woman."

Juan bent to the priest's ear. "But she knew the River Province,

Father! She described the nature of the land and the exact manner in which the river cuts—"

"Haven't you considered that her knowledge might be taken from my own account? Juan, *m'hijo*, what was the date of publication?"

Juan replied that it was last year, 1630.

"And what is today's date?"

"The last day of April but one, 1631."

"She couldn't name all the Indian kingdoms, could she?"

"No, Father."

"The names she has produced for us are garbled, no?"

Juan's brow furrowed briefly.

"Do you agree? You are my help here, Juan, my second pair of eyes and ears. Do you agree the names are garbled?"

"Yes, Father, they are."

Fray Antonio patted Juan's arm at this confirmation, brought his fingertips together, and spoke in an almost normal tone. "Now after today's interview I want to question the community as a whole before I return to her. We shall complete this little side trip and be on our way in less than a week. And your duties—"

Juan smiled. "I promise you I know my duties, Fray Antonio. I am to make sure the horses are rested and well fed for the journey, to find a capable boy to accompany us as servant, and I must be on guard lest bandits rob us of the special copy of the book you are to present the king or any of the gifts from the New World you bring for the bishop of Viseo and others—"

"*Bien, bien.* You seem tired, Juan. Are you well?"

"I am, Father."

"Enough sleep? It's very noisy here. Cats squalled outside my window last night. Did they wake you?"

Juan told him his cell had no window; he was not bothered by cats. Fray Antonio examined Juan's face with some care. Yes, a bit tired. The priest said, "You must be very anxious to be finished with this matter and on to Seville. You'll be glad to see your sister again?"

"Very glad." The soldier's face lighted then dimmed. One sister alone remained to welcome him, and her husband, a sly inspector of cargoes for the Contratación. In the eight years he had been away, his mother and elder brother had gone to God.

The Saint of Bilocation

"We're home!" Fray Antonio clapped Juan's shoulders; for some time they grinned at each other. Then, remembering how soon they would part, a wistfulness came over the priest's smile. It was unlikely, since Juan thought to remain here in Spain, that they would see one another again in this life. Fray Antonio said, "After these years it will seem strange not to have you nearby."

Juan quickly bent his knee and kissed the priest's hand. He continued to press it when he stood again. "Strange," he agreed. "And sad for me."

Fray Antonio had planned his own solemn speech of leave-taking. These simple words—and the tears in the soldier's eyes—surprised him. He turned away, blinking, toward the window that framed a late afternoon slipping into evening, the odd hour Sor María de Ágreda chose for the interviews. When he had recovered, he opened the door to Fray Luis, who pointed the way and started off.

"Here we are, riding out again!" Fray Antonio peered fondly up into Juan's face, and when the soldier smiled at this little joke the priest asked him, under his breath, of course, if he had heard the town's opinion of the abbess's bizarre travels.

"Yes. They believe it. And far beyond this town, they say, people believe."

"And their opinion of Sor María herself?"

"That she is a saint."

Fray Antonio shook his head. Despite his cautionary speech, he also thought this could be so. He had listened open-mouthed, at their introduction, as she described the river kingdom. But he would be more prudent in forming his own opinion. Of course he would give over his materials to his superiors; councils would be called. He was not appointed final judge, but he was required to report. "Do *have* an opinion, Fray Antonio. And *don't* let the woman play you for a fool"; the Jesuit had found it necessary to say that outright. Church authorities had become suspect of supernatural tales. They so often sprouted cults and heresies.

The priest glanced at Juan, whose eyes were averted from him, as though searching the horizon for dangers, a soldier's habit. The horizon before them, however, held only the winding stone hall of the Convento de la Concepción Purísima. Spain. Civilization. Home.

✤

Lately Fray Antonio had experienced a certain stiffness in his knuckles, but today he noticed no discomfort. His pen ready, he cleared his throat.

"As you know, the bishop of Viseo, the archbishop of Mexico, and many learned theologians are interested in your claims. They speak of your bilocation. While you remain here in Spain, you also appear to preach among the Indians. Will you tell us how this feat is accomplished?"

Old Fray Luis sat to one side and behind her in a leather chair supplied with a cushion. He smiled toward her expectantly.

Sor María de Ágreda gazed toward a window of fading afternoon. She told Fray Antonio that her "wings" to the New World are Michael and the blessed Saint Francis himself. She might be at her desk, writing, she said, when a fall of sunlight enters the door. She turns for her cloak and finds herself almost instantly walking down from the hills to join the Indian peoples. While she is there, in the land of New Mexico with them, she knows their languages perfectly. She—

This was the opening. Fray Antonio executed the plan he'd conceived quite on his own, simple though he was. He interrupted her with a greeting in the Piros language.

Her expression did not change. Her shoulders lifted and fell. "I don't know that speech here," she said.

Fray Antonio switched to the Tigua tongue—no response—and then to the language of the Apaches de Navajo.

"I told you. That speech doesn't remain with me here."

Fray Antonio's lips puckered and then drew into a straight line as he marked in the back pages of his notebook, in a chart he had devised. No Indian lang. A disappointment. This, he felt, would have proved the matter quickly and beyond any doubt. He amended himself. At least, she would have convinced *him*, the intermediary to more learned minds.

Next, however, was the question he had been instructed most particularly to ask. Fray Antonio could not deny a certain excitement. He located his cambric handkerchief and touched it to his mustached lip.

"How long does it take to reach the New World? Is only . . . what the theologians name your *spiritual essence* . . . transported? Does your body remain here?"

She did not turn away, nor did she seem to appreciate the import of his words. Her thick eyebrows lowered.

If she knew how detailed, prolonged, and heated the discussion had been on this point! The archbishop's elegant chamber had been loud

The Saint of Bilocation

139

with terms and theories. And she says nothing? Fray Antonio thrust his shoulders forward.

"During sleep or dream, Abbess, does the body dispatch the soul? Or is the soul liberated by the very act of the body's disengagement in sleep? Are your travels more precisely visions of the soul—is this why you say you fly to New Mexico several times in one day?"

Discomfort rippled over her face; again she gave him no answer. Heat rose and settled on his forehead.

"Let me refine. Do you experience a rapture or a suspension, in which you find yourself frozen into a momentary posture? I mean to say, you may be sitting or standing, and suddenly your body is suspended, drained of heat and sensation, barely breathing, while the soul lifts free? Is the body entirely abandoned or does some part of the soul stay? And is your return in a few moments or is it hours or does time pass at all?"

Sor María shrugged. "Time and the body are not questions I must answer, nor are they obstacles to overcome. One world lies without boundaries inside the other, Fray Antonio. I am here, I am there, it does not matter. It is the work which matters and that work is the people whose hearts are opened to God."

The dismissive tone offended him—that was all she would say? He and his brothers in New Mexico had also caused many heathens' eyes to be directed toward God. A great many. When Fray Antonio finally spoke, his voice was more strident than he meant it to be.

"Why were you chosen to perform these miracles, Abbess?"

"That I cannot tell you, for I do not know. Why were you chosen as my interrogator?"

"I know the River Province, and I am given to writing with care about what I have seen." His earlobes burned. "I'm afraid I have no high qualifications."

María de Ágreda bowed the face that caused him such unease. Softly she professed humility; he read in the bent posture of her body a fervent sincerity that swayed him. Until she murmured that when she wrote, she would write of other things.

"*You* would write?"

"Yes."

"That is to say, you would write of things you cannot see?"

"Yes."

In the River Province

Both replies had caused Fray Antonio's jaw to cant to one side. But wait, hadn't he been told of her writing? Some sort of treatise on geography, no? Except that the woman had included the dimensions of planets, calculated the celestial regions! His brow wrinkled; he set aside the subject of bilocation. Descending to the mundane, he asked about one mission in particular. The abbess lifted her head.

"At that mission the priest was an old man, but he was not gray. His hair was still black. His face was long and very red. He was a trifle stooped, but he worked with zeal. This Franciscan waved the people inside, but they were too shy and crowded back into the doorway—"

"José," Fray Antonio whispered, his pen arrested. This was the second occasion the hairs on his arms had risen like grasses in a breath of wind. Involuntarily he glanced behind him at Juan, whose stance against the wall had become rigid. Anyone from the River Province would recognize old José from her description. Fray Antonio did not think he had included this priest in his book, but for a moment his tumbling mind would not recall this point for him. "Fray José Pino, you mean?"

Her palms turned up. She did not know the father's name. Her slender hand drew down below her chin, to indicate a length of face. "A red complexion," she repeated, folding her hands.

Fray Luis sighed in his sleep. His white-bearded chin had sunk to his chest.

"Please continue." Fray Antonio found his place again on the notebook's page.

"The people crowded back into the doorway when the father would have them come forward to be baptized. The baptismal font in that mission is of stone; it stands to the right of the door. The father needed them to align themselves so all could see, so that he could call them forward, one at a time. But they were too shy. So I pushed them."

Her lips curled up ever so slightly, but as she met his intent eyes, her face became again impassive.

"I gave them a big shove from behind. They all turned around to see who was pushing, the ones at the back especially, for they'd felt my shove the hardest. They saw no one, though they often see me. And when they saw no one, they laughed and came forward, arranging themselves as the father would have them. They are a patient people, intelligent, deserving . . . "

The Saint of Bilocation

141

Fray Antonio looked up. "The Indians? I too have had some occasion to find them so. But that is not the common view. Surely you know how many religious have been martyred to the more barbarous tribes."

She allowed that God calls many martyrs.

Fray Antonio realized he was poised on the brink of relating the story he had so mistakenly confided to the Jesuit. The old Indian's song, which had caused in him such confusion, such a desire to know, such a . . . removal from himself and the true world. He held his tongue, though, judging that that matter and his own puzzling over it lay wide of his duty as interrogator. Nevertheless, he sat forward, expectant, hoping despite himself to draw out their little point of sympathy. But she said nothing else; her eyes were gray and steady. He swallowed and went on, "And Fray José?"

"The father baptized many souls that day, mothers, babies, strong men. His mission stands not far from a piece of the river. Large trees border the river there, their trunks wider than the embrace of one's arms. On the one nearest the mission door he has hung a crucifix—not from Spain. His was carved by an Indian. It's curious and beautiful."

Behind him a choking sound as Juan stifled himself. Fray Antonio wiped his brow. He had stood before this crucifix himself, disturbed by the power in its crudeness; the figure seemed to flow from the wood or into the wood. In it the cross and the man were one. The season he last saw it was autumn; the huge cottonwoods' leaves burning gold and amber; if one gazed into them one was dazzled by sunlight and flame. A little ways beyond, the silver river gleamed.

Silver and gold, as the adventurer Nuñez Cabeza de Vaca had promised the crown of Spain.

"Tell me, Abbess, have you seen on your travels any cities of gold?" Fray Antonio ventured the trace of a smile.

"Do you want to know if the Indians cook their meat in gold pots? If they tip their arrows with emeralds?"

Even a provincial nun like this would have read of Cabeza de Vaca's marvelous claims. One of her heavy brows was arched at him. He decided her strong black eyebrows were masculine—the women of his family were delicate. She had no right to the irony he saw in her attitude now; as for claims, hers were the more fantastic.

Fray Antonio's smile dried up. He would try his second test.

"Let me inquire along another line. In Fray José's province, a chief lately requested from him a piece of baize cloth in which to bury his mother. It seems she fancied the gray color; she had seen it on the person who appeared to the Indians. What can you tell me about this?"

Her eyes narrowed. "*¿Una viejita?* And her son the chief carried a scar *así* on his cheek?" The blade of her hand cut sideways across her own rosy cheek.

Blinking, Fray Antonio agreed, "About there."

"*¿Y la viejita está muerta?* Ah." She crossed herself, the slender hands coming to rest in a spire.

"You must know it wasn't gray she admired, Fray Antonio. Someone has told you wrongly. This woman was always touching the cloth. I said to her, 'It's the blue of the heavens.' 'No, maiden,' the old woman pointed upward with her crooked finger, 'the best blue of the earth.'"

The chief had indeed asked for blue; this test she had passed. Fray Antonio sat back. Sor María's eyes, which he had formerly thought gray, brightened to the color of sunlight on leaves. New April leaves, like those beyond her window. He knew somehow that she would smile but for the gravity in his own presence.

"Your habit is gray and white. Your veil is black. How can you claim she is speaking of you?"

Sor María rose from her desk. She crossed the room to a trunk and lifted from it a coarse cloak of a vivid blue color. Fray Antonio took it into his hands. The cloak recalled to him the sky of the river kingdom on an autumn day. The cottonwood trees blazes of saffron against the blue—a lake without ripples stretched above his head, an airy calm lighted from behind. Many days he was happy there; a fragment of that happiness surrounded him, now, in this room in Spain.

"The dye comes from here. It is fixed with alum, or sometimes with urine," she told him. "I wear it on my travels."

He put aside the cloak almost reluctantly, dipped his pen and recorded everything in his notebook. Though he would rather have pressed her again on the mechanics of her bilocation, he asked her to describe the Isleta mission. She did, in fine detail, recalling how the church was laid upon the land and its particular appointments: a copper bell, a painting brought from Spain, which hung, she believed, upon the wall of the common room. Fray Antonio had seen this mission; what she told was almost precisely true.

He rested the pen, closed his notebook. Juan came to stand behind him. At once Fray Luis pried himself from his chair to guide the visitors out, his small eyes bright, watchful. Fray Antonio wondered if the old man had been asleep after all.

In the doorway he turned back toward the abbess. "That painting you mention is the portrait of Mother Luisa de Carrión. It hangs in the refectory, not the common room. Her habit is very like yours."

"Yes." She glanced down at the gray sackcloth, the rough white habit over that, the Franciscan cord at her waist, and looked up at him again. White cloth was wound around her face. That was the first time the hairs raised on his arms, on walking into this plain room to meet her. A little woman whose entire family had gone into the religious life for, he'd assumed, the usual reasons of poverty and superstitious piety. And then.

Then the woman at the desk had turned on him a face of such astonishing beauty that it aroused not admiration but awe and perplexity. A soft wide forehead with a spot of luster at its center, black brows, heavily lashed gray eyes, clear with a tint of rain; shell white skin suffused with a rosy underlayer, rose lips. He must have shown his confusion; he'd stepped back from her. He had not imagined a saint should look like that, for he had never until then seen a woman who had.

Fray Antonio tucked his notebook tightly beneath his arm. He said, "Good night, Sor María. Tomorrow I shall begin to interrogate the community, with your permission."

"With my permission, Fray Antonio," she answered, inclining her head. Fray Luis hovered by her side.

"Why—," Fray Antonio whirled, he must know this, "if you have as you say visited the New World on these many occasions, cannot even one friar report seeing you? Not one?"

"There is no need."

The room had dimmed with evening. He could not make out the color of her eyes, but her cheek in the fading April light was the same rose-tinted pearl, preposterously lustrous. Again her tone was flat. He had stopped in the doorway, twice called her back from her own duties. Her folded hands, the inclination of her head told him she was waiting for him to leave. And so he did.

✛

It was very difficult to settle into making his private notes. He walked about his room, his mind multiplying new questions. Finally he slipped off his sandals, unknotted the cord at his waist, and sat down. Here was something he could do. In the back of the notebook where he had drawn the lines, he inserted the story of José on the side of confirmation. And the crucifix. Her accurate description of the River Province also went there, and the blue cloak. Against her were her misnaming of the Indian kingdoms, her inability to reproduce any of the Indian languages here. His scheme resembled a ledger, and as of that moment it was weighted on her side.

You must form your opinion carefully. But you are not the judge, Fray Antonio reminded himself. You are a recorder of testimony. An instrument.

That was how the idea came to him. He knocked over his bell, picked it up and jingled it, then described what he wanted to the servant. As he waited to receive it, he bored in on the issue again. The abbess did not fear him; he had observed that. To old Fray Luis, however, the trials of the Inquisition were not so far removed. Indeed, though Torquemada was long buried in hallowed Spanish ground, Rome kept the Inquisition alive. The favor she enjoyed with the bishop of Viseo could not help her there. If no one authenticated her claims, what happened to her then? The proofs of her innocence—or guilt—could be prolonged, terrible, and bloody; that face burned and pierced, that pure, unmarked face . . . Not your affair, his intellect chimed. Pues, bien, if she did not fear him, neither did she rejoice in his presence. That was clear. In fact, in the flattened voice, in the shrugs, didn't he detect a suppression of the personality? Deception? Possibly, or even the manifestations of madness.

Or perhaps this saint of bilocation simply did not like him.

The sting he felt at this interpretation brought him to himself again. He pressed his temples and let out a deep breath. He padded over to the window on his bare feet and gave himself this reminder: liking Antonio Jimenez Vera is not a condition to sainthood.

He started when the servant returned with a small brass scale suitable for weighing delicate quantities. She lighted the tapers he pointed to and retired. Fray Antonio prepared to say his prayers, but as he knelt the bright reflection caught his eye. He could not help noting how distinctly all three parts of the flame could be seen in the brass—the blue base, the clean yellow spire, even the shadowy midportion between.

The Saint of Bilocation

145

The door had a heavy key, but again the soldier had not locked it. His candle had not long been extinguished; the windowless cell smelled of smoke and his sweat. Baptista's bare feet floated across a shaft of moonlight. She knelt beside the low, narrow bed. She could make out only an outline of him in the black room, but she could smell his sweat, feel the heat from his body.

"Talk, whoever you are." His low voice was not meant to frighten her. He could have demanded loudly; he could have pointed a knife. She had, the first time, entertained various perils. But he had only asked who was there; she had been sorry not to answer. His naked arm had reached out, and as naturally as a sunflower, Baptista inclined herself toward him. He traced her head, her brow, nose, lips. Before the hand could leave her, she quickly turned her head so that her cheek fit against his palm. Callused and damp, it had kindled her cheek, tightened her stomach, stolen her voice.

But now, on this second secret visit, she answered him, "Someone who asks your help." Baptista wedged her diary against the soldier's chest.

"What is this?" he asked.

Without her permission, her fingertips took the delight of touching him. The soldier's jaw, so hard, his beating neck, his shoulder, his chest, his belly with its arrow of hair. Then she rose and fled.

✤

Yes, of course Juan might attend the interviews of the community as long as he remained as before, impassive. Witnesses might be subtly influenced by an emotional bystander.

Juan touched his lips.

"Very well. Call the first one."

Juan called the nuns, scrutinizing them rather severely, Fray Antonio was amused to see. Oh, they had long been allies, he and Juan! The first nun testified, and the second, and the eighth, and their confessors, Fray Luis and the younger priest, Fray Anselmo. Twenty-one more nuns remained. Fray Antonio had miscalculated badly—this process was more lengthy than he ever dreamed. Each had some marvelous moment that must be heard by Fray Antonio—a time when the abbess's face could be seen through like glass, in the garden when roses seemed to sprout from her fingertips, this and that petty kindness. It was late; the questions became deadly tedious. None of them had witnessed anything conclusive by Fray Antonio's standard, though four reported—he scrupulously noted this—that the abbess's cloak gave off a peculiar odor of comfort. What would be the nature of that odor of comfort? Three squirmed and squinted but could not say. The fourth, Fray Luis, was more articulate.

"It is an odor which calms the soul, Fray Antonio. It may enter *aquí*," he tapped his drooping aquiline nose, "but it settles quickly into the heart."

"What can it be compared to? A floral scent? Rose? Violet?"

Slow shake of the head.

"A warm smell of the hearth?"

Again, the old man nodded No.

"A perfume or an oil, then? Musk or myrrh?"

"No no it's—" The old face, shrouded in thought, shone with relief. "It's like a silent choir."

Fray Antonio could make nothing of this but senility; nevertheless he wrote it down, duly asking, "And how is this odor like a sound?"

The old priest had to consider that weighty matter.

"Shall I repeat the question?"

Fray Luis waggled a finger. "No, no. An odor and a sound . . . both can fill one, no?"

"But how can a choir fill if it's silent?"

Again the old priest assumed a posture of deep concentration. Fray Antonio pulled at his beard until the answer made its circuitous way into Fray Luis's brain. Finally he exclaimed, "*De este modo!* One perceives its music with the inner ear!"

"Ah."

Fray Antonio stood, rubbing his hip. "It's very late, well past the hour for dinner. I think," he told Juan, "we'll continue tomorrow. Fray Luis's profound meditations must conclude our session today."

Fray Luis's smile was as indiscriminate as a baby's and nearly as toothless.

Fray Antonio took his cheese, bread, and chocolate in his cell. Stop thinking about it! he commanded, but the long hours of questioning had overstimulated his mind and left his body restless. If what she said were true . . . if, if, if. He tried to imagine being enveloped in an archangel's wings but failed. He couldn't determine a convincing sensation—hot and feathery? No, that evoked the odor of chickens. Cool like marble? Surely angels had not such density. Perhaps thin . . . yes, of course, translucent as . . . as a seashell, and God's light penetrating the great, boned wings. An enormous figure, human and divine, its face obscured by light but its palms open. Visible, the joints of each curved finger—this, he saw! Frightened, Fray Antonio beat his fancies back and prayed for an hour to quell the disturbance in his brain.

When he sat at his desk again, he copied the blessed odor testimony—there were four of them after all, a valid corroboration—from the record into his back pages. He had nothing with which to oppose this information in her favor. Then he folded the column and tore it out, rolled it into a fat spill. He dropped it on the scale, into the tray holding Fray José and the Indian crucifix. He knelt and eyed it to be sure. Yes. The tray was weighted lower than the one holding No Piros Lang., No Tigua Lang., No Apache de Navajo.

⊹

The next day, Fray Antonio began to pull at his beard much earlier. He had to remind several long-winded witnesses that kindness was quite an ordinary quality in the world while flying in an eye's blink across an ocean was not. One Sister Filomena, an old nun whose mouth drooped unpleasantly on the left side, sputtered that she had witnessed the abbess lit from behind by the glorious light of angels.

The explanation was obvious. "Were you in her study?" Fray Antonio inquired.

"Yes, there."

"I believe the windows there face both south and west. Did the abbess stand before her west-facing window perhaps?"

"Oh just so!" the old woman cried. "Her blessed body was framed in rose and golden light!"

"What time of the day was this vision granted to you?"

"Oh, at sunset, Father."

"Did anyone else witness this event with you?"

Knuckley fingers dabbed at the dribbling mouth, a burst of pride. "Only I. And Father . . ."

"Yes?"

"The angels bore dear little children's faces!"

"Thank you for your testimony, Sister Filomena."

Fray Antonio set his pen on the desk and flexed his wrist. "The next, Juan," he said.

Juan strode into the hall and returned with a girl who seemed too young to have taken full vows, a tiny triangular face bound with vast white. Juan took his place against the wall, but Fray Antonio noticed the soldier studied this girl, like all the others, intently. The priest was touched again by this allegiance on behalf of their mission here; he felt fortified, less alone. He picked up his pen.

"Sister—?"

"Sister Amalia, Father," the girl supplied.

"Sister Amalia." He did not have to read the questions by now; his voice was dull from repetition. "Have you on any occasion seen the abbess fly?"

The little nun blinked at him. "No, Father."

"Have you seen her body rise into the air and hang suspended?"

"No."

"Have you seen her soul escape from the sheath of her body as she sleeps?"

"No."

"Have you see her, perhaps, awake but seeming asleep, frozen into one posture, deaf and dumb to all entreaties?"

"No, I have not seen that."

Fray Antonio sighed inwardly.

"Have you seen any sight that would verify Sor María's claims to visit the New World?"

The girl's brow creased, and her lips pulled back as she considered. Her teeth were unattractive, light gray and uneven and pointed like the pales of a bleached fence. "Could you mean . . . her wounds?"

Fray Antonio glanced up. "Which wounds are those?"

"Once when we could not find that Baptista for a whole day . . . pardon, I mean to say when Baptista could not serve, I acted as the Mother's servant. I saw her come from her chamber bleeding, a cut above the ribs and one at the neck. I went to help her. On those travels the Indians had not welcomed her, and she had been martyred."

Fray Antonio recorded this new information carefully. "And you saw the wound sites? The blood?"

"Blood, yes, Father. I dressed it. But I needn't have. The next day, the

Mother's wounds were healed. When I removed the bandage, the skin was whole, without mark."

"You're certain?"

The triangular face nodded solemnly. "She asked me not to speak of it, and I have not until now, except"—the girl smoothed her habit—"to my own parents, whom I knew I could trust never ever to tell."

"Your parents live in the village below?"

"Yes, Father. They keep a shop."

Fray Antonio tilted his pen back. "So all the village may pass through this shop in the course of a week?"

The girl smiled. "*Todo el mundo.* All the world, it seems like."

The only one to witness the miraculous wounds is the child of the village center of gossip. Her parents would never ever tell? She could not have been a day past her confidences when her mother would have been measuring out flour and salt, whispering the tale. A day later all Ágreda would have heard it.

Fray Antonio turned to the notebook's back pages and copied this story in the confirmation column and its sadly obvious counterpart opposite—he did not consider his investigation advanced. He had many to interview still. Three or four more days? A week? He sent Juan to ask the abbess's permission for an additional period of questioning.

Juan was a long time returning, and when he did return, Fray Antonio was glad to see the soldier smiling. "We were laughing about something that happened today," he told Fray Antonio. "One of the child musicians pocketed the coin her mother had given her to buy candles and instead left the abbess a wedge of cheese."

Fray Antonio rubbed his tight forehead. "How did the abbess respond to this . . offering?"

"She ate it." Juan broke into another smile, which then flickered and extinguished.

✠

It was not accurate to say, Baptista decided, that she waited out the days, but rather that to so close a watcher as herself their course had become minutely visible. Really, all the movement! She went around dizzied. And with a sympathy in her blood, for though to pray was good, to do, to work, to sing, to run, to wave one's arms was only a louder praise.

Which would she rather be—the night or the day? The moon or the sun? Baptista could not choose. The moon drifting away like a boat, morning stars towed after it, the sun shooting up and across in a blazing arc, the clouds' hard traveling. The sun might chase the moon down or the moon wait for the best opportunity to take her dark place, but they had their order, their agreement. Some mornings Baptista discovered them peacefully together, the sun as loud and bright in the treetops as a hundred yellow birds and the wan moon hanging just above the tree, half tucked inside the sky's pocket.

The soldier knew her hair was short and clung to her head in damp, flattened curls. He knew her small round breasts tipped upward, her waist cupped in, her hands were chapped, the knuckles dried and toughened. Sackcloth had chafed her skin. How could he not have thought of prison, excommunication, the punishments for staining a nun? It moved her when he withdrew his hand and flung it over his eyes. So good. Such a useless thing to do. His other senses were flooded with her, as hers were with him.

"Take the book yourself," he said now, his voice muffled by the hand over his face.

"I cannot."

"Why?"

"He won't believe me." Baptista told the soldier how she had mocked the interrogator, how he had chased her and cried after her, What are you?

The soldier made a breathy sound. Baptista's fingers were clenched tight against her palms—was he disapproving? Her fingers uncurled, searched out his hand, and guided it to her again.

He lifted his head, with a groan put his mouth on her breast, sucked the hardened nipple, and at once they were his, her eager hands caressing his cheek, his forehead, cupping his shoulders. These were not soft hands, and she couldn't use them softly. Fingertips rough from scrubbing, nails often traced with garden earth, the creases of the knuckles stained from paints. They belonged to themselves; they did as they wanted. Lips grazed his neck, the hands roved downward. Other words than those about her diary fell out of the mouth he couldn't see: "Juan de Vaca, you have the most beautiful shoulders in the world." That he could not see her both frightened and reassured him, she knew. He pulled at her waist until she slipped her body against his on the narrow planking.

The Saint of Bilocation

151

"No," he said into her ear. "The diary must have an author, and the author must swear. Can you find the courage to go to him yourself?"

Baptista had no answer. How could she answer? As he moved over her, they forgot one might ask or one might offer something to the other. That was impossible because there was no other at all. There was a center they held that held them within itself, no room no bed but a borderless breadth and depth. The darkness shone and the passing hours stopped still.

Until she dragged her body up and took herself away from him.

The slither of the *sayuela*, her nightdress, rough as sackcloth. Then a flash of moonlight, a blink of shadow, and the door shut him into blackness. There was no sound of footsteps. Nothing, though he raised his head from the thin mattress, straining to listen.

Juan leapt from the bed and ground his knees into the stone floor. He believed he was praying after the intense fashion of Fray Antonio, but at the same time in another chamber of himself he was able to imagine the floor warmed from her kneeling there. He thrust his head into shaking arms. His body bowed, curved, stinging in the chill night air, he realized that the prayer had become his own savoring of the woman's wetness, still on him.

✤

Juan called the last of the nuns. These were novices enjoying the drama of the interrogation, who took hours to report trivial observations and to answer Fray Antonio's questions with a choir of no's and folded hands. As the last one sauntered out, a violin and viol began a skillful duet; the priest did not mind. It was enlivening after his long morning. Then Juan called the two boarders, and speaking to the second, Fray Antonio lifted his head to study this person. A man past fifty with deep furrows between the eyebrows and in the withered cheeks. A bruised gaze.

This boarder, a tax collector, answered every question in the affirmative. Yes, he had seen Sor María fly. Yes, he had seen her hang suspended above the . . . sacristy, yes, the sacristy. The sandals fell from her feet. Yes, yes, he had seen it all. Now would the learned theologians of the church believe she is a saint?

"Are you quite certain you have seen these things?"

The tax collector was certain.

"How long have you boarded here at the convent?"

"For five years, Father. On my return from my rounds, I live here."

"Why don't you live in the village?"

The man's face clouded. "It's difficult to find lodgings in this village."

"Surely some widow would be glad to rent a room to you."

He could assure the father that the widows of Ágreda were not glad on this account.

"I see. What is your opinion of Sor María?"

The furrowed face seemed to draw in on itself. The music that had been a vague background to their interview died away; the silence extended. From the trembling underlip, Fray Antonio understood clearly that the man would die for her. But the tax collector replied: "She is fair and kind to everyone regardless of rank or profession."

"Thank you, señor. This is important testimony. Will you sign here and swear what you have said is true? You are aware," Fray Antonio continued dryly, "that to swear falsely is to consign your soul to hell?"

The man's eyes bulged. "*¿Qué?*"

"*Claro,* señor."

The man stood, squeezing his hands. His eyes darted sideways. "I cannot write, Father."

Fray Antonio reddened. "You are a tax collector and you cannot write?"

"I keep the sums in my head. It is my talent."

Fray Antonio jumped to his feet. He roared at the man to demand that he take the oath orally—if he could not write!—and that oath would be as binding as his signature.

The students struck up their concerto. A scratching distracted the priest momentarily, but he turned on the tax collector again. "Swear, señor, if your testimony is true, you have nothing to fear."

Offkey, a violin obbligato like distant sobs, the screech of a hopeless viol.

"Swear!" Fray Antonio shouted.

The tax collector shouted back, "I swear she is a saint!" His face white as bleached linen, the man lowered his voice. "If I make hell my home, Father, you have led me there."

"I?" Fray Antonio squinted at the wretched man, then, grimacing with disgust, shoved him. "Go!"

Juan threw open the door; the student violin screamed, the viol gasped, and after a stick's cruel tapping, both began again from the beginning.

The Saint of Bilocation

Fray Antonio carried his notebook, some bread, and a cup of wine into the courtyard, so as not to be drawn into the storm of confirmations and doubts that roiled in his room. He chewed his bread, dropping bits to the cats that swarmed around his ankles, and deliberately shielded his brain from the whole matter. Out here, the chanting was clearer, rising to the highest notes. The evening was fine and soft. Soon they would mount up and be gone. He would be glad. The hours of sitting had made him long to stride out into some bare distance.

How easily New Mexico returned to him now, when he wanted to think of it and nothing else! In the beginning he had lived in that land as though it were simply the location of his purpose. Conceived his book as a sales tract to win royal support. But he wrote down more—all he could learn about the peoples and their ways. The strange sound of their languages, their dwellings, their family life, even the barbaric dances the Church had forbidden: all held fascination for Fray Antonio. He drank his wine and called up a hot day by the southern leg of the Río del Norte when they shared food with the Manso peoples, who gave them in turn a trout and a lean hare a boy swung by its ears. A winter at the Taos mission when the same river froze like a white road and the people walked on it. An autumn's mass at Tesuque Pueblo when a woman laid woven ears of corn on the altar and a man newly converted, arrows of white flint. The young priest there had smiled, saying that the people gave such trinkets as were common around them. He would have them offer candles yet, when enough could be made, that the altar would blaze with Christian light! Fray Antonio fingered the flint. He had been years in the River Province by then and appreciated the arrows' workmanship, their beauty and utility.

In his last year there he had baptized the Xumanas people. On that day their captains had come out to meet them, sent, they said, by the woman who walked among them preaching. Their faces and arms colored with brutal designs, the captains asked to have the Spaniards' God so that they no longer lived their lives like the jackrabbit or the shaggy cattle, running along the ground. They led Fray Antonio and Fray Jerónimo, Juan de Vaca, and three more soldiers back to their skin tents, their women and children and dogs. An old wizard ran forward to dispute with the captains. "I've seen them at other pueblos, these crazy people, beating them-

selves until the blood is on their backs! They want us all to be crazy too!"
But he could not change the captains' minds, and the wizard charged away,
shouting he would not be a crazy person. He did not run away entirely,
though, but fixed himself a little way off. Fray Antonio watched him
shaking his rattles and lifting his feet, listened as his hoarse chanting rose
and broke. Fray Antonio's ear had been transfixed by that broken chant.
Beneath the rage and impotence he heard a base of purest faith.

He had been moved, and moved to wonder who were these old gods
who today were leaving. The gods whose feet sprang out of this borderless
land, who inhabited the river and the cottonwoods, who presided over
the slanting rain and the long blue slide of the night. He might go to
the gray-haired wizard and, if he could, talk with him, as . . . a fellow
priest . . . oh wicked designation . . . fellow—

Fray Jerónimo laughed so jubilantly Fray Antonio's sinful impulse
was lost, and made the soldiers laugh with him at the wizard, saying the
devil had run fast, for a jerky old man.

They had been astounded, priests and soldiers alike, when a party of
women came forward bearing a cross garlanded with lavender wildflowers. Fray Jerónimo rolled up his sleeves, knowing that Fray Antonio
would hear from each mouth that baptism was desired. Having seen
their numbers, though, Fray Antonio knew this way was futile.

"Juan, take the cross," he'd ordered, and Juan planted it, a slender
thing, where he pointed. He made known through the captains that the
people should lift their arms if they wanted baptism, and when with a
great cry these hundreds and their children did so, Jerónimo with a curt
nod had said, "Good. We have won souls today."

Fray Antonio's legs would not hold him. He faltered to his knees on
the grassy prairie. Because it troubled him, he chose afterward not to
describe how the cry opened his body, made his heart indivisible from
the air and the sun in the sky, transparent, porous, never so much nothing nor so full. He explained his weakness as a visitation of humility. As
it was. And yet, would his life had ended then, pierced by such a blaze!
Juan had helped him to stand again.

Fray Antonio swallowed the last of his wine and set the cup down
hard. That was your work, not this. You are still the mission priest you
have always been, that you were born to be.

It seemed to him that he had been walled away from what he was. He rested his head in his hands for a moment. Then he forced himself to take in the ordered garden with its tended vines, the little, thinned-away moon. The two nights of their trip would be dark ones.

A question darted past his guard. The tax collector's accusation: that Fray Antonio had damned him. Did the Inquisition lead offenders to hell? No, they rooted out people who had embraced that region themselves—though too zealously in the past. Would his report consign the abbess to their zeal? To their sharp instruments, their hoods?

Uneasy, he brushed away crumbs and cats and walked the courtyard, chafing at having to shorten his natural gait to the scale of the garden. The wisteria still suggested a dry perfume; the roses showed plump green buds. The olives were twined about one another, empty of demons.

At last he returned to the bench and took a deep breath. Then he opened the notebook on his lap and prepared the page she must sign.

⁂

Juan took his accustomed place against the wall. Fray Antonio's moist palms dampened the paper. April had given way to May heat. A late afternoon burned through the abbess's tall windows, creating on the stone floor, her one poor carpet, a pool of amber light.

María de Jesus de Ágreda could say she was transported by the two archangels or by horned devils or by the holy mother of God; the phenomenon had not been satisfactorily authenticated by the community of the convent. Now he copied her description of missions in the north of the river kingdom, two he personally had never visited. He set down each detail; upon such points greater minds might decide the matter. The archbishop's secretary had made that clear, and the dry authority of his voice was never far from Fray Antonio's ear. But Fray Antonio could not subtract himself from the process; he was aware that he was far too caught up.

He took out a handkerchief and blotted his face, then dried his hands, sliding the cambric between each damp finger. He poised the pen over a fresh page.

"We have now completed the missions, I think? *Bien.* One final matter. Tell me, please, about your teaching of the Xumanas Indians, a tribe we have lately baptized."

Sor María lifted her eyebrows, then smiled faintly. "They came to your mission asking to be baptized, is this not true?"

"Yes. They were the ones who brought news of a Spanish woman who claimed to walk among the Indians teaching. The archbishop of Mexico had also heard of this woman, and asked us what we knew."

"What did you know?"

Fray Antonio frowned, realizing the interrogation had turned. He was disturbed by this reversal of roles. But he answered her. "Nothing," he said.

"Was it you who thought of asking the Xumanas?"

He nodded. "Fray Estevan, the pastor of Isleta, had mentioned to me how they came, summer after summer, petitioning, though we had not enough priests to go with them. I bid him call the Xumanas in. They pointed to the painting of the old nun. They said a woman dressed like that but with a young face walked among them teaching, urging them to seek out the priests. Fray Estevan asked them why they had not told us this before."

"What did they say?"

She knew the answer to this question, he was sure. His smile was stiff. "They said we had not asked them before. They said they thought the woman must be here with us, also."

"So I was, from time to time."

"So you say. And yet to none of the fathers was granted the blessing of seeing you?"

"There was no need."

The repetition of this answer angered him. He leaned forward in the chair, exclaiming, "To spend one's life serving God, hungry, cold, in a barbarous land—surely that merits a glimpse of God's marvels?"

"I would say just the contrary, Fray Antonio." Her gaze was impatient. "Why do you need to see what you already know? You, who have been given much?"

"I? Given much?" To what did she refer? At this moment he knew only that he had been given this task, this interrogation, and indeed, it did seem onerous and he, unequal to it.

"Let me tell you what sight greeted you when you and the other priest traveled to the Xumanas kingdom. The people met you with a procession, with a wooden cross woven with wildflowers. Your face, Fray Antonio, wore exhaustion and astonishment. I recognized you at once, from that day. And Juan de Vaca, too, who stood close by your side with his arquebus."

The Saint of Bilocation

A grunt of something like pain; Fray Antonio turned to see Juan cross himself, his lips moving.

"Hear me, Fray Antonio." Sor María offered her hands to him. "I wove the garlands for the cross. But you know that, don't you?"

"They told us that was the lady's work."

"There were too many to speak with one by one, so you held high your crucifix and asked the people to raise their arms if they wanted baptism. The people raised their arms in affirmation. Mothers lifted up their babies' little arms."

The exact words he wrote in his book. He had written of that day with fervor because it had shocked his soul with humility. He had chosen not to write of his most personal response—of how he had slipped down clutching the crucifix or of his own whispered exclamations. But the mothers and the babies, oh yes. And in those very words: "Mothers lifted up their babies' little arms." Fray Antonio was invaded by a tendril of fearful ugliness—that his own experience could be so used.

"Later when you confessed some of these people, they brought to you a leather string tied with knots, no? Each knot signified one sin to be forgiven."

That was true, but he shrank back. That detail he had also written in his book, and in the same words.

"That was the day you ask about, Fray Antonio. Do you have more questions?"

He shook his head no.

She exhaled and sat up straighter. "Then we are finished at last," she said.

He did not answer her. Fray Antonio was seeing his hands add the spills to his scale. He would not be able to resist; he knew what the weight would show. Filled with repugnance, he stood and smoothed open the page that she must sign.

He called down upon Sor María de Jesus de Ágreda the obedience of the most reverend Father General, and in that holy name she swore. Fray Antonio had written correctly, she attested. All she had said here, she had done.

At the oath, a horror crawled the priest's spine. This woman before him, whose delicate hand he could reach out even now and touch, would burn in hell.

And he was the agent who led her there.

No, no, not true. She had brought herself to that wide gate.

A leaden sadness took hold of his body, displacing the horror, burdening his shoulders and his limbs, spread in him until it enclosed his heart and became pity for her delusion, for whatever reason she might perpetrate this fraud; it no longer mattered why. He did not care to know. He stared at the page without seeing it, and the stone floor, the walls with their tall windows fell away. The pity pulled apart and broke like a scab, leaving a blank white place, an opening, a nothing: she was as she was, let others dissect and judge, let the council condemn; his purpose was only to take in without censure, to flow into her soul like water or light. He could not move.

For the sake of all he knew to be right, he tried to shoulder his responsibility again, tried to speak. *Sor María*—his lips only formed the words. He strained to make himself audible, but when he did, his exhortation did not befit his office.

"Sor María, I implore you not to swear to some falsehood. These visits may be dreams, only. They may be visions. I do not hold you to your oath until you have signed."

María de Ágreda studied his anguished face. She reached to the wall above her desk and took a crucifix hanging there. Pressing it to her breast, she came to stand directly before Fray Antonio. Her wide gray eyes stared into his. "God, live in me as I live in You," she whispered. It was a prayer, but it sounded like an oath. "You have in this far world no humbler servant."

Fray Antonio's mouth slackened; his arms and neck chilled. These were the words he whispered on the day he baptized the Xumanas. They were written nowhere but in his heart. "How can you know this?" he cried hoarsely, but she had turned from him and stooped to sign the page.

All I have said I have done.
Sor María de Iesu de Ágreda
15 May 1631

The interview was ended, Fray Antonio still stupidly clutching his pen. She retrieved the blue cloak from her trunk, piled it into his arms. "For whatever use you may make of it," she said. *How can you know?* echoed inside his head. She could not. Unless she were truly the boundless thing she said. This was the evidence. Fray Antonio Jimenez Vera sank to his knees and begged her blessing.

⁜

His temples throbbed, his mind raced in the very way he had as a child visualized eternity: fiery circle, fiery track. His tapers burned; he'd lit them all. There was a terrible pain between his shoulders because Fray Antonio had done a terrible thing.

"Juan, *m'hijo*," he'd begun, his chest thundering, his breath shallow, and the soldier had answered him with the devotion he had always shown. All the same—Fray Antonio narrowed his eyes—Juan's face, so brown when they arrived, was paler, the lines cut around his eyes by the New Mexico sun, deeper.

"You were my second eyes and ears. May I have your judgment now?"

Juan's mouth opened in surprise. "She is a saint. Isn't that your own conclusion? You knelt—"

Fray Antonio looked away from him. "I know. But one . . . When I returned to my room, I remembered one thing. The day I baptized the Xumanas, do you recall it?"

"Of course."

The priest bowed his head for a moment then raised it again, bursting out, "Juan, can you have betrayed us?"

Juan's face flickered with a nervous confusion, his mouth worked; Fray Antonio shuddered. "Can you have told her? You stood by my side as always, only you! Did you tell the abbess of my own exclamations that day?"

Juan stared at him. The confusion deepened, and Fray Antonio read also pain and disbelief.

"You want me to swear to you?"

"Please, Juan, I only mean— "

"I swear I told her nothing." Juan angled away, the heel of his hand pushing against his chest. "Home," he said bitterly. "So we are home now, Father?"

And he was gone. Fray Antonio had run after him to the door, but the soldier kept walking, his boots ringing on the stone.

He flung himself down, furiously entering this last evidence into his private notations. He would weigh it with this last testimony in her favor.

In the River Province

For he believed Juan, and since he believed him he must also believe that the abbess had dressed the wildflowers with her unseen hands. Fray Antonio folded and carefully tore the paper down the midline, the side for confirmations. He rolled the long strip into a spill, laying it into its proper side on the scale. So light was the paper it made almost no impression—Fray Antonio groaned; he might have been loading the scale with butterflies, with snowflakes—but he persisted. He crouched down on his hands and knees to examine them on their own level; the brass trays hung evenly. He covered his eyes. *Lost lost lost* circled in fire in his head. Failed interrogator and failed friend, priest without missions, what am I, I am lost.

His door opened of its own accord.

Relief flooded him. "Juan," he cried, "I did not mean to doubt your friendship or your word—"

But it was a nun clutching a book before her face who barged into his room. Seeing him on his knees, the intruder dropped to hers and scrabbled toward him, jerking at her habit, which caught on the stone floor. "*Por favor,*" she was begging, "your honor, please take my diary. It is an accurate account of the abbess's travels. I have dated each occasion. It will verify precisely what she has told you, and I have painted her form as I perceived it, for some years now, each painting will . . ." The nun stumbled then and wrested her skirts out in front of her. She grabbed them up with no thought of modesty, only of scrambling forward. Candlelight revealed her naked legs, scraped knees, and as she lurched and the book lowered, her small, contorted face.

A cry gurgled up in him. It was the face of the creature who had mocked him in the garden. Again it mocked him—it was an uncanny, diabolical mirror of his own loss and shame. He flew at it, pushing and kicking the thing toward his door, a bundle of sackcloth and flailing limbs possibly only in the guise of human arms and legs, tentacles, truly, or the tendons of webbed black wings. When it was driven across his threshold in a heap, he threw himself against the door.

A tiny voice penetrated the keyhole, sailed through the marrow of his bones, and lodged grieving in his ear. "Oh I cannot help her?"

As answer, Fray Antonio struck the door with his fist and, when he was sure the voice had retreated, laid his forehead against the wood.

⁜

Dawn was clammy, his joints rusted iron. He had spent the night on his knees and, when called, had staggered and stumbled before he could raise himself. Limping from a stiffness in the hips, Fray Antonio barely glanced at the boy Juan had found to care for the horses. Juan himself was drawn and silent, except to say all was loaded and ready. He turned away from the priest's attempted apology.

Fray Antonio climbed from a stool onto the horse, which showed no inclination to leave the stable until Juan yanked its rein and guided it out through the gray dawn to the road. They set off in silence. They were hardly removed from sight of the abbess's tall window when Juan wheeled his horse. The soldier slung himself from the saddle to bend to their trailing servant, who rapped his own head, knocking the man's huge cap he wore even further over his face. Shoulders heaving, limp arms dangling, what . . . was the child weeping in the road? Fray Antonio squinted, but the light was sparse and dust swirled about the two figures, shimmering and mingling their forms.

He tugged his sluggish horse back around and waited. Would anything less than a signed proof of the miracle condemn her to the Inquisition? What do the people say? To hear its agent speak these words: "In the Name of the Holy Inquisition . . ." means to be swiftly deserted by father and friends, by the mother who bore you. What would Fray Antonio write, what would he testify to the councils? He did not know. He wanted to shirk his duties and sleep for a while in a field beside the road. But that—he rubbed his burning eyes, shifted in the saddle to relieve an ache in his bones—he could not allow himself. A warmth touched his cheek, the sun, finally.

Riding up, Juan stiffly assured him the boy would calm himself, serve them well enough until they reached Madrid. Turning then for Seville, he would take charge of the boy, see him safely home.

"There's no need for haste," Fray Antonio murmured to Juan's discomfort. Again they started off. After some time, the priest dug into a saddle bag, and Juan twisted to look at the little servant. No more head-knocking; she was plodding more surely now, Juan was relieved to see. Only her lips and chin visible beneath the obscuring cap. Good.

A flapping interrupted Juan's urgent scrutiny, called him back, a blue tip beating against his sleeve. He turned and stared. Fray Antonio had thrown Sor María's cloak about his shoulders, drawn its hood. The priest rode bowed and nodding inside its blue folds.

In the River Province

In sidelong, soldier's fashion, Juan also kept an eye on him. When the priest's horse slowed, Juan fell back and kicked his dusty boot into its flank. He dashed sweat from his temple. This long road! If only desire, if only boldness were wide-winged angels, Madrid would be theirs in a moment.

The River Province of New Mexico

SOME YEARS LATER

Grimacing with pain, Fray Antonio unfolds his fists until the posture of his hands resembles a man's who is about to grasp a globe. He has soaked his arthritic joints in vinegar, rubbed them with the honeycomb fresh from a hive. The latter *remedio* seems to have relieved the swelling to a degree—enough for him to grip his pen. He composes a letter. She will answer; of this he is certain. The council of 1631 had favored her claims: Fray Antonio Jimenez Vera had spoken for her case with whatever crude ability a mission priest might possess.

Indeed her case has become notorious. Information reaches even his far outpost: Sor María had at last been called by the Inquisition to answer on various subjects. And dismissed, on that occasion. It is likely—he has heard rumors of some new work of hers, elevating the Virgin to Co-Creator of the universe!—very likely she will be called again.

He greets her, conveys his sincere happiness that the Inquisition found no fault in her. He inquires after the prosperity of her convent, sends news: *The King has been generous with funds. Forty more Franciscans do the blessed work, which in former years I shared with so few. The missions are much improved and many more souls converted. I tended this week a young man of Ildefonso whose arm was broken by a landowner here and he* . . . Fray Antonio continues long in this vein, telling of this injustice and of another, of a person's curious tale, of a shadow skimming through his body so that he whirled to catch sight of an eagle.

Resting his hand, he recalls almost as an afterthought, his purpose. Laboriously he takes up the pen again and discloses it: a request.

Now that time has passed, now that she has surely, as he has, deliberated—cannot she describe to him more exactly the phenomenon of bilocation? During its course one must be relieved of bodily ills, without weight or bounds, incapable of knowing. Indeed, the flight itself must be exaltation. This is how he puts it to himself as he walks beneath the cottonwoods. Is he very wrong?

The letter travels by foot, by horse, by rough cart, by wagon, by sailing ship. It is two years before he receives her reply.

Fray Antonio asks young Fray Miguel to plump the fire. "Such a sweet-smelling wood, piñon, isn't it?" He never tires of noting this. "And please, light a fresh taper." The April evening is bright and keen with wind, as though spring is sweeping away the winter, but these thick mud walls breathe a chill. Miguel breaks the seal, thoughtfully flattens the heavy paper, and leaves him alone. Fray Antonio weights the letter on the table with his clubbed hands. She greets him, praises his work. Then she remarks on the state of the local harvests and discloses the convent's news. The abbess's letter is phrased with the directness he cannot forget, in the voice that still interrupts his frequent conversations with the cottonwoods: *One world lies without boundaries inside the other, Fray Antonio.*

Her next passage is less direct.

As to your question, I am afraid my poor deliberations will prove of little interest. As I told the grave fathers of the Inquisition, I can say that my travels happened but not how they happened. I do not understand what is said to be so well as what is. God is my mirror but I am only a woman.

Fray Antonio's brow furrows even as he breaks into an incredulous smile. He marvels at this passage. Its beginning constructed with the circumspection one would naturally employ for the ecclesiastical court, but its end, seemingly so modest . . . soars. Her inferior powers of comprehension—limited to life's truest essence. Her daily mirror—the face of God. Over and over, the light!

"Abbess," he cannot help but laugh, he speaks aloud, "had I not been interrogator, what might you have dared to tell me?" What might *she* have dared? Fray Antonio pounces on this absurdity. "The truth is, Abbess . . . I understood this from the moment my letter was taken from my hand . . . Sor María, Traveler, the truth is that I wanted only to speak with you again." He might have dared to tell her of the old wizard, more, of all his private amazements with this New World and its peoples. She, instead of the arrogant Jesuit, might have been the listener he once sought. The ear, the heart in concord with his own, the harmony, however fleet.

Dismissing this vain wish with a sigh, he returns to the script of the letter; a bulging knuckle marks his place.

I too have a request, mi estimado abogado.

He squints: My esteemed lawyer, she calls him! The merry title fills his ears. Fray Antonio starts, his head jerks up. There, across his pine table in the leaping light of the fire. Sor María herself, freed from the constraint of interrogations, her gray eyes clear as rain falling through sunlight. A joyous heat radiates to his swollen joints, to his many pains—he knows each one even as they cease to matter—to his toes, which twitch against the hardened leather of his sandals. Ah, see how she bows her neck . . .

Gradually his eager hand, reaching across the table, cools, his gnarled thumb crabs again. With his fist Fray Antonio bumps the candle nearer to make out this request of hers.

Please bless me, Father, as I know you bless all who dwell in the River Province.

He leans forward and etches the cross on the warm skin of the air.

LISA SANDLIN
came to New Mexico from Texas
in 1974. She's taught at Wayne
State College in Nebraska since
1997, returning summers to Santa
Fe. She is the author of two other
story collections, *The Famous Thing
About Death* (Cinco Puntos, 1991)
and *Message to the Nurse of Dreams*
(Cinco Puntos, 1997), which won
the Austin Writers' League Violet
Crown Award and the 1997 Texas
Institute of Letters' Jesse H. Jones
Award for Best Book of Fiction.